STARTING OVER

an Action! Series Book

By

G.A.HAUSER

STARTING OVER

STARTING OVER

Book 35 of the Action! Series

Copyright © G.A. Hauser, 2018

ISBN Trade paperback: 978-1726-4393-0-5

© The G.A. Hauser Collection LLC

This is a work of fiction and any resemblance to persons, living or dead, or business establishments, events or locales is coincidental.

All Rights Are Reserved. No part of this may be used or reproduced in any manner whatsoever without written permission, except in the case of brief quotations embodied in critical articles and reviews.

WARNING

This book contains material that maybe offensive to some: graphic language, homosexual relations, adult situations. Please store your books carefully where they cannot be accessed by underage readers.

First The G.A. Hauser Collection LLC publication: October 2018

WARNING:
"The unauthorized reproduction or distribution of this copyrighted work is illegal. Criminal copyright infringement, including infringement without monetary gain, is investigated by the FBI and is punishable by up to 5 years in federal prison and a fine of $250,000."

STARTING OVER

Chapter 1

Santa Monica Chief of Police Billy Sharpe left his brand new police cruiser in the secure parking lot. The hot wind blew litter and leaves across the cement. Billy adjusted his heavy duty belt and reached for the secure door which led to the back of the administrative offices of the court house.

An officer was leaving at the same time. The Los Angeles Police officer snapped out of his daydream at seeing Billy there, and held the door open for him.

"Thanks." Billy entered the A/C-cooled building.

"No problem, Chief." The cop kept walking into the July sunshine.

Billy cleared his throat and shut off his police radio, one he had clipped to his epilate. Using the elevator, avoiding eye-contact with civilians riding up with him, Billy pocketed his sunglasses and left the elevator, his black combat boots tapping the linoleum floor as he went.

Standing outside an office, Billy inhaled for strength and rapped the door with a knuckle.

"Come in."

He turned the knob and peered into the District Attorney's office.

"Chief." Dan D'Amico stood from his desk and reached out his hand.

Billy closed the door behind him and clasped Dan's hand in a firm, but quick, handshake.

"Have a seat." Dan gestured to the chair opposite him.

Billy sat down and rested his elbows on the arms of the chair.

Dan fussed with files on his desk, then pressed an intercom button and said, "No calls, Patrice."

"Yes, sir."

Billy sunk in the chair and interlaced his fingers on his lap.

Dan met his gaze and shook his head. "It's not good, Chief."

Billy knew this was coming. He knew it.

~

Mark Antonious Richfield knotted his light blue silk necktie in the full-length mirror in his mansion in Paradise, California.

He tightened the knot to his shirt collar and inspected his hair and face. Another modeling shoot was approaching and Mark had to be in Los Angeles next weekend. Which meant, he had to get to his plastic surgeon for a shot of Botox soon.

"Bollocks." Mark dropped his arms to his sides and gazed at himself. He'd been so busy the past month; getting married in New York, moving here to his family's estate in Northern California, continuing to get his father's corporation up to speed, traveling to London and Paris to meet with the employees there, dealing with his son, worrying about his new husband, learning the surrogate was pregnant...

What he needed was a bloody haircut.

He brushed his mop of hair back from his forehead and exhaled in frustration. Mark stood near his dresser and opened a carved wooden box, removing gold cufflinks. He shook his shirt sleeve down and attempted to push one through the slots.

When it dropped to the floor, Mark tried not to become exasperated. He stepped back and looked around the soft, beige pile carpet for it.

"Mark?"

"In here, love." Mark picked up the second cufflink and managed to get it into his sleeve.

STARTING OVER

Steven Jay Miller, Mark's partner and ex-husband peered into Mark's bedroom. "Almost ready?"

Mark kept looking for the cufflink he'd dropped, dragging his hair back from his face in irritation.

"What's wrong?" Steve, wearing his business suit, his jacket over his arm, entered the bedroom.

"I dropped my bleedin' cufflink."

Steve tossed his jacket on Mark's bed and helped him search. He found it quickly, under the dresser. Steve held it and gestured for Mark to give him his hand so he could fasten it for him.

Mark tried to breathe deeply since he was getting stressed out.

Steve placed the gold cufflink on for him, and the touched the knot in Mark's necktie. "Fuck, you're gorgeous."

Mark took his suit jacket off the hanger and closed his eyes for a moment.

"Mark? What going on?" Steve rubbed Mark's upper back.

Mark dropped to sit on the bed and lay his suit jacket with Steve's. "I can't catch up. I need a bleedin' haircut, I need to see Dr Love, and I need bloody glasses!"

~

Knowing how hectic the last few months have been, Steve sat with Mark on the bed, shifting their jackets over. "Take time off. Go to LA and get things done." Steve interlaced his fingers with Mark's.

"Bloody hell." Mark yawned and rubbed his face. "I just want to get on with it. I feel as if I have tentacles dragging me south."

Steve rubbed Mark's hand in his lovingly. "Babe? I've got Sac covered. Why don't you stay in Bel Air for a few days? Get the loose ends tied up. Meanwhile, I can locate a good plastic surgeon up here, and I can also find an ophthalmologist."

Mark raised Steve's hand to his mouth to kiss.

"Have you talked to Arnold Newhouse about the *Dangereux* contract yet?" Steve stared at Mark's profile, his long, dark eyelashes and full lips.

"No. Not yet." Mark toyed with Steve's fingers.

"Do you want me to?"

Mark turned to look at him.

Steve melted at the sight of his catlike green eyes.

"No. I can do it. Thank you, love." Mark tilted his head and offered a kiss.

Steve didn't hesitate.

After the sweet kiss, Steve noticed his husband, Tadzio, standing in the doorway.

~

Tadzio wore skin-tight designer, shimmering blue slacks with a blue matching blazer, and a white blouse. His white socks were exposed between his trouser hem and brown lace-up dress shoes. While standing in the hallway, watching his husband and Mark talk quietly, Tadzio fussed with his engagement rings, an emerald cut diamond solitaire and diamond band.

Steve smiled at him after kissing Mark.

"Sierra asked me to tell you breakfast iz ready." Tadzio was going with Steve to the downtown office of Richfield-Miller International for the first time.

Mark released Steve's hand and shifted away from him on the bed. "Go, Steven."

"Are you eating?" Steve stood from the bed and picked up his jacket.

Mark rubbed his stomach. "I'll get coffee on my way."

Tadzio said, "I can get you coffee from Sierra."

Steve caressed Tadzio's cheek. "Mark's going to LA."

"Yes. Stan iz still there, yes?" Tadzio was nervous about leaving Los Angeles and Alex and Billy behind.

STARTING OVER

"Come on. I need to eat." Steve coaxed Tadzio away from Mark's bedroom and they walked to the stairs of the mansion.

The home was so large, Tadzio was still trying to get used to it. He ran his palm over the smooth curved mahogany rail of the majestic staircase, and as he and Steve descended it, Tadzio gazed out at the marble foyer, large front door, and the arched entrance to the living room area, which had to be at least forty by twenty feet in size.

Scents of bacon and strong espresso drew them to the kitchen.

Their chef, Sierra, was busy cooking, and smiled when they entered. "Good morning."

Steve draped his suit jacket over a chair and sat at the breakfast nook. "Hi, Sierra."

Tadzio joined him on the bench seat across from Steve and gazed outside at the view; their stable, their three horses grazing in the paddock, their outdoor pool, their tennis courts, and the mountains looming beyond the open fields.

Sierra brought two plates of food for them with a smile. "Is Mark coming down?"

Steve tucked his necktie behind him and picked up a slice of bacon. "He's most likely taking the jet to LA today. I have no idea if he's eating."

Tadzio said, "He would like coffee, Sierra."

"That's fine. What kind would you like, Tadzio?"

"I like ezprezzo, please."

"Same." Steve chewed the bacon.

Sierra stood at her fancy machine to make their drinks.

Tadzio began eating his gourmet feta and spinach omelet and asked Steve, "What am I going to do?"

"I want you to meet the designers." Steve ate hungrily, taking big bites of his omelet with homemade sourdough bread.

Sierra set both espressos on the table and gestured to the stairs. "Does Mark want me to bring it to him?"

"Don't worry about it." Steve sipped the strong coffee.

Tadzio watched her acknowledge Steve, then he stared out of the window as he ate. "Who iz that man?"

"What man?" Steve leaned down to look. "He's Andrew Wilson, our groom."

"Groom for horses?"

"Yes."

Tadzio watched the young man rolling a wheelbarrow into the stable. He sipped the coffee and wondered how long it was going to take for this amazing house to feel like home.

~

Alexander Mark Richfield parked his red Ferrari in the studio lot. He sat with the motor running for a few minutes, the A/C on, and read his phone. His husband, Billy, had gone to a meeting with the DA, and Alex was worried sick about him.

His chief of police had worked for almost a year to document and fire a heavy-handed rookie cop. After he did, that rookie sued the city.

The chief had lost his temper with the rookie after being called a 'fucking faggot'.

Alex nudged his sunglasses higher on his nose and read his text messages.

In a moment of rage, Billy had punched out the window of this rookie's pickup truck- while in the courthouse parking garage…on a surveillance video.

That act had landed the chief in hot water.

Alex wondered how long Billy was going to be dealing with the bullshit. He didn't get a text back from him yet.

Noticing the time, Alex turned off his car and climbed out, walking to the correct studio where his television series was being shot. It was back from its summer hiatus and he had wrapped the production of his last film, *Lover Boy*, one he

STARTING OVER

costarred in with his father's new toy-boy husband, Stan Charles…Richfield.

Alex's long hair blew all over in the wind. He kept his head down, his sunglasses on, and made his way to the entrance. A security guard was manning the door.

"Hi, Alex."

"Hi." Alex didn't know this guy. Since the old man, 'Buddy' had left, Alex couldn't be bothered. He smiled politely and moved his sunglasses to the top of his head, using them to hold his hair back from his eyes.

Making the long walk to the room where he was going to meet with the producers and director to discuss this new season, Alex was happy to get back to a routine. The nighttime cable TV show was stable, calm, and here in LA.

As he thought about the last film, of flying to New York for the location scenes, which were in the Diamond District, a flash of sucking Stan's cock while he was drugged hit Alex.

Alex paused and closed his eyes.

The guilt. The gravity of his deed hit him hard.

Though Alex had begged Stan for forgiveness, had cried to his dad to let it go, what Alex had done had created a wedge between his dad and himself.

"Hi, Alex."

Alex snapped out of his nightmare to see Carl Bronson.

Carl and his husband Keith O'Leary were actors in another cable series, *Forever Young*, which filmed in the same studio, and had the same producers as well as director, Charlotte Deavers.

"Hi, Carl." Alex hugged the handsome man.

"Did the movie wrap?" Carl asked him.

Alex admired Carl's classic good looks. He was six feet tall and had green eyes, and conservatively cropped brown hair. "Yes. Last weekend."

"Congrats." Carl smiled.

"And congratulations to you too. I hear you got a role in a straight romantic comedy?"

"I did." Carl laughed. "I guess the comedy is me playing a straight lead." Carl turned to look over Alex's shoulder and smiled warmly.

Extras came and went around them, grips and crew carried lighting and wiring to sets.

Alex spun around on his heels and there was Carl's husband; blond, boy-next-door-adorable Keith O'Leary.

"Alex!" Keith embraced him and kissed Alex's cheek.

"Hi, Keith." Alex hugged him tight.

"How's your summer been?" Keith asked, stepping back and putting his arm around Carl's waist.

"Busy." Alex wondered what these men would think of him if they knew he sexually assaulted his father's new husband; drugged him while he was alone, and sucked his cock while he was nearly unconscious.

Both men brightened up to a woman approaching them from down the hall.

Charlotte Deavers, their director, a tiny woman, but a powerhouse on the set, wore her hair in a ponytail, dark-framed eyeglasses, and a white cotton blouse and black slacks. She held a clipboard and walkie-talkie.

"Well." Charlotte smiled at them. "A meeting of the minds?"

"Hi, Char." Alex loved his director. She was like a second mom.

"Alexander." She smiled sweetly. "Is your father busy today?"

Alex touched his chest. "My dad?"

Carl and Keith cracked up. "She didn't mean ours!" Keith roared with laughter.

STARTING OVER

"Yes, Alex. Mark." Charlotte appeared to have her tongue planted in her cheek.

"Why?" Alex touched his phone, which was in his pocket.

She glanced at the two older men and smiled wickedly at Alex. "We want him to star in our final season."

Alex parted his lips to comment. Mark had starred in *Forever Young* ten years ago. "Dad? You want Dad?"

Carl asked, "Is he already working for your grandfather's company?"

"Uh. Yes. I think he's in Paradise today." Alex wished he knew for sure. Ever since he'd fucked up, his father wasn't as accessible as he would like him to be.

Charlotte held her phone in her hand, as if texting or calling Mark, since she had his contact information.

Carl gave Alex another hug. "Have fun on the set. See ya later."

"Bye, Alex." Keith kissed Alex's cheek and he and Carl held hands as they walked to their studio.

"Mark? This is Charlotte Deavers. I know you're most likely busy, but can you call me back sometime today? Will Markham and Derek Dixon have asked me to set up a meeting. They would like you to appear in our final season of *Forever Young*. Call or text me as soon as you can." Charlotte looked at her phone and then said to Alex, "Go get the script. I'll be there soon."

"Okay." Alex watched her rush off. He resumed his hike to the correct room and when he stepped inside it, a squeal of excitement went up from his costars, who appeared thrilled to be back at work after the break. As he was hugged and kissed, Alex felt like a fraud.

He wasn't a nice person. He was a nasty deviant who assaulted a man. Biting back his guilt, Alex acted. Acted calm. Acted happy.

It's what he did. Acted.

~

Stan Charles Richfield emptied the coffee pot. While he was in Los Angeles, he stayed in his one-bedroom apartment in West Hollywood. It was close to his gym, close to his friends, and away from Alexander.

Checking the time on his new Patek Philippe, Stan tidied up the kitchen and grabbed his wallet and sunglasses. They had wrapped *Lover Boy*, but he needed to go to a sound studio for ADR work for some of his lines that didn't make it to edits, and to record a new truck commercial.

Stan also had a list of auditions sent to him by Tadzio before Tadzio quit Adam Lewis' agency and moved to Paradise with Steve.

He had decisions to make. If he auditioned and got a new role, that would mean he'd be here, in LA while Mark was in Paradise.

Stan wanted to act, but he wanted to be Mrs Richfield more.

After locking up his unit, he jogged down the cement stairs to the underground parking area of his apartment house. It was cool in the shady morning, but the temperature was due to heat up to the high nineties.

Stan used his key-fob to unlock his green Lamborghini Aventador, one given to him by his top model husband. Wearing his favorite jeans, skin-tight with threadbare holes in them, and a sleeveless crewneck top, also tight on his muscular frame, Stan climbed into the driver's seat and ignited the powerful engine.

As it rumbled, Stan read his phone for the address of the sound studio. A text appeared.

'*you there, love?*'

'*Yes.*' Stan smiled and his heart rate soared.

'*I've odds and ends to take care of in LA. So, I shall be there shortly. I'm with the jet now.*'

"Yes!" Stan pumped his arm in celebration. '*Can I call?*'

STARTING OVER

'Yes.'

Stan relaxed in the low slung bucket seat and touched himself as he called his husband.

"Hullo, pet."

At Mark's sexy voice, Stan shivered and his cock throbbed under the tight material. "Hey."

"I should be in LA in an hour or so. I am getting my hair trimmed, then I've a doctor's appointment, then I must meet with my modeling agent…"

Stan closed his eyes as Mark spoke, dying to be with him.

"…so? What are you up to?"

"I was on my way to a sound studio." Stan squeezed his hard cock. "I need to do some ADR for the last movie, and record a new truck commercial. Luckily they're in the same building."

"Shall we meet? Both my stylist and doctor are located downtown."

"Which doc?"

"Uh…"

"Mark?" Stan didn't think he had to worry.

"Uh…nothing serious, love."

"Can't tell me?" Stan was surprised and stopped touching himself.

"I've a modeling shoot next weekend."

Stan got it immediately. "Oh. Okay. Well, we could meet for lunch or when I'm done we can meet here at my apartment and workout or do hot yoga."

"I probably shouldn't be doing either after seeing Dr Love."

Stan caught his own hazel eyes in the rearview mirror, thinking about Botox. "Whatever you want, Mark."

"I need to board the jet. Why don't I contact you after I land? Perhaps you can come to the salon whilst I'm there. I'll send you the address."

"Sure." Stan watched a woman leave the lobby and climb into her car.

"Okay, pet. Love you."

"Love you too." Stan heard the line disconnect. He waited for the address to appear, then set the phone in the cup holder and backed out of the space, following the woman out of the secure parking area, and driving to the sound studio.

STARTING OVER

Chapter 2

Jack Charles Larsen moved his mouse on his pad, looking over a bridal registry list on his computer. His law partner Sonja Knight was getting married and he and his husband Adam Lewis were invited. As he searched for an item not yet purchased for the happy couple, Jack thought about Mark's New York wedding.

The wedding he had missed on Memorial Day weekend to Stan. Since it had been planned quickly, paper invitations had not been mailed.

Tadzio had helped Stan's mother, Ali, send text and email invitations.

He hadn't gone, nor had he bought Mark and Stan a gift.

While he located a set of china on the list, one that was nearly a grand in price, Jack thought about a gift for Mark.

Had any of them even sent Mark a card?

Wow. That's fucked up.

Mark's decision to divorce Steve, the former cop that had stolen Mark off the altar at Mark and Sharon's wedding, was so sudden and unpopular, Jack assumed that was why no one had even acknowledged it with a card or token gift.

He called Adam on his cell-phone, putting it to his ear as he looked at the price of the china.

"Hey, He-man."

"Hey." Jack loosened his necktie. He was in his law office and needed to head to court. "How much should I spend on Sonya's gift?"

"She's your law partner."

"I know who she is." Jack laughed. He leaned closer to the computer, then found his reading glasses and put them on to see the fine print. "Since I waited so long, there isn't much left on her gift registry."

"Uh huh."

"I mean, there's a set of fine china for nine-hundred-and forty bucks, and a candy dish for twenty."

Adam laughed. "Okay. Well, between the two, pick the china set."

"Ouch." Jack wasn't prepared to spend that much.

"Do you have to buy the whole set? Or is there a way to donate to it?"

"Oh." Jack tapped a few dropdown menus. "You're so fucking smart."

"I have my moments."

"Three hundred?" Jack asked.

"I'm okay with that."

Jack tossed his eyeglasses on the desk and sank in the leather chair. "I had a kickass time at the estate."

"I enjoyed it too."

Jack rocked in the chair. "I came back unmotivated."

"I hear ya. The whining brats are driving me crazy."

"Fuck. Adam. I want to live there."

"I don't know what to tell ya, Jack. I think I'd go nuts not working."

Jack heard Natalie calling Adam to answer a holding phone call. He smiled to himself. Adam may complain, but Jack knew the talent agent loved the work.

"I've gotta go, He-man."

"I do too. I have to be in court." Jack put his glasses back on.

"Love ya."

STARTING OVER

"Back at ya." Jack tossed his phone on the desk and withdrew his wallet from his pocket, using his credit card to help pay for the expensive china set on Sonja's list.

Then, he hunted around the website for a token gift for Mark. Seeing items Mark didn't need, Jack logged off without a purchase for Mark, wondering if the Top Model's wealth was a good reason to not bother with a wedding present.

Taking off his eyeglasses, Jack stood from his desk and picked up his briefcase.

Mark and Stan.

Yup. I'm going to have to get used to that now.

Jack closed his office door and made his way to the parking garage.

~

Upon arrival in LAX, Mark walked through the private terminal to his waiting limousine.

Dean was there, smiling at him. "Hi, Mark." He opened the back door to the car.

"Hullo, love." Mark, his sunglasses on, sat in the back seat.

Dean closed the door for him and climbed in behind the wheel. "Bel Air?"

"No, love. I've an appointment at a salon." Mark read the address on his phone. "It's in Beverly Hills." He showed Dean the address.

Dean wrote it down on paper on a clipboard, and nodded. "Got it. Am I waiting for you?"

"No, Dean. Stan is going to be available."

"How's he doing?" Dean asked as he drove out of the airport grounds.

Stan had been employed as a limo driver in the same company as Dean. It was how Mark had met him.

"He's fine." Mark stared out of the window at the smog hanging over LA. The fires had been brutal and the smoke seemed to linger.

As Dean became quiet, leaving Mark alone, Mark sent Stan a text, '*I have arrived in LA. On my way to the salon.*'

'*Got it. Wrapping up. Will be there within a half-hour.*'

'*Cheers, love.*'

Mark called Arnold Newhouse, putting the phone to his ear and staring out of the back window.

"Actors and Models for Hire, how may I help you?"

"It's Mark Richfield."

"Oh! One moment, Mark."

Mark closed his eyes and tried to relax.

"Mark."

"Arnold." Mark sat up in the bench seat. "I must meet with you to discuss my contract."

"Good. I need to meet with you too. When can you stop by?"

Mark battled to concentrate. "I may be available around two this afternoon."

"I'll clear the time for you. See you then."

"Bye." Mark disconnected the line and tugged on his long hair absently, wishing he could uncomplicated his life. He noticed a voicemail on his phone. Mark put it back to his ear.

'*Mark? This is Charlotte Deavers. I know you're most likely busy, but can you call me back sometime today? Will Markham and Derek Dixon have asked me to set up a meeting. They would like you to appear in our final season of* Forever Young. *Call or text me as soon as you can.*'

"Good lord." Mark sank in the leather seat and rested his head on the back of it.

~

STARTING OVER

Billy pulled his police cruiser up to another administrative building. Alex had sent him a text, just a loving 'hi' and hearts. Billy sent one back.

He climbed out of the police car and walked to the main entrance. Police officers came and went in black and white cars, on motorcycles, in unmarked sedans, as well as the ubiquitous parking enforcement officers in scooters. Billy entered the building, seeing a woman police officer manning a desk. A line of civilians were waiting to speak to her.

She didn't even look up when he entered, tapping keys on a computer keyboard as she helped someone holding paperwork.

Billy stood at the security door. "Excuse me."

She finally raised her head to scowl. When she realized who it was, her expression changed. "Go right in, Chief." She used a button near her phone to unlock the door for him.

Billy opened the security door and entered the offices for the LAPD.

As he went, cops noticed. They stopped what they were doing to stare at him.

Billy didn't bother to look. He knew he was in a jam right now. Cops weren't the most liberal bunch to begin with. So, being out, gay, and a chief, may bring out the worst in the rank and file.

He made his way to one office.

The secretary looked up from her typing.

"Is Chief Bryant in?"

"Yes, Chief." She picked up her desk phone. "Chief? Chief Billy Sharpe is here to see you." She hung up. "Go right in."

"Thanks." Billy opened the door to see an old friend.

Chief Bryant stood from his desk and extended his hand.

Billy clasped it firmly.

"Take a seat." Chief Bryant, his collar studded with stars, mirroring Billy's, gestured to the chair across from his desk.

Billy sat heavily and tugged his gun holster to get it off his hip. "How' you been?"

"I think the more appropriate question, is how are you?" Chief Bryant, his hair completely gray, deep creases on his face, rested his elbows on his paperwork.

"Will you take me back?" Billy wasn't humiliated. He wanted in.

Chief Bryant studied him. "What rank?"

"I have a choice?" Billy laughed. "I assumed officer."

"Fuck no. I'm not going to do that to you."

"Seriously?" Billy sat up higher, excitement stirring. He leaned over the desk. "Who do you have to clear it with?"

"Maybe the council. But, I doubt even that. As far as I'm concerned this is a lateral transfer. I don't need clearance for other cops. Why should I for you?"

Billy didn't hesitate. "Lieutenant. SWAT."

Chief Bryant reached out his hand again. Billy shook it.

"Go meet your team." Chief Bryant's eyes gleamed.

"Yes!" Billy pumped his arm. "Oh, fuck yes."

"I thought you'd be more upset about the demotion in rank."

Billy scanned the paperwork on the chief's desk and gestured to it. "You like doing this?"

"I do. I'm sixty, Sharpe. The fire is gone from my belly." Chief Bryant's blue eyes still sparkled like a young cadet.

"Who's the L-T that I'm kicking out?" Billy interlaced his fingers on his lap.

"Acting. No worries. We lost the last one to AIG."

Billy's smile dropped. He'd worked in the Internal Affairs Group, investigating cops, and hated it. "Poor schmuck."

"We all had our time there. Including you."

"Don't remind me."

"What's your time frame?"

STARTING OVER

"I just came from the DA's office. I put in my resignation with Dan D'Amico. He's going to clear it with the city, and then..." Billy shrugged. "I suppose someone will make a public announcement. My guess is that someone is me."

"Why don't you keep me posted? When you have the exact date, I'll let personnel know."

"Sounds good."

"Do you want to be back on the hostage negotiating team?"

"May as well. I assume I need a refresher course."

"You do." Chief Bryant nodded and made notes on a pad for himself.

"Do you want me to go through the academy?" Billy teased.

The chief stopped writing and stared at him. "You look as if you could. Christ, how much do you work out?"

"If I didn't work out every day, I'd punch more truck windows."

Chief Bryant laughed and shook his head. "Jesus Christ, I'm glad you're back with us."

Billy thumbed behind him to the office door. "Let me go say hi to the boys."

"Go. And welcome back."

Billy stood from the chair and winked at Chief Bryant, then made his way to the SWAT offices, grinning like a fiend.

~

Listening to his own recorded voice in the studio, Stan paused. He had headphones on, and a microphone was hanging in front of his face.

'*You won't find a better built truck in America. This baby can pull a tractor-trailer-load up a mountain pass. Buy America. Buy tough.*'

Stan watched the sound tech behind the glass. He nodded and spoke into an intercom. "Good. It's a wrap."

Stan removed the headphones. He handed them to an assistant and waved at the man in the sound booth. "Thanks, Frank."

Checking the time, Stan jogged down an internal flight of stairs and outside to his Lamborghini. He read the address for Mark's salon, and drove to Beverly Hills.

As Stan slowed down to assess the parking situation, he noticed a valet. He pulled in front of the salon and climbed out. He was given a claim ticket and trotted into the lobby of the chic spa.

Since he had never been here before, Stan paused and was hit immediately with the soothing mood music, scents meant to relax, and low lighting.

"May I help you?" a woman with heavy makeup and plump lips, standing behind a computer attached to a metal frame, asked.

"I'm here to see Mark Richfield." Stan thought about texting Mark.

"Oh. Yes. One moment." She walked off on stiletto heels and in a miniskirt.

Stan glanced around the waiting area. A few women were seated, staring at him discreetly behind magazines. He spotted his own cologne advertisement on the back of one. *Dangereux* Obsession. Mark wasn't the only one who had to model next weekend. He had both his shoot with Mark for *Dangereux* Red, and his own cologne.

The woman emerged and gestured at him. "Right this way."

Stan pocketed his phone and ran his hand over his hair anxiously. He followed the woman through a large, busy salon with stylists at dozens of stations, chatting, clipping, dying, shampooing, and laughing.

STARTING OVER

He entered a private space, one that had been curtained off from the rest. Before the woman left, she asked Stan, "Can I get you a beverage?"

"Water?"

She acknowledged him with a frozen face and left the private area.

Stan had a look into the room. Mark, in a plush, white robe, was sitting in front of a mirror. His longtime stylist, Javier, was trimming his hair while a young woman was sitting on a stool, giving the top model a pedicure, and another beside him, was giving Mark a manicure.

"Hullo, love."

Javier paused and smiled at Stan. "This must be your handsome husband." After putting a scissors into his left hand, Javier extended his right hand.

"Hi." Stan was enthralled. He'd never imagined this when he showed up.

Another heavily made up plastic-looking woman handed him a bottle of sparkling water and rolled in a stool for him.

"Thanks." Stan sat down and opened the screw-top of the bottle. He gazed at Mark being pampered as he guzzled the expensive water.

Before the woman left, she asked, "More coffee, Mark?"

"No. Ta…How was the recording studio?" Mark asked as the woman left.

Javier clipped just the tips of Mark's wet hair, sending small dark bits of fluff to the floor.

"Good. Easy." Stan wondered if Mark was nude under the robe. He had a peek at his own fingernails.

~

Mark chuckled as he watched Stan. The young man looked like he had landed on Mars. Once a month, Mark had his chest waxed, his pubes trimmed, a facial, a mani-pedi, and a haircut.

The two women finished his nails and took their kits out of the room. Javier stopped clipping and blew Mark's hair dry, using his fingers to style.

Stan watched in the noise, holding the bottle between his knees.

Mark was glad he had come to LA because he wanted to be with his husband.

Javier fussed with Mark's thick brown hair, sprayed an aromatic sheen product on it, and then removed a small towel he had placed behind Mark's neck.

"Splendid." Mark inspected his style.

"Perfection." Javier touched the waves of Mark's hair.

Mark stood from the chair and kissed Javier, then he beckoned Stan with him to the dressing room. Stan left his empty bottle and closed the door behind him.

Mark hung up the robe, then stood naked in front of a full-length mirror. He noticed Stan licking his lips in desire.

Mark spun around to face him. "Hullo, baby."

"Oh, geez." Stan squeezed his own crotch.

Mark rested his arms on Stan's broad shoulders. "So? The ADR? The commercial? All went well?"

"Huh?" Stan shifted his weight from leg to leg and held Mark's sides. "Fuck."

Smiling, knowing Stan was in heat, Mark chuckled. "So, you'll take me to Dr Love and my agent, yes?"

"Fuck." Stan went in for a sniff of Mark's neck. "Oh, fuck."

"Then, maybe I can take my big man to lunch. Did you already work out?"

Stan chewed on Mark's neck, cupping Mark's bottom in his large hands.

"Love?"

"I can't think right now. All my blood has gone to my dick." Stan ran his fingers down Mark's ass crack.

STARTING OVER

"You naughty boy." Mark reached to the door and turned the lock on the knob. He slowly crouched down until he was at eye level with an imposing bulge in Stan's tight jeans.

~

Stan was so excited, he was about to come in his pants.

Mark kissed his cock through the material, then as he opened Stan's pants, he gazed up at him.

Seeing Mark's emerald green eyes, his skin glowing, his hair full like a lion's mane, Stan bit his lower lip and his respirations heightened.

Mark exposed Stan's stiff length from his clothing. He touched just the base with two fingers and sucked the head into his mouth. Mark's gaze was still on his, his eyes showing his wicked delight.

"Fuck…" His legs shaking, Stan came. It took nothing.

Mark closed his eyes and swallowed the load. He hummed and used his tongue in the slit, then smiled up at him. "All better?"

"Get the fuck up here." Stan grabbed Mark's shoulders and drew him to his feet, then went for Mark's mouth. Tasting his own cum, Stan dug his fingers into Mark's feathery soft hair and whimpered in agony.

There may come a day when he grew used to being married to this gorgeous man. But, that day had not yet come.

But…he certainly had.

Mark parted from the scorching kiss. "Let me dress."

Stan slowed down his libido and caught his breath. While Mark put on his designer clothing, Stan tucked his –still-hard-cock into his pants and struggled with the zipper.

"Uh…I didn't work out yet…um. Sure. Lunch would be fine."

Mark cracked up with laughter as he tucked his shirt into his pants. "The blood returning to your brain?"

Stan laughed with him. "I can't help it. Every time I'm with you, I'm on fire."

Mark shot him a sexy smile. He sat to put on his socks and shoes, checked his phone, and then nodded he was ready.

Stan opened the door for him and they walked to the front desk.

"Everything okay, Mark?" the young woman asked.

Mark handed her his credit card. "Yes."

"Would you like the same appointment next month?"

Mark took a second to think. "All right."

Stan glanced back at the people in the waiting room looking curiously at him while overtly ogling Mark. Most, if not all, of the fashion and glamour magazines had their ads in them. Not to mention, Mark was on billboards all over Hollywood.

Stan used one finger to hold onto Mark's belt loop, feeling like a million bucks. And, Mark Antonious? He looked like a million bucks.

"Ta, love." Mark hooked Stan's elbow and they left the salon, out into the summer heat.

A valet rushed towards them. Stan gave the man his stub and the young man raced off.

"Doctor's appointment now." Mark checked his phone.

"Anything you want." Stan pulled him into an embrace.

"Are you finished here in LA? Hmm?" Mark used the tip of his index finger to pet Stan's sideburn as they rocked gently.

"I think so. Are we headed to Paradise?"

"I need to be there. *We* need to be there."

"Whatever you want."

The Lamborghini purred as it pulled up. The young man jumped out, and raced to the passenger's side, opening the door for Mark.

Stan gave the young man a tip and sat down behind the wheel.

STARTING OVER

Mark read his phone for the address. "Right. Dr Love."
Stan fastened his seatbelt and shifted gear, grinning excitedly since he and Mark were together again.

Chapter 3

Tadzio peered into a brightly lit office. Designers were working on fashion concepts both on computer programs and with gouache paints and black pens.

Steve escorted him into the space. "Can I have everyone's attention?"

Tadzio felt shy and lowered his head.

"This is Tadzio Andresen. My husband."

The group of men and women stood up and reached out their hands. "Love your runway work!"

"So nice to meet you!"

"That Vera Wang gown you wore for Mark's wedding was gorgeous!"

Tadzio tried to smile but he was not a fashion designer.

"Tadzio may be interested in seeing how you guys work." Steve had his hand on Tadzio's upper back. "He hasn't decided what he wants to do, but he does enjoy fashion." Steve kissed him. "I'll come back for you in an hour."

"Okay, Steven."

"Take care of my man." Steve smiled, waved, and left.

Tadzio felt awkward and anxious.

One of the young men waved him to a computer. "Tadzio. Come sit here."

Tadzio ran his hand through his blond hair nervously and admired the posters of top designers' drawings on the walls, pushpins in sketches, fabric swatches and patterns.

STARTING OVER

"Have you ever used this program?" the young man asked, pointing to the screen.

"I have not."

"Greg? Maybe he'd rather draw on paper for now."

"Or, he can help us decide on a design for the college scholarship winner."

"Tadzio?" Greg asked.

Tadzio looked around at the dozen designers, all staring at him. "A pen? Yes?"

"You bet." Greg chuckled and gestured to a table with hundreds of colored paints to choose from.

Tadzio relocated to the sketch table and sat on a stool.

"Have fun." Greg smiled at him and returned to his own desk.

Before he picked up a thing, Tadzio sent Alex a text, '*You will come to the estate?*' He missed him.

He sent Billy one next, '*When you can come?*'

Neither man sent him one back. Tadzio sighed and observed the group for a few minutes before he found the courage to do anything at all.

~

Billy stood in the back of a stark white room with rows of rectangular desks. The scent of the space was a mix of musky deodorant, gun oil, and sweat. It was filled with big men, young men, men insane enough to want to be in SWAT. The acting lieutenant had been quietly informed he was going to be replaced.

A sergeant who was conducting a briefing on a potential threat of civil disobedience stopped talking. His eyes widened and he shouted, "Sharpe!"

The men in the room spun around in their chairs. A roar of pleasure, like a military 'hurrah!' erupted and Billy was surrounded in men.

His old SWAT buddies, Manny Rodriguez, Bernie Brown, and Jim Hague patted his back enthusiastically.

"You assholes are still in this shitty squad?" Billy teased his best friends.

"Fuck yeah!" Jim puffed up proudly. "Beats what you're doin', ya douche!"

"Wanna know what I'm doin'?" Billy grinned in excitement.

"Recruiting for Santa Monica's sad bastards?" Bernie laughed.

"Nope." Billy crossed his arms over his chest. "Want me back?"

A look of astonishment washed over the men in the room.

"Shut the fuck up!" Jim Hague shouted.

As the men realized it, Billy was mauled with hugs and high-fives.

"Knew you'd come back!" Manny shouted over the noise. "Knew it!"

As the men in the room showed him just how much they loved him, Billy felt redeemed. He was back where he belonged. Back on the front lines.

~

Alex had a break for lunch. Standing outside of the studio set he sent Billy a text, '*How did the DA go?*'

Anxiety hit Alex, worrying for Billy. He read a message from Tadzio and sent him, '*I'm back taping at the TV studio, so, can't come.*' He didn't think he was welcome at the estate anyway.

He brought his dad's contact information up and stared at it. The sense that he had lost him was killing Alex.

He leaned his back against a wall and tried to keep his emotions under wraps. He had an appointment with his shrink tomorrow, but considered canceling it since he was fed up with not only Dr Van Eldon, but himself.

STARTING OVER

He did need more valium, however. So, he'd go to get more pills and sit through the bullshit.

"Alex?" his costar Kerry waved to him. "They have lunch ready."

"Okay." Alex tried to adjust his attitude and approached Kerry.

"How did *Snapped* do on its opening weekend?" Kerry asked as they walked to where their food was being served.

Alex hadn't even thought about his bonus. "Huh." He sent Adam a text, '*Did Snapped hit the projected numbers this weekend?*'

Assuming Adam had to look it up first before he answered, Alex and Kerry walked to the front of the chow line and picked up plates. They were served hot food and salad, rolls and a beverage.

Alex's phone chimed. He set his plate down with Kerry's on a small table and read, '*Close. Maybe.*' Alex showed Kerry the text.

"I didn't see very many advertisements for it." Kerry ate his roll. "Did you hit the talk show circuit?"

"Jeremy did. I was in New York for *Lover Boy.*"

Kerry snickered.

"What?" Alex asked as he tried the ravioli.

"The gossip rags are all over that one. You and Stan."

A cold chill of terror raced over Alex. "Nothing happened."

"I know that. But they love a scandal."

"What are they saying?" Alex felt pale.

"Huh?" Kerry held his fork near his mouth. "The usual. That you two had sex."

"We didn't." Alex shook his head adamantly.

"I know that!" Kerry laughed. "Alex. They used to say you and your dad shared Billy. It's all a load of shit."

"Oh. Right." Alex tried to pretend he was kidding. He tasted the food and wondered if his nutty behavior was creating a lack of interest in his films.

~

Mark pressed a cold pack to his face.

"Usual aftercare, Mark, nothing strenuous and don't rub." Dr Love washed his hands at a small sink in the exam room.

"Yes." Mark sighed and held the icepack on his lap. "This may be my last. I'm needed elsewhere. I can't keep modeling."

Dr Love faced Mark, smiling at him. "You don't need this shit. I keep telling you that."

"Do shut up." Mark climbed off the table and poked the doctor in the shoulder playfully.

The doctor took the icepack and threw it away. He opened the door and said, "See ya next time."

"You really are a cutup, aren't you?" Mark narrowed his eyes at him and removed his wallet as he approached the women behind a counter.

Dr Love laughed at him and entered another exam room.

Stan was in the waiting room with a magazine on his lap, and spotted him. He stood from the chair and dropped the magazine on the table.

Mark handed over his credit card and put his sunglasses on.

"Here ya go, Mark."

He signed the slip and took back his card and receipt. "Ta, love."

Stan opened the door and Mark avoided looking at the two women waiting to see the doctor.

Stan and he walked out of the clinic and into the parking lot. Stan opened the Lamborghini door for Mark and closed it, then sat in the driver's seat.

"Right." Mark exhaled loudly. "Arnold Newhouse."

"Can we stop for lunch first?"

STARTING OVER

"I'm not showing my face in public like this." Mark flipped the visor down and had a look. He was a little red, but that was all.

"I can't tell you've had anything done." Stan backed out of the parking space.

"That's the idea, love." Mark pushed the visor back up and sank in the bucket seat. "Arnold shall only take a short while, then we'll get my hungry man food." Mark ran his hand over Stan's thigh.

"Are we spending the night in Bel Air?" Stan asked as he checked the address of Mark's modeling agent.

"I don't mind if you'd rather be in West Hollywood." Mark sent Steve a text, *'How is it going?'*

'No issues. A huge order came in from Bellatory. Mark? it's 20K.'

Mark sent Steve, *'yes. I know about it. Check with Fiera. She has a special order from Ralph Lauren.'*

'Okay. You coming back this evening?'

Mark wanted to. He wanted to ride his horse. He glanced at Stan as he drove. Stan smiled at him.

Mark asked, "What do you have planned for this week that is here in LA?"

Stan appeared to think about his answer.

"Baby?" Mark rubbed Stan's thigh briskly.

"Tadzio set up auditions for me before he quit. But."

"But?" Mark let his fingers rest on Stan's cock over his zipper.

"I'm not auditioning. If I do, I run the risk of getting a role."

Mark held back a noise of surprise. "You do realize that is why actors audition. To get a role."

"No." Stan rested his hand over Mark's on his crotch. "I'm not getting dragged away from you."

"I see." Mark smiled in delight. "Then, why don't we go to the estate this evening?"

"Drive?" Stan gestured to his car.

"Oh, heavens no." Mark felt his phone vibrate.

"Then, leave my car in the garage in Bel Air?"

"Pet? It will be safe there."

"Okay." Stan shrugged. He pulled into the parking lot of Mark's modeling agent.

Mark waited until he parked, then he unfastened the seatbelt and turned to face him. "Talk to me. You must communicate your feelings." Mark removed his sunglasses.

Stan did the same, unhooking the belt and turning his knees towards Mark. "No car? I can't have my car there?"

"Love? We have a driver and hire car at our disposal."

"And, I'm going to work with you? As your PA?"

"No?"

Stan's gaze became distant.

Sensing Stan had to think about his decisions, Mark patted his thigh. "Come. Let me talk to Arnold and then we'll discuss us." Mark opened the door and climbed out.

Stan did as well, and used his key fob to lock the doors. As he and Mark entered the small office building, Mark glanced back at the sleek sports car. Was it any wonder his young husband was attached to it? Stan had been in love with his classic Ford Mustang, babying it. Now he had a new pretty toy.

He pulled Stan back from the lobby door to speak quietly. "How about this?" He connected their groins, pressing close. "We'll stay in your place overnight, see your mates…then tomorrow, we'll head up with your car."

The light returned to Stan's hazel eyes. "That sounds perfect."

"Give us a kiss."

STARTING OVER

Stan cupped Mark's head over his hair and gave him a scorching kiss.

Mark laughed when they parted and patted Stan's tight rump as Stan turned to open the door for him.

~

Stan entered the dim interior of the lobby. Mark's modeling agent was not Adam Lewis, not by a long-shot.

Adam had a posh office in a high-rise tower in downtown LA. Arnold Newhouse had an entire, tiny, office building outside of the city center. Real estate was cheaper here. The structure appeared dated, as if it were built in the 1960s, with a need for upgrading and paint.

Stan was a little surprised Mark's agent wasn't a major player in the field. An older woman was seated at a desk and greeted Mark sweetly.

"Hi, Mr Richfield."

"Hullo, love." Mark clasped her hand.

"Arnold's expecting you."

"Thank you." Mark opened the door to an office.

Stan waved shyly at the older woman and she smiled at him. As Mark entered the office, Stan realized all of the framed posters in the lobby were of Mark's cologne ads. There was no doubt Mark Richfield was this small agency's top man.

The inner office was modest, loaded with file cabinets, windows with the blinds drawn shut, and a scent of dust or age.

Arnold Newhouse, a man easily in his late sixties/early seventies, stood from his chair. He was a rotund fellow, in a suit and tie, his head was bald, and he had heavy jowls and a happy smile.

"Hullo, Arnold." Mark reached both hands to clasp his, patting it affectionately.

"Mark. Have a seat." Arnold peered around Mark to Stan. "Stan. Nice to meet you. Congratulations on your marriage."

Stan shook the man's hand.

"Sit." Arnold gestured to two worn wooden chairs across from his desk.

Mark took a seat and moved his sunglasses to hang on his shirt collar. "How much longer is my contract with *Dangereux*?"

"It's up for renewal this year." Arnold moved a file in front of Mark across his cluttered desk.

Stan interlaced his fingers and gazed at the framed posters on the walls. Most were of Mark; his cover photo for the World's Most Beautiful Man, and his early ads for *Dangereux*, including one with his son and horses. *Is that Piccadilly?* Stan wondered.

"Love?" Mark pouted at Arnold.

Arnold smiled knowingly. "It's okay, Mark. I'm retiring."

There was no question in Stan's mind that Arnold Newhouse's living wage was derived from this top model. No doubt at all. Mark was enshrined in this place as a god.

"Are you sure?" Mark asked quietly, as if he were concerned.

"Yes. It's time to enjoy the grandkids."

Stan glanced at Arnold as he spoke to Mark. It felt like a father to a son, very sweet, intimate.

"I could ask Alexander if he would like to continue in my stead." Mark rested his elbow on Arnold's desk.

"No need." Arnold shook his head. "The wife and I are going to go on a long cruise. She wants me home before I can't travel any longer."

"So, TJ and Bob haven't harangued you for a new face?"

"I haven't spoken to them about it. They can't replace you, Mark."

Stan stood from the chair to investigate the photos on the walls. Mark appeared to have been modeling for other companies, looking like Alex with his long hair. Those ads must have been years ago. *How on earth did this guy get Mark's contract?*

STARTING OVER

"As long as I'm not creating a hardship for you, Arnold."

"Not at all. I've done well with you, Mark. I'm grateful for all you've done for me."

Stan was enthralled with how many ads Mark had created before *Dangereux* signed him exclusively. Dozens of ads for a car manufacturer, some so racy, they were R-rated; Mark looking orgasmic in the front seat of sports cars with his cock showing through spandex pants. One even had Mark in a red bikini.

When the conversation became quiet, Stan peered at the two men. They were smiling at him.

"Sorry." Stan stuffed his hands into his pants' pockets.

Arnold gave Stan a knowing grin. "Would you like the photographs?"

"Huh?" Stan would.

"Mark? I was going to offer them to you." Arnold gestured to the walls of framed advertisements from Mark's long career.

Stan asked, "Are you going to throw them out?"

Mark stood from his chair and had a look at them with Stan. "Oh, my. You have those ads from the car company."

Stan couldn't believe he'd not seen them. They were so overtly sexual, he was getting a little excited.

"I have all of your work." Arnold stood from his chair and buttoned his suit jacket as he joined them. "A trip down memory lane."

"Can I have them?" Stan wanted them.

"You bet you can." Arnold chuckled.

"What shall we do with them?" Mark asked.

"I'll figure it out." Stan imagined a wall of Mark's photographs in the estate, maybe in the den or study.

"Take them." Arnold gestured to the wall. "Kate?" he called to the door.

His secretary peeked into the office. "Yes?"

"Can you find a carton for Mark's photographs?"

"I'm sure I can." She smiled and walked off.

Stan had a look at each: *Mark in gold spandex? In front of a gold sports car?* He couldn't believe Mark's hard cock was visible through the material.

Arnold began taking the photos down.

Mark backed up and appeared to be preoccupied.

"How's this?" Kate brought in a large cardboard box.

"Fine." Arnold stacked the framed photos into it.

Stan helped until they had them all. There were dozens of them.

"Would you like the posters from the lobby?" Arnold asked.

"Yes!" Stan recalled the first time he'd seen Mark's ads. He had kept all of the ones he'd found, jerking off to them as a teen.

Stan rubbed his palms on his pants, since some of the frames were dusty. He glanced at Mark. Mark's skin wasn't even red any longer. There was no trace of his treatment.

"Okay?" Stan asked him.

Saying nothing, Mark gave him a slight nod.

Stan took another frame off the wall and stood by Mark with it. "They waited for you to get hard?" he whispered.

"It's a dildo, love."

Stan's smile fell. "What?"

"I could not get hard. They had me shove a dildo into my trousers."

Seeing Mark appearing slightly distressed, Stan had no idea what to say. He placed the frame into the box and carried the carton to the lobby, where Arnold and Kate had removed a few more framed ads.

Stan glanced at Mark as they did, wondering what on earth it would have been like to pose for an ad for a car, with a fucking phallus shoved into your crotch.

STARTING OVER

He managed to pack the photos into his Lamborghini. Once he and Mark were seated in the car, Stan asked, "How did Arnold sign a guy like you?"

Mark put his sunglasses on and fastened his seatbelt. "I was unknown when he did. I did freelance work. He had me working with all sorts of clients."

Stan rested his hand on the gear shift as the car rumbled under his bottom. "Judging by your expression, I'm guessing it wasn't the good ole' days."

"Hardly." Mark touched his forehead lightly and brushed his hair back from it.

"What magazines did those racy car ads show up in?"

"Men's motor magazines. They were not published in fashion or glamour."

"They're very homoerotic for men's mags." Stan shifted into reverse and unlocked the emergency brake.

Mark made a noise in his throat.

Stan had a feeling Mark had some stories to tell about his early modeling career. Some, perhaps, not good ones.

As Stan backed out of the space, he said, "So, the car company, *Dangereux*, what else?"

"I had one disastrous shoot at a seedy apartment for Sun-Spec sunglasses."

"I've heard of them. They were a short-lived sport sunglasses line." Stan paused before entering the traffic on the main street.

"Yes, well." Mark shifted in his seat. "I was assaulted and Billy Sharpe, who had been a sergeant for the SWAT division of the LAPD, came to my rescue."

Stan's jaw hung open. "Assaulted?"

"I was roughed up. He and his men kicked in the door, mistaking it for a drug house. That was how I met Billy."

"Holy shit."

Mark glanced at him. "That's why when *Dangereux* offered, I jumped at it. I didn't have the heart to leave Arnold. He has always been a nice man. Good to me."

Stan ran his hand over Mark's leg. "You're my hero."

Mark let out an ironic laugh. "Right. What now, my pet?"

Stan merged into traffic. "There's so much I don't know about you."

"We'll learn more as we go. No worries."

Stan glanced over at him as he drove, wondering what life was like as the World's Most Beautiful Man.

~

Billy left the LAPD SWAT unit feeling his elation drop like a stone. He drove to another administrative building and parked. Before he climbed out of his police cruiser, he took a moment to decompress.

He had been asked to spend the July 4th celebration with his family, which consisted of his two sisters: divorced Tammy and married Kim. Tammy's son, Matt, had finished his tour in the military and was now a cadet in the academy, having been hired by the Los Angeles Police.

He didn't have a good relationship with either sister.

After his own military service, they had shunned him. Tammy had kept Matt away from him, as if being gay was contagious and Matt would become gay if he associated with him.

He didn't want to see them. With the disruption to his life right now, the idea of pretending to be fine and socializing with people he didn't even know any longer, annoyed him. He held his phone and located his sister Tammy's details.

He sent her, '*Alex and I are both going to be working over the holiday. Sorry. We can't go.*'

All he got back was '*K*'. Not, sorry to miss seeing you, not, be careful working the streets for the Fourth.

STARTING OVER

Neither sibling gave a shit about him. If they ever had.

As Billy tried to prepare himself for his interview with media relations to craft his resignation speech, he thought of Mark. Mark.

He fucking needed him.

After peering around the area of his police cruiser, Billy sent Mark a text, '*are you there?*'

'*Yes.*'

A lump formed in Billy's throat. '*In Sac?*'

'*No. LA.*'

"Thank fuck." Billy called him.

"Hullo, love."

Hearing Mark's soft deep voice, Billy rubbed his face in agony. "Where are you?"

"I've just come from my modeling agent's office. What do you need?"

"You. I fucking need you." Billy shifted his body on the seat, the firearm on his hip digging into him.

"All right."

"Fuck." Billy struggled to face that miserable resignation. Battled to deal with the press and public interpreting what he was doing as a defeat, a blow to his ego, a demotion, punishment, admission of guilt and more thug-police behavior.

"Love? Where are you? Are you at home?"

Billy looked at the county building, the flags whipping in the wind: Old Glory and the California State flag.

"Chief?"

Billy climbed out of the patrol car and walked to the street. He gazed up and down the block, spotting a coffee shop. "Can you meet me?"

"Of course. Where?"

The phone to his ear, avoiding gawkers, Billy read the address on the café. He relayed it to Mark.

"I can be there shortly. But, love? I'm not alone."

"Who're you with?" Billy stood with his back to the glass front of the coffee shop, gazing at the pedestrian and vehicle traffic on the boulevard.

"Stan."

"Oh. Okay. It's fine."

"On my way."

"Thanks." Billy pocketed the phone and waited, needing someone to support him, someone he loved, someone he counted on. And, that someone, was Mark.

STARTING OVER

Chapter 4

Tadzio didn't like anything he was drawing. How Steve thought he could do this was a mystery. He left his sketches on the desk and had a look at the other designers. Seeing them working on computer programs, Tadzio became mesmerized.

As Greg worked, he dropped and dragged different fabric colors and options onto his elongated model figure.

Tadzio gave up. "Thank you. I think I will go."

Greg stopped working and faced him. "Can I see your designs?"

"Iz not like this." Tadzio pointed to the computer screen. "I am ama-ture."

Greg stood from his chair and walked closer to Tadzio's desk. He picked up several of the sketches. "Wow."

"I can go." Tadzio pointed to the hallway. "Thank you." He left the office and felt hungry. Tadzio made his way down the long well-lit corridor, seeing a potted palm tree and a wooden bench under a row of framed awards for excellence.

He sat on the bench and sent Alex a text, '*I wish I have you hear.*'

Nothing came back from Alex. Tadzio knew when Alex was at the studio, he didn't have his phone on.

Sinking emotionally, Tadzio had a feeling not working for Adam, not acting, not doing anything, was going to upset him. Yes, he loved the big house, but…doing nothing?

He scrolled through his contacts out of boredom. Seeing Stan's friends listed, Tadzio remembered something. He sent Becca a text, '*You are gay?*'

A text came back, '*Did you mean to send me that?*'

'*Yes. Becka. You are gay?*'

'*Can I ask why you are asking?*'

'*I have woman you will like. I can match you?*' Tadzio looked up as two older women in business attire walked by, each carrying material swatches and discussing placing orders.

Tadzio paid attention to their outfits, knew the designers instantly by their trademark styles. They were chic, and appeared impressive in their smart skirts and blazers. He kept watching as they passed, looking at their leather pumps, their jewelry and their hair styles.

'*You want to set me up with someone?*' Becca texted.

'*I wood like to. She iz very pretty nice.*'

'*Who is she? Is she a friend of yours?*'

'*Yes. She is good for you.*'

'*I guess so.*'

Tadzio smiled. '*Good!!! I thin you will so like each odder!*'

'*You're silly. Do you want to come out to dinner with the gang this week?*'

'*I am in north. I am not in Angelez.*'

'*Darn. Is the woman also north?*'

'*No. She iz same plus you.*'

'*Okay. I've gotta go.*'

Tadzio lowered his phone and tried to remember where Steve's office was. He stood from the bench and walked to the stairs, then headed one level up. Tadzio searched the hallway and grew lost. He sent Steve a text, '*I cannot find.*'

Another chic woman in a gorgeous skirt and blazer outfit, carrying files, walked by him.

"Pardon? I can't find Steven."

STARTING OVER

She looked up from her armload of paper. "Mr Miller?"
"Yes."
She pointed to the end of the long hall. "His office is right there."
"Yes." Tadzio nodded. "I see it. Thank you."
Just as Tadzio made his way, Steve emerged, holding his phone. He spotted Tadzio. "I was coming to get you."
"I lose my way for a moment. But, here you are."
"Let's get a bite to eat." Steve put his arm around Tadzio.
Tadzio reciprocated, his arm around Steve, and held tight. "I don't know, Steven. I don't know if this is what I want."
"It's okay, babe. Take your time." Steve squeezed him affectionately with one arm. "How does the deli sound?"
"Iz good. Yes."
Steve stood at an elevator with Tadzio. Tadzio checked his phone and wished Alex would text him. He was losing his mind without him.

~

Stan located the café Billy had suggested. Mark drew the visor down and inspected his face, removing his sunglasses.
"Mark? You look fine. Not red."
Mark patted Stan's thigh in appreciation.
"Should I hang here?"
"I have no idea what the chief needs me for." Mark unfastened his seatbelt. "He didn't say you should not be here."
"Is this about Alex?" Stan asked, moving with the crawling traffic as lunch hour loomed.
"My impression was no." Mark searched out of the passenger's window. "There he is." Mark pointed.
Indeed, the muscular Chief of Police was waiting, in uniform, and had spotted the green Aventador.
"What should I do?" Stan pulled closer to the curb, into an available metered space.

Billy approached the car. Mark lowered the window.

Stan waited. When Billy leaned into the open window, Stan immediately saw his expression of concern. "Mark? Go. I'll walk around and kill time."

"Hi, Stan."

"Hi, Billy."

Mark leaned over to Stan and kissed him. "I'll text you."

"Okay."

Billy opened the car door for Mark and Mark climbed out. Stan double-checked the parking spot for warning signs, then he shut off the car. Mark and Billy walked to the café, and Billy opened the glass door for the top model.

Stan checked his console and pockets for change. He exited his car, fed the meter so he had an hour, and had a look around the area.

He oriented himself, and then took a walk, letting the beleaguered chief find solace in Mark.

~

Mark moved his sunglasses to the top of his head. Inside the noisy coffee shop, he and Billy waited their turn in line.

So many people were holding up their phones at them, it was distracting.

As he and Mark were given the barista's attention, Mark said, "Double espresso. Tall."

"Got it, Mark." The barista already knew exactly who they were.

Billy ordered, "Iced frap, large."

Before Mark paid, Billy handed the clerk a twenty.

Both men stood away from the chaos as they waited for their coffees. Mark didn't prod Billy. He wanted to allow the man to gather his thoughts.

STARTING OVER

Once they received their drinks, Billy gestured for them to leave the packed café, and get away from the racket and phone-cameras.

Billy held open the door, and he and Mark sipped their beverages as they strolled the sidewalk along the bustling street traffic.

The chief gestured to a small park, one with benches under shade trees. Pigeons pecked at pebbles on the ground, scattering at their approach, while litter blew against the low retaining walls.

Mark inspected the wooden bench and then sat on it, drinking his strong coffee. His sunglasses were back on his nose.

Since Billy was in uniform, pedestrians peered at him curiously.

"Mark."

Mark shifted on the bench so he could see Billy more easily.

"So, what are you guys doing in LA?"

"Love? No need for small talk." Mark rested his cup on his knee, taking off the plastic lid to let it cool.

Billy exhaled and wiped his hand on his dark blue trousers from the condensation of his iced drink. "I was asked by the DA to resign in order to not be charged with property damage."

Mark felt as if he were punched in the gut. He winced.

"He insists I give a public statement about it. I'm supposed to record it with media relations for airing on the news." Billy sipped the frap, taking off the lid, not using a straw.

Mark gazed at the passing car traffic as his mind spun with thoughts.

"I'm humiliated."

Mark held his stomach and battled for strength.

Billy shifted his position on the bench to face him. "Mark. Was what I did that fucked up?"

Mark moved his sunglasses to the top of his head, since he needed Billy to be able to look into his eyes. "No, love. But, you are under a microscope. If civilian Billy Sharpe had done it, no one would have said a peep."

"I fucked up. I fucked my goddamn career up." Billy set the iced coffee on the bench beside him and wiped his hands.

"There was no wiggle room? No negotiation?" Mark drank the cooled espresso down quickly.

"No. The DA tried. Defending myself with a physical act against a verbal assault…well, even I know that's excessive. I became the villain I was trying to fire."

"No. No." Mark shook his head. "Do not equate yourself with that despicable rookie. I won't permit it."

~

Billy sipped more of his frappuccino. He stared at Mark for a long moment. "I can't do it. I can't walk through that door and make a video of me resigning."

Mark rested his hand on Billy's thigh. "I take it you have no choice."

"They won't let me do it quietly. I'll be crucified in the media if I somehow slip away."

"Oh, my pet." Mark rubbed Billy's leg. "Life is so very hard. Challenges we face constantly…" Mark shook his head, his long hair blowing in the wind. "It's enough to wear a man down to a nub."

Billy rested his hand on Mark's, squeezing it.

"What can I do? Tell me. Anything." Mark brought Billy's hand to his lips to kiss lightly.

Billy gazed into Mark's green eyes. "Come with me. Let me see you when I read my statement."

"Yes. Absolutely." Mark nodded emphatically.

"Let me pretend I'm just telling you. Help me forget what I'm doing and get lost in your eyes."

STARTING OVER

"Yes."

Billy checked the time. "I'm late."

"I am with you. I am with you for as long as you need me."

Standing, Billy threw their empty cups into a waste bin. "Where's Stan?"

"He took a walk so we could chat." Mark got to his feet and put his sunglasses back on his nose.

"Can he do without you for another hour?" Billy adjusted his gun-belt on his hip.

"Yes." Mark interlaced their fingers. "Where are we going?"

"There." Billy pointed to the office building.

Mark nodded. On their walk to the administrative office, Mark put the phone to his ear. "Love? Perhaps you can get your workout in." Mark peered at Billy as they went. "I am going to accompany the chief for an hour…Yes, he'll drive me home."

Billy paused at the lobby door.

Mark brushed his long hair out of his face. "Yes. Thank you, pet. I do appreciate you understanding…love you too." Mark pocketed the phone. "I'm all yours."

If only.

Billy opened the glass door and led Mark to the elevator.

The two of them stood quietly as they waited for it.

Mark clasped Billy's hand and interlaced their fingers. They entered the elevator together, alone, and Billy poked the correct button for the floor.

Mark pulled him into an embrace and rocked him. "This too, shall pass."

Billy pressed his face into Mark's fragrant hair and closed his eyes.

~

"Adam Lewis, can I help you?" Adam tapped his earpiece.

"Adam! Charlotte Deavers."

Adam rocked in his chair. "Well! Hello, there. What can I do for you, busy lady?" He smiled.

"You represent Mark, correct?"

Trying to read between the lines, Adam thought about it. "No. His modeling agent is Arnold Newhouse."

"Acting, pumpkin. Not modeling."

"I don't have Mark's contract. I don't think he has one for acting. Why?" Adam moved his mouse and opened up a file checking to see if Mark was listed as one of the men in his stable of actors.

"Will and Derek want him back for our final season. It seems fitting since he was in our first."

Adam laughed. "Oh, boy."

"He hasn't returned my calls. Do you know if Mark's available?"

"I have no idea. He recently purchased his family's estate up north in Paradise. You heard he owns Richfield-Miller International, right?"

"I don't keep up with the world of high finance."

"Why don't you send me the script and I'll see to it he gets it."

"Thanks, Adam. I knew I could count on you."

"Don't be shocked if he says no." Adam opened his email box.

"Mark, saying no? Never!" She laughed.

Shaking his head, Adam spotted the email with the attachment. "So? Nude? In bed with Keith and Carl?"

"You already read it?" She cracked up with laughter.

"Okay. I'll check it out. Char, is this really the last season for *Forever Young*?"

"It is. We had a good run."

"You did. Any awards coming your way?"

STARTING OVER

"I doubt it. We've been around for too long. We're ignored by the illuminati."

Adam thought about finding work for Keith. Carl he had no problem with. "Hey, if you hear anything out there in TV land that would suit Keith, will you give me a heads up?"

"Yes."

"Thanks, Char." Adam opened the attachment with the script. "And, thank you for being the go-between for Mark."

"No problem. How's Alex been doing lately?"

"Okay. We're just now back at the studio. He seems fine."

"Good. His last movie, *Lover Boy,* wrapped."

"The amount of horseshit spinning around Alex and Stan in the rags is vile. I can't even look at them at the checkout line."

"I don't either." Adam shook his head in irritation.

"Later."

"Later." Adam disconnected the call and took a moment to read the television script. When he read what they wanted from Mark, he doubled over with laughter and dabbed at his eyes.

Natalie poked her head into his office. "You okay?"

Adam caught his breath and sent Mark a text, '*you have got to play a role on Forever Young. It's perfect for you.*' He looked up at Natalie. "Charlotte Deavers just called. They want Mark to appear on the season finale of *Forever Young*." He wiped at his eyes. "Fucking priceless."

Natalie smiled. "I love that show. I'm so pissed off they're cancelling it."

"Oh, fuck." Adam kept chuckling and sent the script to both Mark and Jack. "Richfield...he's either going to love or hate it."

"Can I read it?" Natalie giggled.

Adam sent it to her computer. "Have fun."

She rubbed her hands together eagerly and before she took a look at it she asked, "Do you know a friend of Tadzio's named Becca?"

"Yes." Adam noticed more phone lines light up, hearing Logan answering them and putting them on hold.

"Is she nice?"

"Yes. She's very nice. Why?"

"Tadzio's fixing us up."

Adam blinked. "You and Becca? Is she gay?"

"I assume so." Natalie shrugged.

Adam thought about telling Natalie that Becca was going to be Mark and Stan's surrogate, but…was it his place to do that?

He smiled tightly. "She's a good kid."

"Kid?" Natalie asked in surprise.

"I don't know. Twenty something. Anyone under thirty is a kid to me." Adam shook his head.

"Oh. Okay." Natalie returned to her desk and both of them picked up a holding line.

~

Mark placed his phone on vibrate as he stood near a back wall.

The small conference room was filling up.

Billy, holding paperwork in his hand, was seated in the front of the room at a desk as a microphone was placed in front of him.

A representative of the police guild was there, talking quietly to him, a lawyer from the union was also present, as was a cameraman from the police media relations.

Mark received a few raised eyebrows at his presence, and he returned them with scowls.

No outside media, no television crews, no questions were going to be asked.

A bottle of water was placed near the chief, and he nodded, his reading glasses on, the single sheet of paper in his hand.

"Ready?" his guild representative asked.

Billy responded, "Yes."

STARTING OVER

The lawyer leaned out of the door of the small room and into the hall. "Come in."

Mark rested his back against far wall in a room with no windows. Posters about 'aspiring to be your best' were on the walls, which was ridiculous irony in his opinion. Since, the best man for the job, was being asked to resign.

Two civilians were escorted into the room, an older man and woman, dressed casually, yet with an air of menace.

More men in suits entered as well, and Mark had no idea who these people could be.

His focus was on the chief.

Billy removed his glasses for a moment, as if assessing the room occupants. He met Mark's gaze. Mark gave him a determined expression, trying to send positive vibes out.

It grew quiet.

The man working the video camera said, "Whenever you're ready."

The guild rep said, "Chief Sharpe?"

Billy put his reading glasses back on, held the paperwork, and then gazed at Mark for a moment.

Mark kept still, in full view of Billy, behind the two civilians who had been directed to their seats.

"This conference has been called," Billy began, "for me to tender my resignation. It has been my honor to serve the men and women of the Santa Monica Police Department…"

Mark ground his jaw in rage as he listened to what was impossible for him to swallow. *These morons don't know what they are losing.*

"…as the chief of police, it was my job to set a shining example. I realize an err in judgment changed that. I apologize to the men and women of the department and to the community I had the honor to serve." Billy stared directly at Mark, offering his words to Mark, and Mark alone. "It is with deep regret that I am leaving my position as chief, effective immediately. Thank you." Billy set the page down and his stare on Mark did not waiver.

"Cut."

Billy stood, moving away from the table, taking off his glasses.

Mark took a step towards him.

Ignoring the noise, the conversations around him, Billy reached out his hand.

Mark clasped it.

"My God. Is that his queer husband?" the older woman said with a sneer, "That's disgusting."

Rage ignited in Mark instantly. He was about to offer his rebuttal, but Billy escorted him out.

"Who was that nasty creature?" Mark showed his teeth as Billy walked with him to the stairs to head down.

"The rookie's mother."

"Vile. I see where that pig gets his attitude."

"*Got*…his attitude. He's dead."

Mark bit his lip on another snide comment. He and Billy stepped out into the sunshine. Mark hooked his elbow, put his sunglasses on, and they headed to where Billy had parked his patrol car.

Billy unlocked the passenger's side for Mark and shut the door after Mark sat down, then he walked around the back of the car to the driver's side.

Mark looked at the dashboard, the switches for the overhead lights and sirens, the computer on a bracket, the paperwork and supplies tucked into the console, and then at the shotgun hanging over the Plexiglas screen between the front and back seats.

Billy started the car and drove out of the lot. "Thanks."

"It was a short speech." Mark hooked the seatbelt.

STARTING OVER

"What more was I supposed to say?" Billy glanced over at him. "I'm not about to grovel or make excuses. I didn't even want to apologize, but the guild asked me to."

"I take it this was designed to pacify those two monsters."

"Yup." Billy slowed for a traffic signal. "So they won't sue."

Mark tried to relax after the stressful event and rested his hand on Billy's leg over his dark uniform. "Why don't you take time off? Hmm? Go play at the estate for a week."

"Can't." Billy drove towards Santa Monica.

"Why on earth not?"

"I'm working with LAPD SWAT."

Whipping his head around to him, Mark gaped in surprise. "No!"

"Yup." Billy rested his hand over Mark's.

"Already?"

"Already."

"What does Alexander think?" Mark heard the dispatcher's voice over the car's police radio.

"Don't care."

"Are you starting over? Going in as an officer?" Mark gazed at Billy's crisp uniform, at the stars on his collar, his gun on his hip.

"Lieutenant."

"What then? Hm?" Mark squeezed Billy's large thigh muscle. "Back to climbing the ranks?"

"*Hellll*, no!" Billy slowed down as suddenly everyone around them was obeying the speed limit.

"Why SWAT? Why?" Mark was not happy.

"Okay. I'll reenlist in the army."

Mark stared at his profile. "That's not funny."

"Lesser of two evils, Richfield."

"Bloody hell. Why can't you retire?" Mark blew out a loud breath. "Alex makes enough—"

"Eh!" Billy cut him off. "I'm not going to be the stay at home wife, so can it."

Mark sighed and slouched in the seat. Billy moved Mark's hand between his legs.

"Incorrigible." Mark's palm was pressed over Billy's balls and cock.

"I can't believe I'm no longer the chief." Billy veered around the slow moving cars.

"Okay, baby." Mark cupped Billy's package gently. "You got through the hard part. Just keep putting one foot in front of the other."

They stayed quiet for a moment, Mark massaging Billy's soft cock soothingly.

"How long are you and Stan staying in LA?"

"I want to go home tonight, but I need to speak to Dr Van Eldon about Alexander's appalling behavior. His appointment is tomorrow, correct?"

"Yes. I think four." Billy pulled into the police division's parking lot.

"I keep getting dragged back here. I want to be free of this place and stay up north." Mark forgot about his phone and took his hand back from Billy's balls to remove it from his pocket. He read a text from Adam. "Speaking about being dragged backwards." Mark exhaled and unfastened his seatbelt as Billy parked.

"What?" Billy asked.

"I've been asked to appear on the final season of *Forever Young*."

Billy smiled, then roared with laughter.

"Do shut up." Mark climbed out of the car.

Billy leaned on the fender of the police cruiser as cops came and went all around them. "Come here." Billy held Mark's waist and made him stand in front of him. "Thank you."

STARTING OVER

Mark pressed their crotches together as he leaned back to see Billy's handsome face. "I'm glad I could ease the pain."

Billy petted Mark's hair as he stared at him, a contented look on his face.

"You'll be fine, my love." Mark touched Billy's jaw.

Cupping Mark's head, Billy drew him to his mouth. Mark kissed him, feeling a tongue touch his, and then parted and peered at the cops taking notice.

"Give me a minute and I'll drive you home." Billy ran his hands down Mark's shoulders to his biceps.

"Should I come with you?"

"Maybe not." Billy gestured to the parking lot. "My car's right there." He gave Mark his key.

"All right." Mark used his thumb to sensuously caress Billy's lower lip.

"Fuck, you're gorgeous."

Mark lowered his eyelashes modestly and stepped back.

Billy ran his fingers along Mark as he moved towards the rear of the police station. Mark watched him enter the secure building and then he walked to Billy's black Corvette.

He paused to take in the surroundings; police officers in uniform *everywhere*. Mark leaned against the Vette and enjoyed the sight of macho men, all giving him a close inspection as he did the same in return.

Chapter 5

Stan worked out at his gym in West Hollywood. After, he returned to his apartment to shower and change clothing. Stan stood in his living room, looking at his furniture, wondering what to do about this place.

Mark was paying his rent, but it seemed like a waste of money to him now. If he wasn't auditioning, if he was going to work with Mark in Sacramento, did he need this apartment?

His phone chimed with a text. Stan read one from Becca, '*are you in LA?*'

There it was. The reason to stay here. Becca. He sat on his sofa and texted back, '*yes.*'

'*with Mark?*'

'*Yes.*'

'*Dinner?*'

Stan sent Mark a text, '*We're staying in LA overnight, right? driving up tomorrow?*'

'*yes.*'

'*Dinner with the gang?*' He sent Becca a text, '*can I let you know?*'

'*Yup.*'

'*How are you?*' Stan texted.

'*Still pregnant!*' And she sent a laugh emoji.

Stan smiled and then checked to see if Mark had texted back. He had not. Stan had a bad feeling about Billy. The chief may

STARTING OVER

have to resign and that upset Stan. But, chiefs of police can't punch out windows when they're insulted.

Stan certainly didn't have to pack up this place today, since Mark had encouraged him to keep it for now. Before he grabbed his keys and left, heading to Bel Air, his dad sent him, *'How are you doing?'* on a text message.

Stan sent back, *'Okay, I guess.'*

'Can I call?'

'Yes.' Stan stood from the sofa and picked up his wallet from the nightstand, then pocketed his car key.

His phone chimed. "Hi, Dad."

"Hi, Stan. How are you feeling?"

"I'm trying to draw a line behind me and move on." Stan stepped into the bathroom and checked his face and hair quickly before he drove to Mark's place.

"Do you need counseling?"

Stan stared into his hazel eyes in the mirror. "I don't think so."

"Are you still working with Alex?"

"No. We wrapped. I'm avoiding him." Stan left the bathroom and stood by his dining room table, resting one knee on a chair. "Please tell me you haven't told Mom."

A low exhale came from Michael. "No. I haven't."

"Good." Stan paused then asked, "How are you doing, Dad?"

"I'm exhausted."

"Fuck." Stan sat on the chair he was kneeling on and sank over his lap. "I don't know how you do it."

"I have to. We're the last line of defense."

"Jesus. How did it come to this?" Stan thought about the disastrous political climate.

"It's a pendulum, it swings from time to time."

"I'm terrified my marriage will be nullified."

"Don't be terrified. You'll be fine."

As Stan thought of all the work his dad was doing in both New York and in DC, as an attorney general, he said, "Hey, in case you don't hear it enough, thank you. And I don't mean just for being my dad, I mean for all the work you do behind the scenes to keep our democracy."

"Thanks, son. I appreciate the pep talk, even though I called to give you one."

Hearing his dad laugh, Stan smiled. "I'm so lucky I have you."

"Same here. I'm very proud of you."

"I should go. Mark is with Billy Sharpe. They're making him resign."

"I'm sorry to hear that."

"Me too. I swear, it's as if all the good men have to leave, and the politicians who have done so much worse, don't."

"Don't be so sure about that. The courts may work slowly, but we're weeding them out."

Stan smiled again. "You're awesome."

Michael chuckled. "So are you. Okay. Enough sharing compliments, just call me if you need me."

"I will. Love you."

"Love you too."

Stan disconnected the call and found a text from Mark, '*anything you want, baby.*'

Stan grinned and sent Becca and his friends a text, '*dinner in Bel Air?*' His phone lit up with enthusiastic replies. Stan got to his feet and made sure he had what he needed, then walked to the parking garage and his Lambo.

~

Steve checked the time on the wall clock in his office. He sent Mark a text, '*are you coming back here tonight?*'

'*No. I am staying in Bel Air since I would like to speak with Alex's doc tomorrow at his apt.*'

STARTING OVER

Steve leaned back in the large leather swivel chair as he thought about it. *'Does that mean you're not going to be here tomorrow either?'*

'We are driving up after the apt.'

'And what time is the apt?' Steve glanced up at Tadzio who was leafing through a book of fabric samples while seated in the lounge area of the big office.

'four.'

"Are you fucking kidding me?" Steve said out loud. Tadzio turned to look at him curiously. He called Mark.

"What is it, lovely?" Mark asked when he answered.

"If you drive up here at four, you're not going to get here until nearly midnight."

"I am well aware of the time frame."

"Why do you sound pissed off? What did Alex do now?" Steve leaned his elbows on his desk. He had loosened his necktie and rolled up his shirt sleeves.

Tadzio placed the fabric samples down on the low coffee table and walked closer.

"Steven. Really. Using that tone with me?"

Steve rubbed his face in exhaustion. "I'm drowning here, Richfield. I'm flying by the seat of my pants. Get your ass back here."

"I am trying desperately. Do you know how much I want to be there?"

Steve calmed down and reached out to Tadzio. The sweet twink stood beside him and leaned on the arm of the chair. Steve rubbed Tadzio's back gently. "Talk to me, Richfield. What the hell have you been up to all day?" *Besides coddling Stan.*

"I'm with the chief. Can I call you later?"

"What are you doing with Billy?" Steve became jealous. Tadzio nuzzled his neck.

"Steven! You are exasperating me! You can't manage one day?"

"Jesus Christ! Why are you yelling at me?"

Tadzio backed off and pouted.

Steve heard Mark conferring with someone, probably Billy. *If you two fuck…I'm gonna kill someone.*

"Steven." Mark exhaled loudly. "Billy had to resign. He asked me to accompany him to the taping at the administration building. Early this morning I saw Arnold Newhouse to end my contract with *Dangereux* so this weekend's shoot is my last. I also went to see Dr Love, as I have already told you, and Javier for my hair appointment."

"Oh." Steve's anger deflated. "And you'll be done in LA after Alex's shrink."

"Until the weekend when I have the photo shoot for the cologne."

"Oh." Steve glanced at Tadzio, seeing his frown.

"All right?" Mark said in frustration, "Can I go now?"

"Mark? Come on. Don't be like that. I just don't know this business like you do. I feel as if I'm waiting for you to make any major purchasing decisions."

"Why? Steven, you are perfectly capable. Don't think I will second guess you. There are so many employees there to assist you. Ask them. Don't be so full of pride you can't ask for help. They know you are new to the business. Just ask."

"Fine." Steve ran his hand over Tadzio's chest.

"Steven."

"What?"

"I'm trying. I'm trying to tie things up here. I feel as if I can't get free."

"Okay. I get it. Sorry I was so angry." Steve found Tadzio's nipple through his silky shirt and pinched it. The pretty model smiled and crouched down behind the desk.

STARTING OVER

Steve blinked in surprise and looked up at the door to his office.

"So, plan on me being at the estate sometime late tomorrow. All right?"

Tadzio moved between Steve's knees and opened the zipper of his suit trousers.

"Steven?" Mark asked over the phone.

"Huh?" Steve peeked at his office door and then Tadzio who drew his cock into his mouth.

"Later." Mark hung up.

Steve put the phone on his desk and spread his legs, resting his head on the chair as Tadzio hummed and sucked him off.

~

Alex read his TV script while sitting by his pool. His sarong on, topless in the heat, he memorized his lines for the first episode of the fall season.

He sent Tadzio a message, missing him too, but Tadzio hadn't sent one back.

He didn't get one from Billy or his dad either.

Alex set the script aside and stared at the pool and the view beyond of the Getty museum. The smoke had cleared a little and the smog was less. He missed his dad. A lot.

~

After the call from Steve, Mark grew irritated and tired. Billy had collected his belongings from the Santa Monica division, and was wearing jeans and a T-shirt- and his gun. He placed a box of uniforms in his trunk. As Billy navigated the afternoon traffic, Mark wanted to be in Paradise. He was upset with Steve for questioning his motivation.

Billy glanced at him.

Mark tried to sit up in the low bucket seat. Billy drew Mark's left hand to his lap, running his finger over Mark's wedding ring absently.

"Steve giving you a hard time for being here?"

"Yes." Mark tugged at the chai charm on his necklace and then gazed at Billy's legs as they worked the pedals.

"Do you ever feel as if you have three husbands?" Billy drew Mark's hand closer to his crotch.

"Three?" Mark thought about Steve and Stan. "Jackie?"

Billy adjusted Mark's hand so it lay between his legs again.

"You?" Mark laughed. "Bloody hell."

"We need you in our lives. All of us." Billy slowed for the stop and go traffic.

Mark used his fingertips to trace where Billy's soft cock was tucked behind the denim fabric. "I am aware."

"What are you and Stan doing for dinner?"

"Why? Do you think I want Alexander in my presence?"

Billy appeared frustrated with the highway traffic and merged to the right lane to get off the jammed interstate. "Fuck, I hate LA."

Mark did as well. He tried to keep the chief calm by stroking him where he wanted to be stroked, as Billy located a main street and dealt with lights instead of a parking lot freeway.

"How long are you going to shun Alex?" Billy massaged Mark's hand between shifting gears, keeping it where it was.

"I don't know. I'm so angry with him. I can't look at him."

"You realize that's going to crush him."

"Alex needs to understand there are consequences for his actions. He's become a spoilt brat."

"Mark." Billy stopped for a red light and drew Mark's hand back when he tried to move it away. "Alex had a fucked up childhood."

Mark scoffed. "Who didn't?"

"The amount he craves your approval and attention is high. If you think avoiding him and not allowing him access to the estate is good for Alex's ego, you're mistaken."

STARTING OVER

Using more force, Mark drew his arm back from Billy, fuming angrily that he had to make concessions when no one else seemed to be. Mark said, "The fact that your husband has committed sexual assault, and you are not as deeply horrified as I am concerns me."

Billy shifted into first and kept driving. "Look. The act of sucking Stan's dick for a few minutes isn't going to traumatize him. I don't approve of the drugging him, however. I think all Alex had to do was ask."

Mark sat up higher in the seat. "Are you joking? Do you think for one minute what he did was excusable?"

"Mark? Come on." Billy shook his head. "Alex is a gay man's wet dream."

"We discussed this on the drive to Paradise." Mark ran his hand through his hair and tried to keep his voice controlled. "When will you realize it does not matter who the perpetrator of the act is. What is relevant is that it was unwanted. The fact that Alex had to drug my husband to gain access to his body should be your first clue." Mark shook his head in upset. "You, of all people. You. You are a law enforcer. Are you telling me that you judge sexual misconduct solely on the basis of the desirability of the attacker?"

"No. Stop putting words into my mouth." Billy drove down their street after a long snarled commute. "But, Mark. This is Alex and Stan. The two of them had sex scenes from the film they just did. Do you think after we see it, see them kiss, grind all over each other with hard-ons, and perform fake sexual acts, you're going to feel the same way?"

As Billy paused on the driveway while the garage door elevated, Mark said, "Let me out." He unhooked his seatbelt.

"What?" Billy grabbed Mark's arm. "Come on. Stop it."

Mark was about to explode. "Have you ever been the victim of a sexual assault?"

Billy pulled into the garage beside Alex's Ferrari. "No. Not sexual but—"

"I have!" Mark yelled at him. "You were there! Sun-Specs! Do you think if those men were posh? If they were in business suits it would have been excusable?"

Billy turned off the engine. "Mark…"

"Do you think it would have been acceptable if Drew Persley had been young? Hmm? Young and fabulous? Then, all right, have a grope of my cock?"

"Mark? Calm down." Billy tried to coral him.

"No! I don't like what you're implying! Not one bit!" Mark breathed fire. "So? I am a model? Hmm? I may touch people at will? Since I am attractive I have permission to sexually touch men? Are you out of your bleedin' mind?"

"Mark…" Billy reached out to him.

"Perfectly useless." Mark tried to find the door handle. "Here I am, foolish enough to back you when you have committed a crime. Where are you when my husband becomes a victim?"

"Mark…" Billy grabbed Mark by his wrist. "Mark Antonious! Look at me!"

Mark growled and tensed up.

Billy shook him.

Mark glared at him.

"If you continue to punish Alex, he will not be able to handle it." Billy pulled Mark nearer in the closeness of the car's compartment. "I know Alex, and so do you. You! You, Mark Antonious, are his fucking world! His universe! If you continue to act coldly, to refuse him entrance to the estate, even after Alex has apologized, groveled, begged forgiveness, you will *kill* him! Do you hear what I'm saying!"

Mark stopped resisting and caught his breath.

STARTING OVER

"He's already on valium! He's seeing your shrink!" Billy battled to control his volume. "What's next for him, Mark? Want me to tell you!" Billy yelled, "Suicide!"

Mark crumbled inside. He trembled and shook his head in denial.

Billy lowered his voice. "I see it in his eyes. Mark, he's dead inside. He died the day you kicked Steve out, and no matter what we do, he isn't back to us yet. If you avoid him, if you cut him out of your world, Alex will not survive."

"Dad?"

Mark spun around in the Corvette's seat. Alex was standing in the doorway of the home.

~

Stan made the bed with fresh linens. Since the movers had come, there wasn't much left in the house in Bel Air. It felt like a hotel with only some toiletries, bare essentials of clothing, nothing left on the walls, and few electronics and kitchen items.

Stan left the framed ads for Mark in his car, since he was going to take them to Paradise tomorrow with him.

He checked the time and finished making the bed so they had clean sheets to make a mess of when they had sex later.

Stan trotted down the stairs and looked out of the front window. His friends were expected for dinner, but he had no idea what Mark wanted to eat.

He sat on the sofa in the still-furnished living room, and propped his bare feet up on the coffee table. Mark's hardbound books had been packed and transported, so they no longer were on display.

All of the photographs were gone, nothing was left on the mantle place.

Stan looked up food delivery options on his phone, not wanting pizza and not sure he wanted Chinese food either.

He checked the last text he'd received from Mark, and it was nearly an hour ago, saying he was on his way home. The traffic was always bad in LA, so Stan didn't worry.

He heard a car door and stood up to have a look outside. Fred's car had pulled in front of the home. Stan opened the door and smiled as his friends walked up the paved path.

"Hey!" they called in greeting.

He hugged and kissed them as they entered the house.

Oswald immediately commented on the missing items. "It's emptying out. When's this house going to be for sale?"

"I don't know. It's Steve's house, not Mark's." Stan looked outside for Billy's car before he closed the door.

Lou, Antwon, Fred, and Becca also inspected the bare walls and strange sense of vacating.

Becca placed her purse on the sofa and asked, "Is Mark here?"

"He's on his way. He was with the chief most of the day." Stan gestured to the sofa and loveseat in the living room.

Lou sank low in the sofa cushions and held his phone. "That vid went viral. The one taken at the karaoke place?" He held up his phone. "Seriously. He's an icon."

"I don't think that's going to help him much." Stan joined Lou on the sofa and propped his feet on the coffee table again. "What are you guys hungry for?"

"Stan?" Becca, her hair in a high ponytail, wearing denim shorts that came to her knee and a white cotton top, asked, "Do you know a lady named Natalie Cushman?"

"No." Straining to look behind him out of the window, Stan became anxious for Billy's Vette to drive by. "Why?"

"Tadzio's trying to set us up." She read her phone. "Natalie sent me a photo." She held it up to him.

Stan reached for it. "She's cute."

"Dude?" Antwon said, "She looks at least thirty."

STARTING OVER

"So?" Stan handed Becca the phone.

Lou laughed loudly. "Antwon? You're talking to a dude with a sugar daddy."

Fred wandered into the kitchen. "So? There's no food?"

"What are you in the mood for?" Stan called to him. "Mark's not my sugar daddy," he said to Lou.

Oswald and Lou fell over laughing.

Becca pretended her phone was fascinating and Antwon covered his mouth to hide his smile.

"Not your sugar daddy?" Lou choked with hilarity. "He says, as he reads the time on his Patek Philippe and parks his Lamborghini in a million dollar home in Bel Air while he packs to move to a gazillion-dollar estate."

"An estate with a thirteen-room mansion and servants," Oswald coughed with laughter, "A stable, two pools, a tennis court..."

"And he stars in a major motion picture with his sugar daddy's son, Alexander Richfield," Lou dabbed at his eyes as he spoke.

Fred returned, holding a can of mixed nuts.

"Where did you find that?" Stan asked, rolling with the good-natured teasing, since it was true.

"In a cabinet." He popped one into his mouth and made a face, then checked the label.

"Stale?" Stan assumed so, since Mark didn't keep many 'snacks' in the home.

"Gross." Fred returned to the kitchen.

Stan focused on his crazy friends again. "Does everyone say that? Does everyone think that Mark's my S-D?"

Becca sunk down even lower in the loveseat cushions, her face behind her phone. Antwon, as if to avoid the topic, joined Fred to search for food.

"Dude!" Oswald teased, "You are! Come on. Duh. He's like…what…Thirty-something?"

"Thirty-something?" Lou snickered. "You moron. Alex is our age! Mark wasn't ten when he had him."

"Holy shit." Oswald stopped laughing and blinked. "How old is Mark?"

Since Stan wasn't talking, both men focused on their phones, trying to find out.

Fred returned, this time holding a bottle of tequila. "Ya still got booze, dude."

Antwon flapped a paper menu that Stan had left on the refrigerator. "Chinese?"

"Wow." Oswald touched himself as he searched his phone. "There're so many nude pics of Mark. Is that photo-shopped or does he have a dick that big?"

"I found a vid he did on a cable TV show. He's in bed with two men." Lou sat next to Oswald and they looked at each other's phones. "Fuck! Is that his real dick?"

"Where did you find his vid?" Oswald asked, "That's that two guys from the cable TV show, *Forever Young*."

"Look at the date." Lou leaned on Oswald's shoulder. "Ten years ago?" He stared at Stan. "How old is he! Come on! He's not like in his fifties, is he?"

"Mark? Fifty?" Fred asked, sniffing the contents of the tequila bottle. "No way. He looks thirty." He held it up to Antwon, who shrugged indifferently.

"He ain't thirty." Oswald kept moving his thumbs on his phone.

"Guys?" Stan wondered where Mark was. "So, uh. Food?"

"Anyone want tequila?" Fred held up the bottle.

"Not me." Becca asked, "So? Should I go on a date with this Natalie-lady?"

STARTING OVER

Stan stood from the sofa and took the menu from Antwon. It was for Chinese food they had ordered before. He brought it into the living room. "What do we want?"

Becca was texting. Oswald and Lou were leaning their heads together getting off on naked photos of Mark, and Fred and Antwon were looking for shot glasses.

Stan set the menu down and sighed.

Chapter 6

"Dad?"

Mark climbed out of the Corvette. Billy opened the trunk and picked up a box and his uniforms, which were on hangers.

"What's going on?" Alex asked.

Mark touched Alex on his shoulder lightly as he entered the kitchen of the home, bypassing him. Alex waited for Billy and took the box from him. "You quit?"

"Yes." Billy carried his uniforms into the house and kept walking through the large, spacious open-planned rooms with his armload.

Mark tapped a text on his phone as he stood near the back sliding door.

Alex set the box containing police gear on the floor by the door to the garage and approached his dad. "How bad was it?"

"He'll live." Mark looked up from his phone. He did a sweep of Alex's attire. "Please tell me you did not wear that outside."

Alex touched his gold sarong. "Does everything I do piss you off?"

Mark gave him a look of irritation. "I am going with you to Dr Van Eldon's appointment tomorrow. I will not argue with you about it."

"Why? Why are you going?" Alex took a bottle of water out of the fridge.

"You know why." Mark narrowed his eyes at him.

Alex drank from the water, inspecting his father's face. "You had Botox." He drew closer. "And a haircut."

STARTING OVER

Mark took the water from Alex and drank it thirstily. "Your husband is going through hell. I suggest you behave."

"What have I done!" Alex yelled.

Billy appeared, wearing shorts and white socks, topless. He crouched down and slipped on his running shoes.

"Is Steve here?" Alex asked, trying to take the bottle back from his dad.

"No," Billy said, tying his laces.

"Who are you running with?" Alex asked, as his dad finished the water in the bottle.

"No one." Billy left through the front door.

After Billy vanished, Alex crossed his arms over his bare chest. "What did you talk about with him to piss him off? Why are you even here?"

Mark shoved the empty plastic bottle at Alex, making him take it. "I shall expect you to pick me up on your way."

"Dad. No. I'm going from the studio in Burbank. It's out of my way."

Mark shook his head at his son. "Put some bloody clothing on. You look ridiculous."

"I was out by the pool!" Alex screamed and threw the empty bottle against the wall. It clattered to the tile kitchen floor.

Mark sneered at him and walked to the front door.

"Dad." Alex chased after him, grabbing at him. "Dad!"

Mark paused and appeared to count to ten to control his rage.

"Why were you with my husband?"

Mark faced him, looking livid. "When you grow up perhaps then your husband will seek you out for his needs. Until then, I suggest you do some soul searching, Alexander, because I cannot tolerate you at the moment."

Alex felt sick inside. "Is this because of my outfit?" Alex held the gold material and pulled on it.

Mark parted his lips and his eyes widened. "Are you joking?"

"Needs? What needs? Did you suck Billy's cock?" Alex began to disintegrate.

~

The urge to slap Alex's face for that accusation was almost irresistible. In a measured voice, Mark said, "Only you, Alex, suck other men's husband's cocks."

"Dad..." Alex pouted. "I said I was sorry. Come on. He didn't hate it."

Mark's rage hit a new high. "What did you just say?"

Alex shrugged. "I said, he probably liked it."

Hearing his own son using a lie that sexual predators claim about their victims drew out the ire in Mark. With his jaw clenched, Mark advanced on his son.

Alex appeared stunned and backed away, holding his hands up defensively. Mark kept stalking Alex until Alex's back hit a wall.

"I don't know who you are any longer." Mark battled to keep his tone reasonable. "The more I listen to you, the less I like you."

"Wha-at?" Alex began to hyperventilate. "You don't like me? Dad! I'm your only son!"

Coming within an inch of Alex's face, Mark snarled. "How dare you? How dare you fake your remorse, your apology for my benefit? For Billy's benefit, when you feel nothing."

"Dad..." Alex shook his head. "Come on."

"Stating that my husband liked it?" Mark sneered and wanted to smack Alex. "Are you a sociopath?"

"Dad..." Alex tried to touch him.

Mark slapped Alex's hand away from him. "Keep this up. Keep up this irrational behavior and see how far apart it will drive us."

"I said I was sorry! Stan is okay with it. Dad...come on. Stop it."

STARTING OVER

"I will see you at the doctor's office." Mark backed up and made his way to the door.

"Dad! Come on…I'm sorry! How many times do I have to say it?"

Mark paused and glared at him. "Until I am certain you mean it." He opened the door. "But, hearing your filth, your smugness about Stan wanting to be drugged and sexually assaulted is revolting. No son of mine behaves this way."

"Dad." Alex interlaced his fingers to plead.

"Grow the bloody hell up!" Mark left the house and slammed the door behind him.

He was so enraged he was shaking. Mark inhaled deeply several times to calm down. He made it as far as his driveway, and sat down on the retaining wall. Fred's car was out front and Mark wanted to adjust his attitude before he entered the house.

He stared at the neighborhood, the trees waving in the wind, the birds soaring from limb to limb, as he battled to unwind.

What he wanted was his horse. What he wanted was to be in Paradise.

The tentacles that were wrapped around his life here in LA were strangling him.

Mark heard heavy footfalls and looked up from the tarmac of his driveway. Billy was returning.

He paused near Mark and caught his breath, looking as if he'd sprinted the entire three mile route. Sweat poured out of the chief, running down his chest and neck.

Mark met his gaze. "I have no idea how this is going to resolve itself, love."

"It has to. Mark. Don't give up on him." Billy dabbed at his temple.

Mark heard talking. He glanced at his front door and Stan was there, looking out.

Both he and Billy turned towards him. Stan made his way over, followed by his friends.

Mark smiled through his anguish and reached for him. "Hullo, baby."

Stan kissed Mark. "What's going on?"

"Hi, Chief." Becca stood in front of Billy and grinned at him.

"Hi, hun." Billy greeted Stan's friends.

Antwon asked, "Chief? Are you having dinner with us?"

"I don't think so." Billy pointed down the street. "Have fun." He jogged off.

Mark stood from the wall and held Stan's hand, walking to the front door. "How are you all?"

They were quiet as they entered the home.

Mark ran his hand over his hair and hadn't had consumed anything but coffee all day. "Did you order food?"

"We didn't yet." Stan closed the door behind them.

"Go ahead, love. Let me…" Mark gestured to the top floor.

Fred produced a joint. "I've got one."

Antwon pointed to the patio. "Outside?"

Mark nodded and walked to the slider, opening it, while Stan ordered their food. Fred lit up, handing the rolled joint to Mark.

Mark took a hit, his back to the breeze, and gave it to Antwon.

Becca crossed her arms and appeared unhappy. Mark drew her closer, kissing her hair. "How are you, lovely?"

"I'm okay, but you seem upset."

Lou took the joint next and handed it to Oswald.

Mark rocked her in his arms, closing his eyes. He had another chance. Whether it was a son or a daughter, Mark had another shot at bringing up a human being with standards, with morals.

"Mark?" Oswald offered the joint to him. Mark took one more hit, and held the smoke in.

Stan stepped outside. "Thirty minutes delivery time."

STARTING OVER

Mark gave him the joint and squeezed Becca close, dancing to music in his own head.

She held onto him and rested her cheek on his chest. She sighed deeply and waltzed with him across the patio.

~

Billy removed his running shoes and noticed Alex sitting near the pool. He dropped his socks onto his shoes, opened the slider, and stepped outside.

Alex pouted at him.

"Come in." Billy tilted his head to the house.

Alex stood from the lounge chair, wearing that vile sarong. His head lowered, Alex obeyed.

"Move." Billy urged him to keep walking.

Once Alex was in their bedroom, Billy tugged off his running shorts and briefs. "Get on the bed, face down."

Alex parted his lips for a second, then thought better of a reply. He knelt on the bed on his hands and knees.

Billy jerked himself hard, gazing at Alex. He pushed the material up and exposed Alex's tight ass.

Alex spread his knees.

Once he was hard, Billy picked up the lube, using it liberally. He moved closer to the bed and aimed his dick at Alex's rim.

On target, Billy tangled his fingers into Alex's long hair and pulled it, making Alex gasp and arch his back. Billy thrust in deeply.

"Ah! Fuck!"

Billy hammered into him. "Like that, babydoll?"

"Fuck!" Alex dug his fingers into the bedding with white knuckles.

That fucking sarong. Billy hated it. He pulled out, grabbed Alex by the legs and flipped him over. Alex's cock was engorged.

Billy held the gold material on either side, and tore it, ripping it open over Alex's body.

"Billy!" Alex flinched.

Billy dove on him, grabbing Alex by his throat and forcing his legs back. He slammed his cock back into Alex.

"Ah! Fuck!" Alex winced and clenched his fists.

"Want it?" Billy sneered.

"Yes!"

"How much?" Billy choked Alex.

"More!" Alex panted loudly.

Propping his hands on the bed on either side of Alex, Billy watched the act, his slick cock driving inside his man.

"Oh, fuck…" Alex threw his head back into the bed and coughed on his gasp.

Billy pulled out and stared at him.

Alex blinked. "Huh?"

"Want it?"

"Yes!" Alex touched himself.

"How much?" Billy sneered this time as he said it.

"Huh? A lot!"

Billy used the sarong to wipe the lube off his cock. "Suck it."

"Billy…" Alex pressed his palms into the bedding and pouted.

"Suck it!" Billy roared like an order.

Alex quickly got to his hands and knees on the bed, drawing Billy's cock into his mouth.

Billy dug his fingers into Alex's hair, gripped tight. "That's it."

Alex closed his eyes.

Once Billy was on the edge, he shoved Alex back on the bed. Alex caught himself and gasped in surprise.

Billy landed on him, pinning Alex under him. He aimed his dick for his rim again and hammered in.

STARTING OVER

"Ah! Fuck! Billy!"

"That's it." Billy pinched Alex's nipple. "That's it..." Billy came, sliding in and out of Alex as he did.

"Ah! Fuck!" Alex held his own cock in both hands and cum spattered his smooth chest. "Fuck! Ah! Holy shit!"

Billy watched the cream coat Alex's chest. "That's it, doll."

"Oh, God..." Alex nearly convulsed under him, milking his dick.

Billy moved in and out until he was soft, then he stood beside the bed and stared at Alex. He picked up the horrible sarong and used it to wipe his cock and Alex's cum, then balled it up and threw it on the floor. "Get up."

Alex appeared woozy.

"Up." Billy reached out.

Alex clasped his hand and was hauled to his feet.

"Go." Billy nudged him to the bathroom.

Alex stood at the sink and rinsed his mouth, spitting and catching his breath.

Billy slapped Alex's tight rump with a crack! and turned on the water in the shower. Alex shut off the sink tap and gasped as he recovered.

"Get in." Billy pointed to the tub.

"Yes, Billy." Alex climbed into the shower.

Billy entered it with him and held out a sponge. "Clean my back." Billy faced the spray and relaxed.

Alex, like a good husband, obeyed.

I will break that willfulness, babydoll. I will break that ego, that nasty pride.

Billy relaxed and thought about LAPD SWAT. It was like starting over...

But this time, he was in control.

~

Tadzio nodded off on the drive from Sacramento to Paradise in the limousine. Steve was beside him, his arm around Tadzio's shoulders.

The car entered the ruddy lane and Tadzio became more alert as it rocked and shifted on the uneven surface.

The chauffeur parked in front of the stately mansion and opened the door for them.

Steve thanked the young man and walked with Tadzio to the front door.

Before Tadzio tried the knob, Warren opened it from within. "Hello, Steve, Tadzio."

"Hi, Warren." Steve smiled at the older man. He held Tadzio's hand and they walked together to their private bedroom. As they went, Tadzio peered into the kitchen. Sierra was busy cooking and tantalizing scents came from the stove.

Steve closed them into their bedroom, then entered the walk-in closet to remove his suit.

Tadzio sat on the bed and took off his shoes, then sighed and watched Steve undress. Steve put on shorts and a tank top. He emerged and then stepped into the bathroom.

"You are working out, Steven?" Tadzio asked.

"I was going to run the trails."

"Oh!" Tadzio thought that sounded fun. He hopped off the bed and undressed, putting on spandex shorts and a sleeveless tee.

Steve finished in the bathroom and paused. "You want to come?"

"I do." Tadzio put on a pair of white socks and entered the bathroom. The toilet lid raised up as he drew near. He shook his head at it because he thought it was absurd, and relieved himself. "Steven?"

"Yes?"

STARTING OVER

"If I do not design clothes, what can I do?" Tadzio stepped back to flush and the toilet did automatically. "This iz so strange," he said to himself and washed his hands. After he did, he pinned his hair up in a ponytail. Tadzio returned to Steve, who was reading his phone, standing near the dresser.

"Steven?"

"Hm?" Steve used his thumbs to text.

Since he didn't get an answer, he asked again, "If I do not design, what can I do?" Tadzio looked at Steve's phone. He was texting his sister about his parents' reaction to Laura's visit here last weekend.

Steve chuckled at something he read on his phone, then set it down. "Okay. Sorry. So, you don't want to design."

"I am no good." Tadzio shrugged.

Steve crouched down to tie his shoelaces. "That's not what I heard."

Tadzio found his running shoes and sat on the floor to put them on. "Not what you hear?"

"Greg told me your designs were fantastic." Steve finished tying his shoes and waited.

Tadzio blinked in surprise. "He did?"

Steve gestured to the hallway. "Let's go."

Tadzio walked to the back of the house, through the kitchen where Sierra was cooking.

"Hi, Steve, Tadzio."

"Hi, Sierra. We're going to run on the trails before dinner." Steve opened the back door.

"No problem." She smiled.

Tadzio tried to see what she was making, but couldn't figure it out. Steve and he left through the back of the mansion, and Steve began jogging. They followed the paved path, running by the paddock where the horses were grazing. All three perked up, ears high, to watch.

Tadzio laughed as he noticed their attention on them.

The two high-strung horses, Piccadilly and Shadow, paced with the two men in excitement along the fence rail until they reached the end, then they blew out noises and whinnies in the wind. Bull kept grazing on the long grass outside the fenced paddock.

He and Steve passed the barn and took off across the open field on a dirt trail that had been used by the horses. The temperature at the base of the mountains was cool and refreshing. Running on soft clay dirt was easier than tarmac and cement.

"Steven!" Tadzio inhaled the fragrant air. "This iz wonderful! Billy and Alec would so much enjoy this!"

"Ha!" Steve was glowing, beaming with light.

Tadzio kept up with his energetic pace. "So? Greg say he liked my drawings?"

"Yup."

Tadzio couldn't believe it. He thought, compared to the designers working on the computer programs, his were trash. "Huh." Tadzio wasn't sure what else he could contribute, at least, until a baby was born. "Okay, Steven."

"Mark said there's a waterfall out there somewhere. Want to find it?"

"Yes!" Tadzio responded with enthusiasm.

"Cool."

"Cool!" He and Steve raced over the fields in delight.

~

Steve inhaled the fresh mountain air and floral scents. His goal was quite a distance away. Maybe on horseback this was a quick jaunt, but on foot?

It was a haul. And he loved every second of it.

STARTING OVER

A half hour later, the tree line loomed closer. He slowed up, trying to find the trail. Tadzio breathed heavily beside him, but had no trouble keeping up.

Steve pointed to a gap in the thick brush. "That has to be it."

They followed the steep incline, and as they did, Steve heard the noise of water crashing.

Energized by the sound, he grappled his way over rocks and ferns and stood at a ledge. Tadzio scrambled behind him and caught his breath.

"Steven!"

"Wow." Steve craned his neck to the top of the cliff where the water cascaded off the rocks. Below was a deep crystal clear pond. "This is paradise all right." He made his way over ferns and moss to a flat surface of granite rock and had a look around. "Now I know why Jack and Mark came here so often."

Cooling off in the spray and breeze, Steve couldn't get over how gorgeous it was here. No sound other than the falls, no pollution, no crowds, no chaos…just peace.

As he thought about stripping and diving in, he noticed a carving on the stone's face. He approached it.

'*Jack & Mark July 1st 1998*'

"Oh. My. God." Steve crouched lower and touched it.

Tadzio leaned on Steve's back to see. "Oh! Mark! Mark iz here wit Jackie!"

Steve plopped down to his bottom to think about it. He could just make out a heart around their names.

Tadzio sat across from him, the rock's message between them. "I think Jackie wish he and Mark had married."

Steve had an image flash of the day he had crashed Sharon and Mark's wedding. A memory of Jack Larsen, his devastation, hit Steve.

As Steve zoned out to the soothing noise of crashing water, Tadzio picked up a stone and began scratching the smooth surface, writing his name inside a heart, with 'Steffen.'

Steve cracked up laughing and shook his head.

Tadzio looked up at him and said, "I know iz with 'V'. Iz so funny this way."

"I fucking love you."

"I fucking love you too." Tadzio giggled.

STARTING OVER

Chapter 7

The group of young people ate their dinner. With the help of medical weed, Mark managed to consume some of the gourmet food.

"Mark?" Becca asked.

"Yes, love?" Mark sat up in his chair, drinking from a glass of water.

"Do you know Natalie Cushman? Adam's assistant?"

"Not well, but I do know of her. Why?"

"Tadzio set us up. I'm going on a date with her."

Mark tried not to show his confusion, because sexuality was fluid and he had assumed since he had 'sex' with Becca...that she may be straight. "All right." Mark set his empty water glass down and began stacking plates.

"When?" Oswald asked, appearing full and helping Mark gather the empty dishes.

"Friday night." Becca picked up the plates to bring to the sink. "Mark? She said you were asked to star in *Forever Young*."

"I love that show!" Antwon brought the rest of the plates to the sink and he and Becca began to load the dishwasher.

Stan stood and cleared up the empty food cartons. "What? When did this happen?"

Mark gathered the silverware from the table. "Uh...today. Adam sent me a script but I haven't read it yet. I don't know if—"

"Oh! You have to!" Becca said, her hands under the running sink tap as she rinsed plates. "Mark! You have to!"

Lou cracked up with laughter. "More three-way sex with the two leads?" He wiped the counters with a small dishrag.

"Oh, my." Mark hoped not. He threw the empty cartons into the kitchen trash bin.

Fred said, "That's one of my favorite nighttime cable dramas." He wrapped leftover food.

Antwon loaded the plates into the dishwasher efficiently. "Me too! Remember when that guy's father was in a coma?"

Mark wiped his hands on a towel and moved the chairs under the kitchen table.

"Yes!" Becca said, "He woke up to find out he had a daughter, Cheryl, who was really his son, but had a sex change?"

Fred placed the leftovers in the refrigerator. "But, that son had a twin, and was left at the orphanage when he was two…and then the twin needed a kidney transplant?"

Mark wondered if they knew Tadzio was 'Cheryl' for one, maybe two episodes. Obviously not since he had been replaced quickly.

Antwon dumped the utensils into the dishwasher basket. "But, the kidney was rejected, so they had to use that criminal's kidney when he died after that knife fight."

"And then," Becca dried her hands on the dishtowel as she said, "That woman got pregnant when she had sex with that married doctor, whose wife was having an affair with the mechanic…"

Mark did not watch the show any longer, but listening to the typical trashy soap opera storylines was not making a case for him to appear.

Antwon finished loading the dishwasher. "Yes! That was when the mechanic drove the getaway car for that bank robbery, but the robber was the same man as the kidnapper, who had stolen the baby from the maternity ward—"

STARTING OVER

Stan stared at Mark, and he stared back, both of them were on the verge of hilarity over this absurd storyline.

Fred added soap to the dishwasher and started the cycle. "And, then, the baby ends up being the lost child from that royal couple, who is now the heir to the throne of that country…uh…"

"Palostan!" Becca pointed at him, as if happy she remembered.

"Yes!" Antwon wiped his hands on the dishtowel. "But, then, they did that DNA test, and it ended up the two royals weren't having sex, because they were both gay? So, the baby was used to fake their son's birth?"

Stan couldn't hold it in any longer. He roared with laughter.

Mark choked on his hilarity and shook his head. "Oh, bloody hell, no."

Lou appeared stunned. "This is the real storyline of that show? I should watch it for the comedy alone."

Oswald folded the dishtowel and draped it over the stove handle. "You can binge watch the episodes. I did."

Stan drew Mark into his arms. "Did you read the script?"

"Do I want to?" Mark held onto him.

"…and then!" Becca said, tugging on her ponytail, "That alien abduction happened, and all of the people in the town were zombies."

"That was awesome." Antwon shook his head. "I'm gonna miss that show."

Oswald asked, "When are you going to star in it, Mark?"

"I…" Mark had no idea if he was interested after hearing the ridiculous plots.

Becca stood near him and Stan. "You have to! Oh, Mark, seeing you on TV? That's so cool."

"He is on TV," Stan said, rocking Mark against him. "His commercials. Mark flying on the Ducati."

"Nah." Antwon shook his head. "It's not the same."

Lou grinned wickedly at Mark.

Mark tried not to laugh as he read the comic's mind. "Go on, Mr Comedian. Say it."

"I can't wait to see you in a clingy, nylon, green alien suit." Lou bent over laughing, dabbing at his eyes.

Becca hugged both Mark and Stan together, and said, "I guess I need to go home. I'm beat."

Mark parted from Stan's embrace. "Then, we must get you home, young lady."

Fred yawned and held his car keys in his hand. "So? This weekend, are you guys at the estate?"

Stan walked them to the door. "No. Mark and I have a modeling shoot on Sunday."

"But, we will be in Paradise hopefully for the rest of this week and back here possibly on Saturday." Mark waited for Becca to pick up her purse, then walked her outside to Fred's car.

"So? Dinner Saturday night?" Antwon asked.

"We'll see. Maybe." Mark drew Becca into his arms. "Oh, my pet. Do keep taking care of yourself."

She squeezed him close. "I am."

Mark cupped her pretty face.

She batted her long eyelashes at him sweetly. "I'm fine, Mark."

He pulled her tight to his body and closed his eyes, trying not to be worried about her.

When he released her, Stan was there, smiling at him adoringly.

Mark gave the young men a kiss on the cheek, and he and Stan waited for Fred to drive off, waving as they did.

Mark walked with Stan back into the house. He stood for a moment staring at the bare walls. He did not want to be here. He wanted to be up north.

STARTING OVER

"Mark?" Stan paused at the base of the stairs and reached for him.

"I'll be right there, pet."

Stan nodded.

Mark entered their home office. Steve's older computer was still here. Sitting in front of it, Mark booted it up, then found the email with the script attached to it.

He opened it up.

His lines were highlighted, and there were few.

He read a paragraph while it was an open file on his computer, so he could enlarge the print. Thankfully, he was not an alien or a zombie.

Mark read the scene he had been cast to star in.

When he saw what they wanted him to do, he choked and tried to find humor in it. *They must be joking*.

Since he was tired, Mark didn't read the entire script. He left it, imagining he could read it tomorrow while he worked from this home office before he went to Alex's appointment.

Mark shut the computer down and secured the home, heading up the stairs.

His stunning young husband was naked on the bed, waiting.

"Oh, my." Mark stood at the foot of the bed to admire him.

"Want in?" Stan gradually drew his knees back and spread his legs.

Bloody hell! Mark dropped his pants and yanked his shirt over his head. He crawled from the bottom up, kissing Stan's ankles, inside his knees, and then pressing his face between the gorgeous man's legs. A fragrance of soap, clean and appetizing, let Mark know, his man had prepared.

Mark drew Stan's cock into his mouth and sucked, humming in delight.

"*Awfuckyeah…*" Stan relaxed on the pillow.

Thinking about dominating Stan drove Mark insane. He sucked Stan's cock until it was rock hard, seeping pre-cum, and blushing.

Mark caught his breath and took the lube from the bed, where Stan had placed it. He used it on himself, and moved one finger full of gel inside Stan's ass.

Stan's legs trembled, and he held onto his own knees.

Mark inched closer, aiming his cock at that glistening pucker. He pushed the head of his cock against it, and slid past the tight muscles.

Stan's toes curled and his eyes closed, as if he wasn't quite happy about it yet.

"Okay, baby." Mark eased in, eager to bang away. Stan's cock became slightly soft. Mark used his slick fingers to tease it. "Open your eyes, pet."

Stan did, as if he hadn't realized he had shut them.

Those hazel eyes, golden-green, and sexy as hell, drove Mark insane. He managed to get enough of his cock inside Stan to create friction, and then began a rhythm.

Stan licked his lower lip as his gaze on Mark became intense.

Mark kept shifting his angle, trying to light Stan up. When Stan's body went tense and his cock pulsated strongly, Mark knew he was on the spot. "That's it."

"Oh fuck." Stan clenched the bedding tightly.

"That's it…" Mark began to rise as he stared at Stan's amazing body and gorgeous face.

"Fuck!" Stan choked and cum spattered his tattooed chest.

A rush of pleasure jolted through Mark's groin. He slid in with short, fast thrusts, and came. "Ah! Yes!"

"Oh! FUCK!" Stan arched his back and grabbed his cock over Mark's hand, jerking it vigorously. Roping strings of cum coated Stan's broad chest, splashing and painting his skin.

STARTING OVER

Mark shivered down to his toes and stilled his hips. His cock throbbed inside Stan's tight heat and the two of them gasped for air.

Mark pulled out and sat on his heels, staring at his cock, slick with lube and his cum.

Stan stretched his legs out, running his heels over the bedding and catching his breath. Stan held his chest as he recovered, staying still.

"That's my man." Mark was thrilled Stan had opened up to this type of sexual play. Mark crawled over Stan's prone body on his hands and knees, and took a wide lap of his tongue into Stan's cum from off his chest. "Mmm."

Stan gazed at Mark for a moment. "Holy shit that internal orgasm is intense."

"I believe you enjoyed it." Mark used the tip of his tongue to tease Stan's erect nipple.

Stan dragged Mark to his chest and kissed him. He rolled Mark over, so he was on top, and whimpered as they swirled tongues.

Mark felt his big man's hard dick slide between them on the stickiness. He shifted his hips side to side playfully to coat that delicious cock in cum, and then reached between them to aim it at his rim.

"Oh, fuck..." Judging from Stan's expression, the young stud appeared to have achieved nirvana.

Mark let Stan's hard length glide inside him.

"Fuck!" Stan braced himself on his hands and pumped into Mark's body.

Mark pinched both of Stan's hard nipples and could not believe how virile and gorgeous his young husband was. "Yes. Yes!"

Stan shivered visibly and Mark felt him climax inside his ass. "God! Oh, *myfuckinggod...*" Stan moaned and hung his head.

Mark exhaled and savored the sense of union. Loving when Stan was inside him, loving when he came, and was rock-hard. Mark relaxed his tightly wound muscles and gazed at Stan as he recovered.

Stan knelt upright between Mark's knees and shook his head. "I...I have no words."

"I do." Mark smiled. "Love. Love... love you."

Stan dove on him and snaked his arms around Mark's back, pressing their hot, sticky bodies together, messing up the clean sheets, and kissing Mark like it was their first date.

~

Alex had finished memorizing his lines for tomorrow's rehearsal. He set his sides down and looked for his chief.

Billy was in the home office, working on the computer.

Alex noticed he had taken down the photos on the wall of his swearing in as chief of police. They were in a stack on the floor. Alex leaned on Billy from behind, over the chief's shoulder and read the computer screen. It was LAPD personnel forms.

"Huh? What?" Alex kept reading. "You...you're already ...Wait. What?"

Billy kept entering information into the form.

Alex read the rank. Lieutenant.

Billy's start date. Effective immediately.

Unit. Special Weapons And Tactics.

"You..." Alex felt anxiety hit. "You already talked to them?"

Billy, his eyeglasses on, continued filling out the employment forms for his pay grade, his direct deposit, his address...

"But...but..." Alex knew Billy wanted to go back to the Los Angeles Police Department, but...already?

Billy appeared to review the forms, scrolling down as he checked his work.

"I...we haven't discussed this." Alex rested his chin on Billy's shoulder.

STARTING OVER

Billy, obviously satisfied with the information, hit 'send' and then 'print'. He tossed his glasses on the desk.

"I…" Alex wondered if this had all happened over the weekend. When? With his dad? "I thought we'd discuss this. Maybe you could be my private security or…"

Billy stood from the chair and took the pages off of the printer. He set them on the desk neatly, and then turned to face Alex.

His big police lieutenant wore his old LAPD T-shirt, and a pair of worn jeans, bare foot.

"I…" Alex pointed to himself. "I thought maybe there was wiggle room."

Billy did not smile. His steel blue eyes were intense.

Feeling an attack looming, Alex backed up a step.

Billy picked Alex up off his feet, tossing him over his shoulder like a fireman's carry.

"Uh…" Alex bounced on his back. "Maybe discuss it? A little?"

Billy threw Alex on their bed and took off his own T-shirt as he stared at Alex.

Alex felt his cock grow thick as he gazed at Billy's powerful body.

Billy stepped out of his jeans and stared at Alex like he was a hungry wolf. "Ya gonna tell me how to live my life, Alexander?"

Alex stared at the engorged veins of Billy's biceps, how they roped around his forearms and big hands. "Uh."

"You gonna tell me what I can and can't do?" Billy grabbed Alex's shirt by the neck and pulled it off over Alex's head roughly.

"Maybe?" Alex inched back.

Billy landed on him, pinning Alex to the bed. "Maybe?" Billy reached between them and opened Alex's pants.

"Uh…wow." Alex's skin broke out in chills.

"*Maybe?*" Billy said with biting sarcasm as he stripped Alex's clothing off and dropped it on the floor.

"Um." Alex panted to gain air.

Billy stood from the bed and showed Alex the lubrication, swinging it between two fingers teasingly. "Maybe? Maybe I wanna fuck."

"I…didn't mean to tell you what to do."

Billy made a show of coating his erection in gel. "Uh huh."

"I just thought, maybe we can discuss it."

Billy tossed the lube on the nightstand and dragged Alex to the edge of the bed. He forced Alex to face down, then urged Alex to kneel on the carpet.

Billy then, used his feet to coax Alex's knees apart.

Alex rested his head on his arms on the bed.

Billy knelt behind him, using the head of his cock to ride up and down Alex's ass crack. "Maybe I don't need your permission."

Alex closed his eyes.

"Maybe, I'm a grown man who makes his own decisions." Billy swatted Alex's ass, hard.

He flinched and clenched his fists.

"Maybe I didn't ask your advice." Billy grabbed Alex by the hair and jammed his cock into Alex's ass.

"Oh, fuck." Alex gasped.

"*Maybe…*" Billy sneered, "I don't need your opinion." He slammed his cock into Alex.

"Fuck." Alex clawed at the bedding.

"*Maybe* you need to be reminded of your place, Alexander. *Maybe* you need to shut the fuck up about my work. My career."

Alex winced as Billy hammered in.

"*Maybe*, Alex?" Billy slapped his body against Alex's.

"Sorry." Alex tore at the bedspread, dragging it into a bunch near his head to gnaw on as he stifled his scream.

STARTING OVER

"Ohh, yes, *sorry*, your new favorite word." Billy jammed his cock into Alex while pulling his hair.

"Ah! Holy shit!" Alex lit on fire from the internal friction.

"How sorry are you, Alex?" Billy amped up the speed of his thrusts.

Alex knew what this was about. Oh yes. He knew.

His father didn't have a method or way to slap the smug out of him. His macho policeman? Uh…he did.

"Ah! Billy." Alex winced and tore at the bed.

"Sorry now, Alexander?"

"Ah! Oh, fuck!"

Billy pulled out, without coming. Neither of them had. He released contact from Alex.

Alex groaned and tried to see Billy from over his shoulder.

Billy grabbed the golden material, left in a pile on the floor from earlier. He used it to wipe his cock off, then dropped it.

Alex caught his breath and slid to the floor, sitting on the carpet facing Billy.

Billy straddled him, aiming his dick at Alex. "I need to finish." Billy's sneer was chilling.

Alex cleared his throat and ran his hands over Billy's cock a few times.

"I don't want a fucking hand-job, Alexander."

Alex closed his eyes and parted his lips.

Billy used a hand on either side of Alex's head, pulling on his long hair, and fucked Alex's mouth.

Alex relaxed his jaw and held Billy's thighs for balance and leverage, trying not to gag.

Billy came, pulling out and spattering Alex's face and neck. Alex choked for air and sank lower on the carpeted floor, spitting into his palm.

Billy released him, entered the bathroom, and washed up.

Alex wiped at his chin, tasting the cum and other not-so-pleasant flavors. He needed to keep spitting out his saliva.

Billy returned, getting dressed in just gym shorts. "*Maybe...*" he snarled, "You should throw that vile rag out." He pointed to the sarong, and left the room.

A little shell-shocked, Alex stayed still as he listened to his husband. The sound of Billy punching the shit out of the hanging bag behind the house made its way to him.

Some lessons in life were harder to learn than others. Thinking that what he had done to Stan was trivial, excusable, or not criminal...

His police lieutenant husband was going to make damn sure Alex paid. That he learned, being forced to perform sexual acts you weren't particularly fond of, well...

There was no 'maybe' about it.

And as far as Billy's career choices? Alex knew now, he had to shut the fuck up. He had lost his power here. And he knew, he deserved this.

He was lucky he wasn't arrested and charged with a crime.

Unsteady and brooding, Alex stood, picked up the gold sarong, and stuffed it into the trash in the bathroom. He rinsed his face and hands, spitting into the basin, using mouthwash to clean his mouth.

Then, he looked at himself in the mirror over the sink. He did not like the man looking back.

STARTING OVER

Chapter 8

Tuesday morning, LAPD homicide detective Jeff Chandler, sipped coffee in his townhouse. The television was showing the weather and morning commute. Jeff, wearing a suit and tie, his gun inside his shoulder holster, glanced up to his husband Detective Mickey Stanton coming down the stairs of their loft.

Also wearing a business suit and holster, Mickey worked in the robbery follow-up unit in the LAPD. He kissed Jeff as he walked by to get his own cup of coffee.

Jeff paused to catch the headlines before he dropped bread into the toaster for breakfast.

'*And, in local news, the much beleaguered chief of the Santa Monica police, William Sharpe, has resigned...*'

Jeff choked mid-sip.

"What did I just hear?" Mickey asked from the galley kitchen. He walked closer, holding a steaming mug of coffee. It was a 'Mickey Mouse' shaped mug, one his sister Aura had given him.

'*...the media relations unit from the Santa Monica Police Department released this video of the chief of police giving his resignation.*'

Both Jeff and Mickey paused to watch the short clip. There was Billy Sharpe, eyeglasses on, wearing his dark uniform, holding a sheet of paper.

'*This conference has been called for me to tender my resignation. It has been my honor to serve the men and women of the Santa Monica Police Department...*'

"Shut the fuck up." Mickey shook his head. "No way."

"Goddamn it. I knew it." Jeff looked for his phone.

'*…as the chief of police, it was my job to set a shining example. I realize an err in judgment changed that. I apologize to the men and women of the department and to the community. It is with deep regret that I am leaving my position as chief, effective immediately. Thank you.*'

Jeff held his phone in his hand after setting his coffee down and watched Billy on the TV.

The anchorman returned to the screen after the video. '*Our reporters reached out to Chief Sharpe's office for further comment, but we were informed the chief has already left. According to the city council and district attorney's office no charges will be filed against the chief for his actions in damaging a pickup truck window.*' The video from the parking lot surveillance camera was rerun.

Mickey snarled and shut off the TV. "Fuck, I hate people."

Jeff tried to think clearly since he was so enraged. He sent Billy a text. '*Hey. Just saw your press release. Are you okay?*'

Mickey dropped four slices of bread into the toaster.

'*yes. I'm fine.*'

Jeff leaned on his husband to show him Billy's text.

"Of course he's going to say that." Mickey removed butter and jam from the fridge.

'*Come out for dinner tonight?*' Jeff asked.

'*I'll let you know.*'

Jeff tossed his phone on the counter and ran his hand over his hair in frustration. "Mick?"

"Yeah?" Mickey tugged two paper towels off a roll to use as plates.

"What's he gonna do? Huh? Retire?"

"He can. Alex is rich." Mickey picked up the 'mouse' mug, since that was Aura's nickname for him, 'Mouse'.

STARTING OVER

Jeff had another thought. He grabbed his phone again and sent Mark a text, '*I take it you heard about Billy?*'

'*Yes.*'

'*Are you in Sac?*'

'*No. In LA at the moment.*'

"Oh!" Jeff watched Mickey remove the toast and put two slices on each paper towel. "Wanna see Mark tonight?"

"Is he in LA?" Mickey buttered the four slices.

"Yes." Jeff sent Mark, '*Dinner?*'

'*Perhaps. Can I get back to you?*'

'*You bet. How is the chief dealing with this?*'

'*He will be fine. No worries.*'

Jeff watched Mickey eating the toast as he stood near the counter. "Fuck." Jeff felt like shit.

Mickey gestured to the buttered slices of toast.

Jeff set his phone down and picked up a piece to eat. "If you were a movie star, and made millions, I wouldn't work."

Mickey chuckled. "I'll keep that in mind when I'm discovered."

Jeff thought about Billy having to make that resignation video and didn't know if he could have done it. If what Billy had done had warranted it, maybe, but...

For punching an inanimate object after a hateful homophobic slur? Nope.

After gobbling the toast, Jeff brushed off his hands and checked the time. "Let's go."

Mickey nodded, dropped the butter knife into the sink and jogged up to the loft bathroom.

Jeff grabbed his car keys and shut off lights and the TV, sighing deeply about the changes going on around him. It was as if everyone he loved, was starting over.

~

Stan drove with Mark to his gym in West Hollywood.

Since they were stuck in LA for the day, at least until Mark attended Alex's shrink appointment, Stan figured they should make the best of it.

On their way from Bel Air, Mark, his sunglasses on, wearing spandex shorts and a sleeveless top for the hot yoga, rested his hand on Stan's bare leg. Stan, in gym-shorts and a tank top, was going to lift weights so he looked his best for the weekend shoot.

His car's trunk was still filled with the framed photos from Arnold Newhouse's office. As they drove to his apartment building in WeHo, Stan noticed Mark texting on his phone.

"Love?"

"Hmm?" Stan lowered the music blasting from the speakers.

"Would Becca consider living at the estate until the baby is born?"

"I don't think so. She's working here in West Hollywood. She really loves her job."

Mark appeared anxious.

"Hey." Stan cupped his hand over Mark's as it rested on his thigh. "Maybe in her last trimester?"

"Yes. All right." Mark squeezed Stan's quadriceps.

Stan stopped the car as the security gate to his apartment building rolled open. "Don't worry about her. Trust her, Mark. She has an amazing support group. Not only us, but at her work."

Mark glanced at him as Stan drove under the building to his reserved parking spot. "Could we pop in? Could I meet her coworkers?"

Stan rolled into his assigned space and shut off the Lamborghini's engine. He held his phone and sent Becca a text. *'Mark wants to meet your coworkers.'*

'okie dokie.'

Stan laughed and showed Mark Becca's text.

STARTING OVER

"Very good." Mark smiled at him and climbed out of the car. They left their change of clothing in it, and exited through a security door. The gym was a block away, on Santa Monica Boulevard.

Holding Mark's hand, Stan and he plodded down the steep decline in the warm wind. "So, the plan is to head to Paradise after Alex's appointment?"

"Jeff has asked to meet for dinner. I thought perhaps it may be too late if we go tonight. Why don't we wake up early and drive tomorrow?"

"I'd prefer that." Stan surveyed the crowded boulevard as their presence was noted. Phones were held up overtly to film them.

"I'll see what Jackie and Adam are up to." Mark waited as Stan opened the gym's door for him.

"Cool." Stan walked with Mark to the front desk, where they scanned their keychain ID tags to get in.

~

Alex slid his sunglasses to the top of his head as he walked the length of the studio to his set. Tugging at his tight jeans, Alex could still feel the echoes of Billy's lovemaking. The chief had asserted his dominance three times last night.

Alex struggled to walk without chafing.

"Alex."

He paused and tried to straighten his features. "Hi, Char."

"Have you spoken to Mark about the role in *Forever Young*?"

"No."

"Did he get the script?"

"I guess so."

"Any news on when *Lover Boy* is going to get through post?"

"Nope." Alex tried to loosen the stranglehold his briefs and jeans had on him today. He yearned for his sarong.

Charlotte, her dark-framed eyeglasses on her nose, her brown hair in a ponytail, raised an eyebrow at him. "Rough night?"

"Uh."

Charlotte laughed as she walked away. "Oh, to be a fly on your bedroom wall…ten minutes to get on the set, sugarplum!"

Alex felt his face go red hot and headed to his wardrobe department, needing to get a different, loose-fitted, pair of pants.

~

Steve knotted his maroon necktie in the full-length mirror in his walk-in closet. He tugged his shirt cuffs down and buttoned them. When he emerged into his bedroom, Tadzio was there.

Steve stopped short.

Tadzio, holding a compact and applying pale pink lipstick, closed the compact and slid it and the lipstick into a purse that was lying flat on the dresser. He turned to look at Steve. "What, Steven?" Tadzio looked down at his own outfit. "Iz Coco Chanel."

Tadzio wore a black and white tweed houndstooth jacket and matching skirt, hose, and black pumps.

Steve blinked as he inspected it. He had seen the women working in his office dressed this way.

Tadzio had painted his fingernails hot pink, had lined his eyes with black and shadowed his eyelids in pale blue, his hair was in soft golden ringlets to his slightly padded shoulders, and he was deciding on a scarf or a chunky white beaded necklace.

"This, Steven?" Tadzio tied a silk black and white scarf around his throat. "Or dis?" He removed it, and held up a necklace with large round opalescent beads.

"Yuh…uh…" Steve had no clue. "Either." He thumbed to the direction of the kitchen. "We have to eat and get going."

Tadzio nodded and fastened the necklace, then picked up white cotton gloves and put them into his purse. "I am ready."

STARTING OVER

Steve grabbed up his suit jacket, folded it over his arm, and then remembered his phone. He followed Tadzio out of their bedroom and shook his head at Tadzio from behind, since Steve would never imagine from this angle, Tadzio was a man.

~

Jack stood in the courthouse, holding a brief he needed to file. He ran his hand over his closely cropped blond hair and felt tired, as if he couldn't shake a fatigue or jetlag he'd had since he returned from Florida.

While he waited his turn, his phone vibrated. Jack took it out of his suit jacket pocket and put his reading glasses on. Mark had asked if he and Adam were free for dinner.

'*Yes.*' Jack kept alert to his surroundings since he didn't want to hold up the line of attorneys waiting to do what he was doing. '*Where?*'

'*We could go to the place in Malibu, near you.*'

Jack moved up in the line. '*Why don't you two just come to our place?*'

'*Jeff and Mick are also coming.*'

'*That's fine.*'

'*All right. When?*'

Jack battled to focus since he was tired and distracted. '*Seven?*'

'*See you then.*'

Jack was about to send Adam a text letting him know, when, the clerk said, "Please don't use your phone in line."

"Sorry." Jack handed him the paperwork. "This needs to be filed."

The clerk slapped a stamp on it and entered it into a log book.

Jack couldn't deal with this today. He battled for almost a week trying to get his head back into the game, but ever since his father had died, he struggled.

"Here you go. Next!"

Removing his glasses, Jack took the stamped form and backed away from the line. He called Adam, since he was too tired to text.

"Hey, babe."

"Adam." Jack plugged one ear as the noise level increased in the room. "Mark is coming to dinner with Jeff and Mick."

"Okay. What should we make?"

"Just barbeque something. I'll bring food home on my way."

"Okay. What time?"

"Seven."

"Okay."

Jack disconnected the call and left the chaotic courthouse. It took him a few minutes to get his head cleared enough to locate his car and remember what he had to do next. Jack sank in the Jaguar's bucket seat and closed his eyes for a moment, trying to figure out why he was struggling.

~

Wearing jeans and an LAPD T-shirt, Billy Sharpe pulled his Corvette into the parking lot of the SWAT training facility. He picked up his holstered firearm from the passenger's seat and walked to the classroom.

The parking area was loaded with pickup trucks and Detroit muscle, dogs barked from kennels nearby.

Billy opened the door to the building and as he stepped into the room full of men, they appeared to have been waiting for him.

Holding a fake microphone, Bernie Brown was in the middle of the gang of SWAT-thugs, and the entire room of men broke out into song. While they did, the sergeant turned on a TV screen which had Billy's karaoke number cued up.

The gang of crazy cops 'sang' with Billy's video, belting out the lyrics like a flash-mob of teenagers.

STARTING OVER

As they serenaded their new lieutenant, Billy shook his head in amazement. He was so flattered, he dabbed at the corners of his eyes as he laughed, since they were awful.

They finished singing, and took exaggerated bows and yelled, 'Ta-Da!'

"I fucking love you guys." Billy could not be happier.

"Woo!" Manny Rodriguez pumped his arm. "A million hits! L-T you've gone viral!"

"Check it out!" Jim Hague used a TV remote control to show Billy how many other police officers had paid tribute to him, singing that same song after announcing why; to support him. To stand behind the 'beleaguered gay chief of police' no matter what.

"Well. Fuck me." Billy watched the montage of police karaoke videos from across not only the nation, but the world. Cops from England, Ireland, Australia, South Africa, Germany, Norway, Greece, Portugal, Mexico...

The men in the room pumped their fists in unison, giving Billy a militaristic cheer.

After what had been pure hell...Billy was finally finding heaven.

Chapter 9

Finished running on the treadmill while Stan completed his heavy weightlifting, Mark and Stan enjoyed the hot yoga class together.

Then, they returned to Stan's apartment and showered.

Blowing his hair dry as Stan shaved in the basin next to him, Mark thought about this appointment with Dr Van Eldon and wanted to get it out of his head. It was bothering him to such an extent, he wasn't up for sex.

Mark set the blow-dryer into the vanity cabinet and took a moment to calm down, since he was running a dialogue in his mind about what he wanted to discuss with the doctor.

As he imagined Alex's denials, his excuses and his half-assed apologies, Mark's anger grew.

At a light touch to his shoulder, Mark woke from his thoughts.

Stan pulled him into his embrace.

"Sorry, love. I'm so bloody distracted." Mark ran his fingers down Stan's smooth, broad back to his bottom and cupped it in his hands. "Do you want a climax?"

Stan touched Mark's chin and stared into his eyes. "Later."

The fact that Stan could read his moods so well gave Mark some relief. He backed up and tried to gather his thoughts. Mark entered Stan's bedroom and picked up his pair of Rag & Bone white skinny jeans, putting them on with a pale green Salvatore Ferragamo short-sleeved top and Alexander McQueen black loafers. "Right."

STARTING OVER

Stan dressed in blue jeans and a white cotton sleeveless crewneck top.

"So..." Mark ran his hands through his hair and sat on the foot of Stan's bed. "My word. I can't think."

Stan sat next to him, shoulder to shoulder. "We'll stop by Becca's workplace, then I'll drive you to Alex's appointment, wait for you, and then we'll go to Jack's place."

"Yes." Mark asked him, "Did I tell Jeff?"

"Can I check?"

Mark looked for his phone. He picked it up and scrolled his texts. "Can you?" Mark handed it to Stan because he struggled to read the tiny print.

Stan used his thumb on the touch screen as Mark tugged at his necklace, running the chai charm along the gold chain.

"You did." Stan handed the phone back to Mark.

Mark kissed him in gratitude and stuffed his wallet and keys into his pockets. "Oh. Pet. You haven't had anything to eat."

"I'll grab a protein bar. It's fine." Stan left the bedroom.

Mark tried to relax but this ordeal with his son was infuriating him.

He gathered his workout clothing to wash in Bel Air this evening and met Stan in the kitchen. He was chewing a healthy nut and berry bar as he read his own phone.

Mark checked the time. "Right. Shall we?"

Stan stuck the bar in his teeth and picked up his keys, shouldering their gym bags. He left his apartment, double-locked the door and the two of them made their way to the parking area. Stan finished the snack and threw the wrapper into a small trashcan in the lobby.

Mark sat in the Lamborghini and found he was tensing his back, his neck, and his jaw. After the relaxing yoga class it was annoying. Stan started the engine and backed out, waiting for the security gate to roll open.

Mark exhaled loudly. "I don't know what to say. I don't know how to discuss this with Dr Van Eldon. I want to slap Alex in the mouth."

Stan paused as he emerged onto the city street, then said, "I'm okay, Mark. I mean, I have to move on too. I'm not interested in stewing over it, of keeping it fresh in my mind. I'm trying to let go."

"Perhaps you can. If so, you're a better man than me."

"Mark? I'm not saying it wasn't awful. I just need to get over it. I can't keep thinking about it. I need to just start fresh and live my life."

Mark gazed at Stan while he drove them to Becca's workplace before the doctor's office. "Baby. Alex wants to come to the estate. I'm not sure I want him there. But, I do want Billy to come. Billy needs us. He needs that home to unwind."

Stan said, "If Billy's with Alex, Mark, he won't fuck up. I got the impression Billy is furious with Alex. Do you think Alex will ever try that again?"

"I will bloody murder him if he does." Mark showed his teeth.

Stan slowed for a traffic signal. "Mark? Go ahead, talk to the shrink. But, don't dwell on this. Alex said he's sorry. He most likely is, but for himself. I know he doesn't really care about my feelings."

"That's just it!" Mark growled, growing furious. "He is sorry for how this is hitting him. Sorry for himself." Mark shook his head. "I cannot believe my own son behaved this way. I cannot believe it."

"See what happens with the shrink, but, Mark?" Stan rubbed Mark's leg. "Let it go. Please. Seeing you so hurt, so angry. I can't take it."

STARTING OVER

"Oh, my pet, my pet." Mark held Stan's hand and kissed his knuckles. "Here I am worried for you, and you are worried for me."

Stan chuckled. "That's love, Mark Antonious."

Mark met Stan's warm smile with one of his own. "Yes. You are right. Give us a kiss."

Stan pecked Mark on the lips and drove through the LA traffic to Becca's natural healing center.

~

Becca finished placing fresh linens on a massage table. She took the dirty linens out and then glanced into the lobby. Mark and Stan were there, looking around.

Becca placed the sheets into a bin and rushed towards them. "Hey!"

"Hey!" Stan picked her up into his arms.

"Hullo, lovely." Mark gave her a hug.

"Come meet everyone!" She dragged Mark over to a receptionist. "This is Lena. This is Mark and Stan."

"I recognize them from their ads." She shook their hands.

"Bev!" Becca called to her.

"Hi, Stan." Bev, who had joined them for paintball and other events, hugged Stan. "You must be Mark."

"Hullo." Mark shook her hand.

Becca was beaming in excitement as Mark greeted her staff. Anything she could do to help Mark feel less stressed about this pregnancy, the better.

As the massage therapists and acupuncturist became available, Becca introduced them.

"No worries, Mark, Stan. Becca is in good hands."

Mark gave Becca a warm smile. "Yes. I believe she is."

~

By four pm, Alex parked his cherry red Ferrari in the lot of his doctor's office. He wasn't keen on his father coming. Alex wasn't planning on telling the old doc about his deviant deed.

After reading the call time on his paperwork for tomorrow's rehearsal and seeing which scenes he had to work on tonight, Alex heard a rumbling noise. Stan's green Aventador pulled into the parking lot.

Alex folded the paperwork and climbed out of his car.

Stan parked in a shady spot in the lot. His father leaned over to give Stan a kiss and then exited the car looking model-ready in his costly designer clothing; the perfect leading man. As Mark approached him in tight white pants and a pale green top, Alex was so envious of his dad's fabulous sex appeal and gorgeous looks, he battled to stop feeling inferior.

Alex also wasn't used to getting a sneer every time his father saw him. "Hi, Dad." He went for a kiss.

Mark turned his cheek away from Alex and opened the door to the lobby. Alex gazed at his father's clothing. He looked down at his own, and wondered if he needed another visit to Rodeo Drive to embellish his wardrobe. Competing with his father was exhausting.

Since Mark had seen Dr Van Eldon for decades, he knew where to go. Alex tugged at his clothing, which felt ill-fitted since he was wearing baggy pants to keep comfortable.

Mark opened the door to the doctor's office and sat down on the brown leather sofa.

Alex paused to gaze at the tropical fish tank, tugging at his waistband.

"What on earth are you wearing?" Mark asked, picking up a magazine from the side table.

Alex ignored him and didn't sit, since, well, Billy had been rough on him.

STARTING OVER

Mark flipped pages of a magazine, appearing irritated. "Alex. Sit."

"No." Alex tried to pull off looking fascinated by the colorful fish.

The inner door opened and the older, spectacled, bald man said, "Come inside. I'm ready for you."

Mark threw the magazine on the table and entered the office.

Alex inhaled deeply and tugged at his pants as he followed.

~

Steve read invoices as he sat at his desk in the Sacramento office. Yes, he could manage, but…he needed Mark's input.

He didn't grow up with this company like Mark did. Steve was a cop, not a fashionista. Even his work with Parsons and Company's advertising agency couldn't prepare him for this.

He had emails, voicemails, as well as employees here in the office, all coming to him for final approval on purchases. Some orders with costs in the hundreds of thousands.

He struggled to contact Mark. First he called, then he texted. "Goddamn it."

Steve gave up trying to deal with it himself and stood from his desk. There were employees that had worked here for years. He knew when to wave the white flag and ask for help.

He put his suit jacket back on, buttoned it after smoothing his tie, and headed out to find help. As Steve made his way to the next level in the chain of command, the buyers, Steve passed offices with men and women busy at work.

He paused. Steve walked over to a glass wall, seeing a dozen women working on both computers and fabric samples, holding up swatches to patterns. They were wearing similar outfits to Tadzio; blazers and skirts, nylons and pumps, chunky accessories and lipstick.

Steve looked down at his suit, one he'd worn for years while working at Parsons and Company. It dawned on him. He was clueless. He'd purchased this suit for his interview with Harold Parsons. It was a decade old. He'd gotten it on sale at a rack in a men's clothing warehouse store.

Holy shit.

Steve forgot his mission for the moment and took the stairs to the lower level. He made his way to the designers.

There was his Tadzio, looking just like the gorgeous female employees from the administration offices.

"Yes. This iz the fabric pattern." Tadzio worked with Greg picking swatches. "I think wit narrow pinning, on the waist, yes?"

As the designers noticed Steve, they smiled and greeted him.

"Steven!" Tadzio brightened up. "Come see the design Greg use from me on his computer."

Self-conscious now of his outdated wardrobe and lack of style, Steve ran his hand over his tie and entered the room.

"Look. Greg make my drawing on his computer."

Greg said, "Steve, Tadzio's amazing. His designs are so out there."

Tadzio laughed. "Out dare iz good, Steven."

"Can I borrow Tadzio?" Steve asked.

The designers laughed sweetly at Steve, since well, Steve owned the company, and Tadzio was his hubby.

Tadzio, confident on his heels, approached him. "What iz it?"

Steve held Tadzio's hand and kept quiet until he had returned, up the stairs, to his own office. He said, "I need your help while Mark is gone."

"Of course."

Steve sat Tadzio at his big desk. "I have this invoice for Bellatory wool. This is the designer asking for it. This is cost." Steve showed Tadzio the computer file. "What do I do? I know the order has arrived in San Francisco."

STARTING OVER

"Yes." Tadzio used the mouse to scroll over the invoice. "You see the markup. Iz the same on this past sheet. The higher the fabric cost, Steven, the lower the mark. Look. See this fabric? Iz very in-nexpens-eve. So, we make higher mark to double."

Steve got it. "Thanks."

"Iz okay. I know dis from so many years in fashion industry." Tadzio adjusted the invoice to reflect the profit margins.

"Babe?"

"Yes, Steven?" Tadzio gazed up at him.

Steve touched his jacket lapel. "Um."

Tadzio became more attentive.

"Can you go shopping with me?" Steve felt like a moron.

Tadzio's pale blue eyes went wide. "Yes! I would love to dress you. Steven, you are so handsome. But…you are more macho than style."

Steve ran his hand over his tie, one he'd had for a decade. "Shit. I'm embarrassed."

Tadzio gripped Steve by his necktie and pulled him downwards. "Let me dress you. I will make you look like a model."

Steve peered at his office door. He scooted the desk chair back, knelt down, and pushed Tadzio's skirt up his thighs.

"Steven!" Tadzio giggled and exposed his cock from his panties and nylons.

Steve drew Tadzio's cock into his mouth and sucked, grateful for the backup.

~

"No! You are not sorry!"

"I am! How many times do I have to say it!"

"You're sorry about yourself! You're sorry you got caught!"

"No! I'm sorry I ever touched him! It was one of the lousiest nights of my life!"

"Of your life? *Of your life?* So, this is about you?"

"Oh, my God! I can't say anything right!"

"I don't know what to do with him! *I do not know what to do with him!*"

"Mark." Dr Van Eldon held up his hand. "I want you to stop shouting at each other for a moment."

While seated on the stiff brown, noisy, leather sofa, Mark ran his hand over his hair. The water bottle he was drinking from was now empty. "Please stop pacing!" Mark screamed at his son.

"Alex?" the doctor asked quietly, "Please sit."

"I don't want to." Alex crosses his arms.

Dr Van Eldon, seated in his wingback chair, a yellow legal pad on his knee, wearing a tweed suit and bowtie, studied them carefully.

Mark brooded. "This is perfectly useless." He checked the time.

"I said I was sorry!" Alex yelled.

"Why did you do it! Why!" Mark could not stop his fury. "You seem to think everything that is mine is yours by default! I've got news for you, Alexander. It isn't."

"Alex," Dr Van Eldon's voice was calming. "Why can't you sit down?"

"My ass is sore!" Alex growled.

Mark blinked. "Bloody hell."

The doctor stood and opened a wooden cabinet. He withdrew a pillow and handed it to Alex.

Alex snatched it, then sat on top of it at the farthest spot on the sofa, away from his dad.

The doctor returned to his chair and picked up his pad. "Alex. I think you owe Mark an explanation as to why you did what you did."

"Ya wanna list?" Alex snarled at Mark.

"Yes!" Mark screamed.

"Alex?" the doctor spoke softly.

STARTING OVER

Mark clenched his jaw in fury.

Alex held up his index finger. "One." He snarled in utter sarcasm. "I wanted you to think Stan and I had an affair so you'd divorce him and get back with Steve."

Mark winced and shook his head as he stared at the doctor.

"Two." Alex held up two fingers to his dad in a British, 'fuck-you', which Mark doubted the doctor realized. "Every fucking man in our life wants you! Every fucking one!" Alex shrieked.

Mark battled for sanity as his son told him how much he hated him.

"Three!" Alex shifted on the pillow as if it wasn't helping. "You fucked my husband so many times I don't even know how many!" Alex covered his face.

There it was.

The truth. Finally.

Mark sank into the stiff, noisy leather cushions and closed his eyes.

Dr Van Eldon paused, then asked, "So this was revenge for what Mark did?"

Alex stood from the couch, as if he needed to. He ran his fingers through his long hair and appeared to be in agony. "Yes. He did. He made love to my man. *He* did!" Alex aimed a loaded finger at Mark.

"You made love to my Steven." Mark felt like vomiting he was so sick of this bullshit.

"Once!" Alex held up his finger. "One time in Rome! He came at me! He and Jackie! They came to me!"

"Alex?" Dr Van Eldon kept his voice low, "What do you want from your father?"

Alex turned his back to them.

Mark became guilty about what he had done with Billy. He had no idea that it haunted Alex to this extent. The first time the chief had pushed him into sex, Mark went into a suicidal tailspin that nearly put him into the grave. After that, Alex nagged Steve and Billy to get them to fuck to entertain him. Next, Alex had an affair with a costar, Diesel VanDen, and since he felt guilty for cheating on Billy, he gave Mark and Billy the green light to fuck.

"Alex? Mark is right here. Tell him."

"I want…" Alex sniffled. "I want to be like him." He lowered his head. "I want people to respect me like they do him."

"Respect is earned," Mark said.

"There!" Alex aimed that loaded finger at Mark again. "You think I'm so much less than anyone else in your life. I'm a superstar! I'm the 'it' boy in Hollywood! Me!"

Mark had no idea what he expected, but this surely wasn't it.

Alex loomed closer to where Mark was seated. "Me. I'm the one making millions per film. I'm the one. Not Stan. Not your 'pet'."

"Leave him out of this." Mark shifted to sit higher on the uncomfortable, noisy sofa.

"Tell me, Dad." Alex crossed his arms defensively. "How many times did you fuck Billy? Suck his dick? Had him suck your dick?"

"Oh?" Mark narrowed his eyes. "Whilst you were humping Diesel VanDen? Whilst you told your husband to go ahead and make love to me out of guilt?"

"Mark." Dr Van Eldon shook his head, obviously wanting Mark to stop.

Mark stood from the horrible couch. "Alex, it was a blip in our life. If I made love to him three times, I'd be surprised. You behave as if Billy and I had an affair that lasted years. That couldn't be further from the truth."

Alex showed his teeth. "Who does he call when he needs someone to help him?"

STARTING OVER

Mark crossed his arms. "He calls Steven, he calls Jeff, Mick, Jackie. And, Alexander, if you would *bloody grow up*!" Mark roared, "He would ask you!"

"I hate you!" Alex screamed, "I hate you!" He covered his face and wept.

Mark felt so ill at the moment he was about to fall over. "There it is," Mark whispered, "The truth."

"Alex? Is that the truth?" the doctor asked, "Do you hate Mark?"

Alex dropped to his knees and wailed in aguish. "I hate that I can never be you…I hate the way everyone adores you and tolerates me."

"They don't bloody tolerate you, Alexander." Mark shook his head. "Billy worships the ground you walk on, but you're so self-involved you don't even recognize it." Mark exhaled deeply. "Jackie and Adam love you like a son. Steven is so mad for you, he'd kill for you."

The doctor handed Mark the tissue box, and he brought it to Alex.

"Tadzio would have married you, if you weren't already Billy's." Mark tapped Alex with the box. "He's loved you for a decade."

Alex lowered his hands and took a tissue.

Mark dropped the box on the coffee table. "Josh and Tanner adore you. Jeff and Mickey, Blake and Hunter, all love you to death. You foolish boy. What more do you want from us? How high a pedestal do you need?"

Alex, his eyes red-rimmed, stared at him. "High enough to see you at eye level, Dad. That's all."

"Stand up, Alexander."

After blowing his nose and wiping his eyes, Alex did.

"Come here."

Alex fell against him.

Mark rocked Alex in his arms and kissed his hair. "So, this is revenge for Billy." Alex nodded against him. "Then, let me apologize." Mark shook Alex so he met his gaze. "I am truly sorry. Billy was under the impression you gave him permission. He thought after your affair with Diesel, he had a free pass."

Alex's lower lip quivered.

"Be assured, Alexander, Billy and I have not had sex oral or anal, in years. And, you, my pet, coaxed my Steven and Billy to perform together for your entertainment."

Alex winced and peeked at the doctor.

"All right? Can we get beyond this chaos?" Mark needed to get out of this stuffy room. "Have we had enough?"

Dr Van Eldon stood from his chair. "I suggest we meet on Friday for another group session."

I'm sure you do. Mark did not want one. "I will be living up north in Paradise. I will not be available."

"Dad." Alex dabbed at his nose with the tissue. "Come on."

The doctor read his appointment book. "So, you're no longer going to be in LA?"

Alex replied, "He is. He's got a modeling shoot on Sunday here."

"I would prefer not coming back here after. Alex, the shoots are taxing." Mark checked his phone.

Alex stood near the doctor's desk. "Um. I'll come back. And...I need more pills."

Thinking about what Billy had said, Mark spun towards the doctor. "No."

"Huh?" Alex cleared his throat and threw away the tissue. "Dad? I need them."

"What for?" Mark approached the desk, seeing the doctor writing out another prescription for valium.

"For...ya know. Keeping sane." Alex inhaled deeply.

STARTING OVER

"No." Mark shook his head. "Doctor, I don't think giving Alex those pills is wise."

"Why not?" the doctor asked, holding the piece of paper.

Mark didn't know what to do. "Do you mean other than the fact that Alexander used those pills to drug my husband?"

Before the doctor reconsidered, Alex took the prescription and folded it.

"Alex?" The doctor narrowed his eyes behind his round eyeglasses. "Those pills are only for you. Understood? You are not to abuse them."

"I know." Alex tucked the prescription into his pocket.

Mark asked, "Are you suicidal?"

His son glared at him. "No!"

"Alex?" Dr Van Eldon studied Alex.

"No!"

While Alex and the doctor scheduled an appointment, Mark sent Stan a text, *'five minutes.'*

'okay.'

It had only been an hour, but to Mark, it had felt like a week.

Alex pocketed his written appointment reminder and he and Mark walked to the door of the waiting room.

A woman was seated there, and on her lap was a magazine.

When Mark emerged he spotted his cologne ad in the centerfold. The woman looked up, then down, then up with her mouth hanging open.

Mark touched Alex's shoulder, nudging him to the door. Alex had seen the woman's reaction as well, and the two of them left the waiting area and walked towards the lobby exit.

Mark stopped Alex before they stepped outside.

Alex appeared as exhausted as Mark felt.

"I am going to Jackie's for dinner. Would you like to come?"

"Yes." Alex cleared his throat.

Mark checked his watch. "It's just after five. Why don't you go home and freshen up, then you and Billy come by at seven."

"Okay." Alex tugged at his jeans in back.

Mark asked, "Why is he being so rough on you?"

"Why do you think?" Alex pouted.

"Your police officer has imposed your penalty?"

Alex muttered under his breath.

Mark used one finger to raise his son's chin, making Alex search his eyes. "Do you truly hate me?"

Alex lunged at him, holding him tight, pressing his face into Mark's hair.

Mark rocked him gently. "All right, baby. This too, shall pass."

"Dad…" Alex hiccupped. "I fucking love you. I'm so sorry. I mean it."

Mark held his baby boy in his arms and squeezed tight.

STARTING OVER

Chapter 10

Stan spotted father and son leaving the building. He lowered the loud music he was playing and stuffed his phone into his pocket. Mark opened the passenger's door and dropped heavily on the bucket seat.

Instead of hitting Mark with questions, Stan said, "It's only five...should we go home first, or still head to Malibu?"

"Home." Mark put his sunglasses on.

As Stan backed out of the space, Alex had as well. Now they were both going to the same place. Stan followed the fiery red Ferrari, wondering what happened inside that office.

After a quiet moment, Mark seemed to unwind and rested his hand on Stan's leg. "So." He squeezed Stan's quadriceps. "Becca's coworkers seem very capable."

"They do. I think if she needed something, they would be there. And that one women, Lena? I think that was her name. She just had a baby."

Mark appeared to be listening, but also preoccupied.

"And Bev is a good friend. She's come out with us before." Stan hit Interstate 10 since it wasn't at a full stop at the moment. Alex did the same, still in front of him.

Mark sounded hoarse, as if he had been shouting, "Becca is gay?"

After driving on the highway in the speed lane, Stan merged over to the right lanes as his La Cienega Boulevard exit drew closer. "I don't think she identifies with either gay or straight.

She once told me she just likes people. I don't think she has a preference."

"How bizarre." Mark took his hand back from Stan's lap and read his phone.

"What I think is bizarre is that the guys are all gay, live in the same house, and I don't think they have sex. I don't know why, but I think *that's* bizarre." Stan stopped for a traffic signal at the bottom of the highway ramp. Alex was still in front of him.

"Really?" Mark glanced at him as he drove through the busy intersection. "Have they ever made advances on you?"

Stan shook his head. "Nope."

"Huh. I wonder why that is? I mean, they are all attractive smart young men."

"No clue." Stan glanced at Mark's lap, at the way the white fabric hugged his body. Being able to see the outline where Mark had tucked his cock to the right side, made Stan horny.

"I do know a bit about Natalie Cushman. She would be good for Becca. To be honest, Stan, if they do date, Natalie would do wonders to ease my mind about our sweet Becca. When Adam had a terrible time with his former agency partner, Jack Turner, Natalie was a godsend, helping him get through it."

"That's good news. Anything to ease your mind, Mark." Stan followed Alex as he indicated the turn onto their street. Stan glanced at Mark's cock again and then focused on the road.

Alex continued on, to his own home. Stan pulled into the driveway of the house they were staying in. Steve's house.

He tapped the remote on his visor and the garage door opened. The two-car garage was almost completely empty. Mark unfastened his seatbelt and touched himself casually as he waited for Stan to park.

Those white pants were driving Stan to distraction. "What's Steve going to do with this house?" Stan shut the engine and unhooked his seatbelt.

STARTING OVER

"Sell, I'd imagine." Mark opened the car door and climbed out. He looked just as good going as he did coming.

That ass. Fuck me.

Stan picked up their gym bags and followed Mark into the house. He stopped to dump the damp workout clothing into the washing machine and then entered the kitchen.

Mark was drinking from a bottle of water, he had set his phone and sunglasses on the kitchen counter.

Stan could not get over him. After the Botox and hair cut, Mark looked thirty, easily. And the body on him...

Stan tugged at his tight crotch as his cock thickened.

"My big man." Mark licked his lips after he drank most of the water. "You must be ravishingly hungry."

Stan tossed his keys and phone on the counter near Mark's and drew Mark closer, using one arm around the model's narrow waist.

"Well. Hullo." Mark set the bottle aside and gave Stan a sexy smile.

"Fuck, you're gorgeous." Stan pressed his cock against Mark's and went for his neck, tasting his salty skin. Mark's scent was intoxicating.

"Mmm." Mark purred and wrapped his hands around Stan's biceps.

"I can't believe how lucky I am." Stan chewed his way to Mark's lips.

Mark met his kiss and they enjoyed each other's tongues as their cocks thickened.

Feeling Mark was receptive after the doctor's appointment, Stan ran his hands down Mark's back to his ass. He parted from the kiss and looked at Mark's crotch.

Mark's cock had engorged and he could see where it was trapped down one leg, under the tight white fabric.

"Oh, geez." Stan's dick pulsated, dampening his briefs.

"What do you want, you gorgeous stud?" Mark teased, running one finger over Stan's erect nipples.

"I want to chew on that." Stan pointed.

Mark stepped back and looked at himself, touching his cock through the white pants sensually.

Stan slid his hand into his own, straightening his dick, touching the seeping slit before removing it quickly.

Mark smiled and sucked on one of Stan's fingers, his green eyes gleaming with sexual potency.

"Oh, fuck." Stan was about to come.

Mark drove him out of his mind. The scent coming from the top model was so appetizing Stan was about to dry hump him.

"Someone wants a climax." Mark chewed on Stan's earlobe and neck.

"Fuck." Stan was riding the edge as Mark sent chills racing all over his body from his teething on his skin.

Mark cupped his palm over Stan's jeans, pushing against his erection.

Stan battled to hold back. "Mark."

"Mmm." Mark stuffed his hand down the front of Stan's pants and tugged at Stan's lower lip between his teeth. When Mark wrapped his fingers around Stan's cock, he couldn't hold back if he wanted to.

"Fuck!" Stan raced to open his pants before he came in them.

Mark dropped to his knees and took the head of Stan's damp cock into his mouth. Stan went into an orgasm instantly.

He gripped Mark by his shoulders and nearly fell over. Biting his lip, stifling a scream of pleasure, Stan's legs trembled as he climaxed.

Mark hummed and milked his cock gently into his mouth.

"Holy fuck." Stan was still hard as a rock. "You get me crazy."

STARTING OVER

Mark stood tall, pinched the soft head of Stan's cock, and craned his finger at him.

Still delirious, Stan staggered to follow, holding onto his open pants.

Mark's ass swayed in front of him as he climbed the stairs. Stan remained hot and bothered.

The gorgeous model paused near the bed, opening his shirt while giving Stan a look that made Stan's skin tingle and the hair rise on his forearms. Stan tore his own clothing off and watched Mark.

Mark dropped his shirt and when he unzipped his white pants, Stan knew there was nothing under them.

"Oh, fuck." Stan stared at the dark groomed pubic hair on Mark's pelvis as the model took off his shoes and lowered the white pants.

The second Mark stepped out of the clothing, Stan lunged at him. He picked Mark up by his waist and threw him to the bed.

Mark laughed in a sexy chuckle and relaxed, bending his knees.

Stan burrowed between Mark's legs and inhaled him, rubbing his face all over Mark's hard length. "Fuck!" Stan flexed his muscles and grabbed the lube, unable to hold back his craving to be inside Mark.

"That's it, baby."

Stan trembled with excitement as he covered his cock in gel, then, he didn't hesitate. He advanced on Mark like a wild animal, aiming his cock between Mark's legs.

Mark held his own knees and opened up.

"Oh, fuck." Stan pushed the head of his cock against Mark's rim and thrust in. "Damn. Damn!"

Mark gasped and arched his back.

Stan tried to control his breathing, but he was in an altered state, being run over by his raging testosterone and powerful need for sexual satisfaction.

After heavy weightlifting workouts, Stan needed release, and pairing that up with a man like Mark Antonious? Stan was going out of his mind.

Deep inside tight heat, Stan pumped his hips. "Oh, fuck, that's amazing."

"That's it, baby." Mark cooed and touched himself.

Stan stared into Mark's face, at his smooth skin, his full wild hair, then at his sculpted chest. His gaze wandered down Mark's cut torso to his Adonis belt and treasure trail, and then…that cock.

As he watched Mark touch himself, manipulate his erection, Stan came, again. "Fuck…oh, fuck."

Mark amped up the friction from below, then he released his hold on himself and clawed at the bedding. "Ah!"

"Oh, fuck!" Hearing Mark about to climax drove Stan wild. He braced himself and thrust in, giving Mark an internal climax.

"Ah! Yes! Ah!" Mark coughed on his gasps and cum spattered his smooth chest. "Ah! Stan! Ah!" Mark threw his head back into the pillows and creamy ropes of cum sprayed out of his slit.

Stan kept up the rhythm until Mark's cock stopped pumping out its load.

"Oh, my God…" Mark bent his knees tighter and curled his toes.

Stan thrust in once more, and then pulled out, seeing his cock still rock hard, coated in sticky gel and his own cum. He panted to gain air and sat up, one leg tucked under him, staring at Mark. "Jesus."

Mark caught his breath and touched his chest. "Bloody hell." He went limp on the bed.

STARTING OVER

Stan walked on his hands over Mark and stared at him.

Mark finally opened his eyes and blinked his long dark lashes at Stan. "That cock on you. That flamin' cock."

Stan chuckled. "He loves you."

"Get the bloody hell over here." Mark grabbed him by his face and drew him into a scorching kiss.

~

Alex was home first. He took off his clothing and opened the medicine cabinet in the bathroom, searching for something to soothe his sore butt.

He located some ointment and dabbed a little on, then washed his hands and checked his face. "You look like shit, Richfield."

He opened his drawers, trying to find something to wear, missing his sarong. Finding one of Billy's big LAPD T-shirts, Alex slipped it on, and then kept his lower half naked as he hunted for food. Standing in the kitchen, Alex searched the fridge, then the cabinets for a snack.

He missed Tadzio. Missed Steve.

Alex couldn't find anything to eat, so he stood at his back sliding door and stared at his pool, at the view of the Getty Museum, and at the distant hills.

The noise of the garage door opening drew his attention. The Corvette's roar, the door closing, and then noise at the connecting door. Alex tugged the shirt lower on his hips and waited.

Billy opened the door. He had a large duffle bag over his shoulder, and was wearing his black combat boots, black cargo pants and a black uniform shirt with dark LAPD patches on the shoulders.

"Hi." Alex walked closer, pushing the toes of his left foot, onto his right.

"Hey, doll." Billy smiled broadly and dropped the duffle bag, which sounded as if it had bricks in it.

Alex ventured closer. A whiff of sweat, gunpowder, and mud came from his happy man.

Billy's hands were black with dirt, and his shoes were coated in dry mud. Billy crouched down to unlace them.

Alex leaned over the bag and peeked into it. It was loaded with uniform gear, and a gun with ammo. There it was. 'SWAT' on a bullet proof vest.

"I'm going to take that into work tomorrow." Billy tugged off his combat boots. "I just didn't want to drive downtown in rush hour." Billy, still crouching, touched the edge of the T-shirt Alex was wearing and peeked under. "Oh? Naked?"

"Yeah. Well." Alex crossed his legs and backed up. "Kind of chafed."

Billy stood tall, washed his hands in the kitchen sink, and untucked his black shirt from his pants. "From me?"

Alex choked. "Yes, from you! Who do you think I'm having sex with?"

Billy gave him a sarcastic chuckle and walked towards their bedroom.

Alex followed.

The big lieutenant changed from his work clothing to shorts.

"You're running?" Alex asked.

"Yes."

"But…you look as if you were training all day. I can smell the gun oil and dirt on you."

Billy shot Alex a grin of pure delight. He inhaled. "Mmm. So can I." Billy laughed and entered the bathroom.

Alex touched his bottom, wondering if he could run. "Want company?"

Billy washed his face, then raised the toilet lid. "Can you run with a sore ass?"

Alex crossed his arms and leaned on the doorframe. "Why did you smirk when you asked me that?"

STARTING OVER

Billy flushed and washed his hands quickly. "Huh. You mean being forced to do sexual acts you don't want isn't fun?"

"All right. I get it." Alex watched the lieutenant shoot himself a dazzling smile in the mirror. "I can't recall seeing you this happy."

Billy swung Alex around to get out of the bathroom and sat on their bed to put on white socks. "Ya coming?"

Alex touched his bottom. "Maybe one more day."

"How was the shrink?" Billy stood and checked his phone.

"Meh. Dad and I yelled at each other for an hour."

Billy looked up from his phone, his expression dead serious.

Alex tugged the long shirt lower and felt stupid. "So, uh… we're invited to have dinner at Jack's place."

"Are we?" Billy scrolled through his phone.

"Yes."

"I see it. Seven." Billy set the phone down. "Let me get this done."

"Okay." Alex followed him to the door. "Is Dad running with you?"

Billy stopped. "Is he here with Stan?"

"Yes. I just told you Dad went to the doc with me. Stan drove."

"Okay." Billy opened the door and jogged off.

Alex stood by to watch him, seeing him run right to his dad's front door. Alex closed the door and returned to the kitchen. He crouched beside the duffle bag and had a closer look. "Holy fuck."

There was a disassembled military-grade rifle in it, with a long curved clip and boxes of bullets. Alex removed the black vest with the SWAT and POLICE tags on it. It was Billy's bulletproof vest.

Alex ran his hand over the Kevlar and sighed.

~

Mark stood at the sink in the bathroom, washing up. His doorbell rang. Stan, who was doing the same at the second basin asked, "Alex?"

"Possibly." Mark dried himself and slipped on his white pants, then trotted down the stairs. When he opened it, a macho police lieutenant was there, his smile, a mile wide. "Hullo, handsome."

"Mark." Billy gave Mark's body a sweep. "Would you and Stan like to go for a run?"

"I'm knackered. We went to the gym and I just came back from Alex's appointment." Mark called up the stairs, "Stan, love?"

"Yes?"

"The…lieutenant," Mark grinned at Billy as he said it, since his urge was to say 'the chief', "From the LAPD SWAT unit would like to know if you would care to run with him."

"Yes!"

Mark chuckled. "You got a resounding, yes." Mark crossed his arms over his bare chest. "Come in."

Billy did.

"Where's Alex?" Mark peered outside before he shut the door.

"Nursing a sore ass." Billy looked around. "What are you guys going to do with this house?"

"It's Steven's." Mark shrugged. "Ask him…Why were you so hard on Alex? Hmm? He couldn't sit."

"I wanted him to know what it's like to be dominated, when you don't want it."

"I assumed so. But, really, Billy. Don't hurt him."

"He's not hurt. He's a little chafed. He's fine." Billy softened his tone, "He said you two spent the hour with the shrink screaming at each other."

"Yes. Well." Mark ran his hand over his hair.

STARTING OVER

"Did that quack get through to him?"

"I hope so."

Both of them looked up when Stan descended the stairs wearing tiny blue gym shorts and white socks.

Billy poked Mark in the shoulder. "Fuck he's hot."

Stan located his running shoes and sat near them to put them on. "How're you doing, Billy?" Stan asked.

"Fan-fucking-tastic." Billy smiled.

Mark blinked in surprise. "Oh! You already officially returned to the LAPD?" Mark reached for one of Billy's hands, inspecting his fingernails. "Is that gunpowder?"

"Yes!" Billy grabbed Mark by his hips and picked him up in the air.

"Augh!" Mark flailed and held on. "Okay, macho man!"

Stan cracked up with laughter. "Ready, Ch—I mean, Lieutenant."

Mark was set back on his feet, breathless. "Oy! LAPD brute!" Mark swatted Billy's chest. "You and Alex are coming to dinner with us in Malibu at Jackie's."

"Ten-four." Billy jogged off.

Stan kissed Mark, smiling brightly, and caught up to the lieutenant.

Mark watched them go, and kept his smile as he closed the door.

~

Stan paced with Billy as they jogged through the picturesque neighborhood. It was good to see Billy happy. "So, Billy, are you off the hook for that Santa Monica crap now?"

"I am." Billy smiled at him as he ran.

Stan noticed the dark tattoo scrolled on Billy's biceps, making the macho man even more masculine. Ironically, Stan knew Alex had a lieutenant badge tattooed on his pelvis, from the nude scenes from last film they had done.

It had Billy's name on it, and 'forever' and had to be covered in makeup.

"Were you a lieutenant when you met Alex?"

"Yes. Why?" Billy asked as they crossed a street.

"His tat."

As if it took Billy a moment, possibly to think of how Stan knew, he nodded he understood. "I was thinking of a way for him to make it into a chief's badge. I'm glad he didn't."

"Will you try to climb the ranks again?"

"Fuck no." Billy shook his head. "I was willing to go in as a beat cop. It was the LAPD chief of police who told me he wanted me to be a lieutenant."

"Really? A patrol cop? You'd have started over?"

"You bet I would."

Stan thought about it. That move would have taken guts. Billy may be tough, but he wasn't consumed by ego. "I fucking admire the hell out of you."

Billy glanced at him quickly. "Thanks, Stan…Get this."

"What?" They came to their usual turnaround in fifteen minutes, and looped back.

"That video from the karaoke bar? The guys had it cued up and when I walked into the training center, I got a serenade."

Stan cracked up. "Oh, fuck. I wish I could have seen that."

"I had no idea it went so viral. They showed me clips on Youtube from departments all over the globe supporting me, and my decision to resign…or not, I guess."

"It's a brotherhood, isn't it? I mean, cops all over the place all feel connected."

Teasing Stan, Billy used an even deeper voice than his normal baritone, "May the police force be with you."

Stan exploded with laughter. "That's classic. I wish Lou could have heard that joke."

STARTING OVER

Billy glanced at Stan and winked sweetly. "I need to see his act one day."

"Ya know, Billy? Lou would love that."

"Thanks for running with me."

"You bet. Anytime." Stan adored him. Absolutely adored him. He wondered if Alex knew just how lucky he was.

Chapter 11

Jeff and Mickey stood in a checkout line at a grocery store. On their way to Malibu, they stopped off to buy a six-pack of beer and a bag of tortilla chips. While Mickey set the two items on the conveyor belt, Jeff eyed the gossip rags that were on display near the candy and last minute impulse purchases.

"Shut the fuck up." Jeff grabbed a magazine and laughed.

"What?" Mickey handed the cashier money.

"He did it again." Jeff held up the magazine.

'The Sexiest Man Alive' was featured on the cover.

Speaking to the cashier, Mickey thumbed at Jeff, "And that."

Jeff handed it to the woman to scan, and then she gave it back.

Mickey picked up the beer and chips as Jeff read the text on the magazine cover.

"Wasn't he the *World's Most Beautiful Man* last time?" Mickey asked as they walked to his pickup truck in the parking lot.

"Shit. That's right. It was a different magazine." Jeff waited as Mickey unlocked his truck doors with his remote. He climbed in, reading the two-page article.

Mickey placed the six-pack and chips by Jeff's feet and started the truck. "Let's see it."

Jeff flipped the page back to the cover photo. There was Mark Antonious Richfield, topless, in a picture that appeared to be from one of his modeling shoots.

STARTING OVER

Mickey held the magazine to stare at it. "Can you imagine looking like that?"

"No." Jeff leaned on Mickey's shoulder to drool. "They have a few of his wedding pics inside, but, the one they chose for the cover is just 'wow'."

Mickey flipped pages quickly. Jeff grew excited as he looked at the photos of Mark in a white tuxedo. Under the wedding photos were credits for the photographer from *Vanity Fair*.

"Can you believe we're friends with him?" Jeff asked, pushing at his hard dick.

"Fuck, he's so hot." Mickey went back to the cover. "Do you think everyone assumes his photos are retouched?"

"Probably."

Mickey gave Jeff the magazine and backed out of the parking spot.

Jeff read the article's text while Mickey drove to Malibu.

'*Mark Antonious Richfield, the CEO and owner of Richfield-Miller International, the nation's top male model, once chosen LA's most eligible bachelor, then selected as the World's Most Beautiful Man, is still one of the sexiest men alive.*'

Jeff peered up at the highway, and then went back to the text. '*Mark, who was recently wed to his modeling partner, Stan Charles, a man twenty years younger than the top model, continues to reign as the top trending celebrity on all social media.*'

Mickey glanced over at him. "What's it say?"

"It says Mark has always fantasized making love to a police detective named Jeff Chandler."

Mickey cracked up.

Jeff smiled and then read the last line out loud of the tiny text box near Mark's stunning photographs, "It says, *Dangereux* cologne struck gold when it signed Mark to be exclusive. The cologne company is now the number one brand in fragrances, worldwide." Jeff closed the magazine to stare at Mark on the cover. "Motherfucker, look at that body."

"He's still got it, Jeff." Mickey slowed down as he drew closer to the beach house.

"He always will." Jeff held the magazine on his lap and smiled.

~

Jack filled ceramic bowls with the prepared salads he had purchased on the way home. Adam was busy mixing a marinade for the meat, making skewers.

Since they were now eight for dinner, Jack set the food out buffet style, because their dining room table only sat six comfortably.

A crackle-like pop! made both men look towards the beach. The closer July 4th got, the more that noise echoed in the warm air.

Adam made a sound of irritation and left the meat to marinade while he mixed a margarita cocktail in a glass pitcher. "You'd think with the fires around here, they'd make them all illegal."

"I agree." Jack stacked the plastic containers from the salads and set out napkins and plates. He checked the time.

Since they had all the windows open, and the breeze was cool and fresh from the Pacific, Jack heard a car's idling engine out in front of their home.

He wiped his hands on a towel, kissed Adam's cheek, and walked to the front door. A black limousine had pulled in front of his driveway. Jack watched as Mark, Stan, Billy, and Alex, climbed of it. While they were talking to the driver, a handsome young man in black, Mickey's pickup truck parked in the driveway beside Adam's BMW.

Jack opened the front door as everyone greeted each other.

STARTING OVER

Adam came up behind Jack and waited with him at the door. "I take it Steve's in Paradise."

"Yes." Jack smiled as the men made their way towards him. They were laughing and sharing something.

"Hi, Jackie."

"Hi, Alex." Jack kissed him and then greeted Billy. "Hey, how are you, chief?"

"Lieutenant." Billy laughed.

"Huh?" Jack focused on Jeff as he held a magazine in his hand and mimed jerking off.

"Hey, Jack." Mickey entered the home next, holding beer and chips.

"Hey." Jack kissed his cheek as Adam took the beer and led the others into the kitchen.

Stan was smiling and shaking his head as he approached Jack. "Hey, Jack."

"Hi, Stan." Jack kissed his cheek. "What's up?"

Thumbing over his shoulder, Stan said, "Mark did it again."

Jack had no idea what that meant. Jeff was all over Mark at the moment, pulling him into his embrace and kissing Mark's neck. Mark was tolerating the playful teasing.

"Hullo, Jackie." Mark kissed him.

"What did you do again?" Jack asked.

Jeff held the magazine up in front of Jack's face.

Jack took it to inspect. "Wow. Nice pic."

"I don't know why anyone reads that silly trash." Mark continued into the home.

Jack stood with Jeff as they ogled the cover photo.

"Damn." Jeff held onto Jack's waist as they stared at it. "Could ya die?"

"Yours?" Jack forced himself to stop drooling over it. He had the real Mark.

"Yup." Jeff snatched it and made his way to the kitchen.

Jack shut the front door and couldn't believe Mark was once more on the cover of a magazine; the sexiest man alive.

~

Alex tried not to wince.

Sure. Whatever.

It's all about Dad. Of course.

He hung out with Adam as he placed the beer Mickey had brought into the fridge. "Is that your margarita mixture?"

"Help yourself." Adam pointed to glasses and a dish of salt. "Mick? You want a beer?"

"Yes, please!"

"Anyone else?" Adam took iced mugs out of the freezer.

Billy and Jeff responded, "Yes, thanks."

While Adam set out three chilled mugs, Alex tasted the margarita. It was superb, of course.

The men were still gushing over the magazine. Alex rolled his eyes.

"Stan?" Adam asked, "Beer, wine?"

"Uh. I'm good."

Alex leaned on the island counter as Adam tipped the beer from the bottles into the mugs without creating a big foaming head.

"How are you, Alex?" Adam asked, looking handsome in his cargo shorts and white polo shirt.

"Meh. Okay." Alex licked his top lip from the tangy cocktail.

Jack stood near them, handing the beer to the three cops.

"Thanks, Jack. Can you heat the grill?" Adam asked.

Jack said, "Sure. And, by the way, Billy did resign, Adam. He's back in LAPD SWAT."

Alex cringed and stared outside the sliding doors, to the ocean while finishing his drink.

"Is that good or bad?" Adam asked as he put the bottles into recycling. "He appears to be in good spirits."

STARTING OVER

"He's elated." Jack chuckled. "Hey. Alex? When's the new film coming out?"

"Dunno." Alex shrugged, thinking about getting drunk.

Adam said, "It'll be in postproduction for a while, Jack."

Alex watched the men hover around his dad while Jeff read the article in the magazine out loud.

Stan had his arm around Mark lovingly and was holding him close.

Alex tipped the last drop of the cocktail onto his tongue and then sent Tadzio a text, *'you there?'*

'Yes.'

Alex left the house, through the glass slider, and sat on a chaise lounge that faced the beach. He called Tadzio.

"Hi, Alskander."

"Hi, Tadzio." Alex sank in the padded lounge chair. "What are you up to?"

"I am just home from working wit Steven. When can you come?"

"Maybe soon. I don't know. Dad and I had it out today at the shrink's appointment. Man, that was brutal." Alex watched surfers and body-boarders ride the waves.

"Iz Mark still mad at you?"

"I guess not. We're getting there." Alex heard laughter seeping through the glass door and ignored it. "So, this is it? You there, me here?"

"I work wit Steven, Alec. I am now enjoying it. I love dis house. You know it. You have been here."

"Fuck. I miss you."

"I miss you too."

Alex pouted and sank on the chair.

~

"Yes! Yes!" Jeff pumped his fist when he learned Billy was back with the LAPD, where he and Mickey worked. "Sharpe, I am thrilled for you!"

Billy was so tickled to be back, he was giddy. He guzzled the beer down quickly and since he wasn't driving, craved another.

Mickey said, "Damn, man. We thought when we saw that surveillance video from the courthouse lot, you were a goner."

"Jack?" Adam called to him, "Can you start the grill, please?"

Appearing preoccupied, Jack nodded. "Shit." Jack snapped his fingers as if he had forgotten. "Sure."

Stan asked, "Need help, Jack?"

"I've got it." Jack smiled at him and left the kitchen.

Billy noticed Alex was outside on the deck as Jack joined him to light the grill.

Stan kissed Mark's cheek. "Want something to drink?"

"Water, love?"

"You got it." Stan headed to the kitchen.

Mickey took Billy and Jeff's empty beer mugs. "I'll get us refills."

"Thanks." Billy wiped his damp fingers on his jeans.

Jeff finally tossed the magazine on the table in the living room.

Billy thought this beach house was gorgeous, with southwestern terracotta floor tiles, stucco walls, Native American wall hangings and potted plants. From the front of the home, you could see through to the back, to the Pacific Ocean's wild crashing tide.

After spying Alex and Jack on the patio, Billy noticed Jeff had Mark in his arms. He shook his head at the crazy homicide detective and joined Mickey, Stan, and Adam in the kitchen.

"What can I do?" Billy asked Adam.

STARTING OVER

Mickey was filling mugs with beer and Stan set two bottles of water on the counter as he checked out what Adam had on offer for dinner.

"Um." Adam shrugged. "Nothing. Just relax." Adam opened a bag of tortilla chips and filled a bowl with them.

After taking the mug from Mickey, Billy joined Alex on the patio.

~

"You gorgeous, fuck." Jeff chewed on Mark's neck.

"Behave."

"I can't believe I have you in my life." Jeff moaned and drew Mark's hand to his cock.

"Oy!" Mark laughed when he felt Jeff's erection.

Jeff kept Mark's body against his. "How long are you and Stan going to be in LA?"

Mark noticed the other men chatting together in the kitchen; his son, Billy, and Jack were on the back deck. "Stan and I are driving north tomorrow, but we both have a modeling shoot this Sunday."

Jeff backed Mark up to a wall and rested against him. Mark felt Jeff's cock pulsating on his hip. "Calm down, lovely."

Jeff leaned back as he stared into Mark's eyes. "How do you do it? How do you look so goddamn young?"

Mark made an exaggerated gawk aimed at Jeff using his hand to rub against his hard-on. "Love? Why don't you ask your husband for a nice hand-job?"

"Can you do it?" Jeff gave Mark a wicked smile.

"No." Mark laughed. He turned to look into the kitchen, and there was Stan, smiling at them, holding two bottles of water.

Jeff cleared his throat and stepped back. "Sorry, Stan."

"He's irresistible. I know." Stan gave Mark one of the bottles.

"Damn. Damn." Jeff walked off, tugging at the crotch of his pants.

Stan shook his head at Mark.

Mark straightened his shirt and then tilted his head to the magazine. "What rubbish."

"Maybe not. I think they have great taste." Stan drew Mark into his arms. "I think Jeff's in blue-ball hell."

"He has a perfectly good husband to fix that." Mark tipped the bottle up, then said, "I need to smoke. I'm not hungry in the least."

"The food spread looks great. Jack started the grill."

Mark kissed him and walked to the patio. He and Stan stepped outside and Mark felt the cooling breeze and spotted surfers on the choppy tide.

Alex was on the phone, Jack was setting skewers of meat and vegetables on the hot grill, and Billy was standing near the crashing waves gazing into the distance with a beer mug in his hand.

"…I don't know, Tadzio, it depends on Dad." Alex peered up at Mark.

Knowing what Alex was doing, Mark said, "Yes. If you come with Billy. But, no, if you do not."

Stan smiled at Mark.

Mark set his bottle of water on the patio table and held Stan's hand. He walked towards Billy, and took a rolled joint out of his shirt pocket. Before they met up with the lieutenant, Stan lit a lighter, cupping his hands in the wind. Mark drew on the joint and puffed it, inhaling a hit and handing it to Stan.

Billy spun around and watched them.

After three hits, Mark had enough. So had Stan. They put out the joint and Mark dropped it into a small tube-like holder he had brought.

He blew the smoke out in the wind and joined Billy as they gazed at the soothing tide and body-boarders.

STARTING OVER

Mark put his arm around Billy on his right, and around Stan on his left, and enjoyed the relaxing sight, and the calming effects of the medical marijuana.

~

Jack turned the skewers on the grill, the marinade sending up a plume of aromatic smoke. He noticed Stan, Mark, and Billy standing near the water, and glanced behind him at Alex, who was talking to Tadzio on the phone.

Adam was inside, laughing with the two crazy cops.

"...I don't know. Why don't you and Steve come here this weekend? Dad's going to be here modeling."

Jack thought about this weekend, having Sonja's wedding on Saturday.

"I have no idea, Tadzio...If Dad's here, he may not want me to go to the estate."

Adam opened the slider and the cops stepped outside with him. "Jack? The meat is burning."

Jack used tongs to remove the skewers, putting them on the platter. "Sorry. I don't know where my mind is."

Mickey peered over Jack's shoulder. "They're not too bad. I like my meat well done."

Jeff sat on the foot of Alex's lounge chair. "Who are you talking to?"

"Tadzio."

"Hi, Tadzio!" Jeff leaned closer to the phone Alex was holding.

Alex held onto Jeff as he giggled with Tadzio.

Adam took the platter from Jack. "Are you all right?"

Jack shut off the gas grill and wiped his hands on a paper towel. "I'm fine."

Adam shot him a worried look.

Jack called to the three men, "Mark! Food's ready!"

"Gotta go, Tadzio. Adam's magic marinade is ready."

"Magic?" Mickey asked, "As in weed?"

Adam shook his head. "No. No weed…Open the door, Mick?"

Mickey slid the glass slider back.

Jack waited for Mark to return from the water's edge. Billy hauled Alex off the lounge chair, Stan gave Jack a sweet smile, and Mark paused to gaze at the horizon.

Someone on the beach was shooting bottle rockets into the sky, the crackle and pop floated on the wind.

Everyone was inside but him and Mark.

"Jack?" Adam called through the open door.

"Okay." Jack acknowledged him.

Mark spun around and faced Jack. His smile fell. "What's wrong, Jackie?"

Jack wished he knew. He couldn't put his finger on it.

"Love?" Mark pulled Jack into his arms. "What's happened?"

A tidal wave of emotions hit Jack. He crushed Mark into his embrace.

"Baby?" Mark rubbed his back. "Talk to me."

From inside the kitchen, Adam spoke through the patio slider. "Jack?"

"One minute." Jack turned away from the house. He heard the slider close.

Mark rocked Jack gently. "All right, Jackie-blue…" Mark rocked him side to side. "It's all right."

Jack choked up and started to cry. The sadness was so intense, this emotional wave, he had no idea what was going on.

~

Mark held onto his best friends, his lover, his 'brother', and squeezed him close. "Let it out, baby. Let it out. Yes. It took you forever…let it out."

"Oh, God…" Jack moaned as if he finally got it.

STARTING OVER

"I wondered when it would hit you." Mark kissed Jack's neck and cheek. "Cry, my love. Cry."

Losing a father. Losing a father that you loved. One that adored you. One that was good to you...

It had taken the gym-junkie-lawyer over a week to finally let go. Jack sobbed heavily, hiding over Mark's shoulder.

"Okay, baby." Mark cooed and caressed him.

"Mark..." Jack sniffled and took a deep breath. "Why did I wait so long to tell him I was gay?"

"No matter, lover. Your father adored you unconditionally."

"But, I hid from them." Jack choked up. "I missed out on ten years of visits, of letting them get to know Adam."

"Hush. Stop tormenting yourself. He knew you adored him." Mark kissed the salty tears from Jack's cheek.

Jack took a deep breath and leaned back from their tight hug, still pressed close at the hip.

Mark smiled affectionately into his watery blue eyes. "He loved you, was so proud of you."

"Why didn't I come out?"

Mark searched Jack's gaze. "Love. We do the best we can at the time. Please. There is no use wishing things had been different. They simply are what they are." Mark wiped the tears from Jack's cheeks.

"Fuck." Jack inhaled a few more deep breaths, calming down.

"Okay, baby. It's okay." Mark dabbed at more running tears. "You're a good man. A wonderful son. Jackie, you meant the world to him, and you mean the world to me."

Jack crushed Mark in his arms. "Thank you. Thank you for always knowing what to say."

"I love you, He-man. Ever so much." Mark squeezed tight.

Chapter 12

Adam had a feeling he knew what was going on out there.

Since they were six, they sat around the table as Mark consoled Jack, rocking him in his arms.

"What's that about?" Mickey asked, using his fork to pull the food off the skewer and onto his plate.

"Jack hasn't had a chance to grieve." Adam tasted the roasted garlic quinoa salad Jack had purchased.

A low, 'Ahhh' came from the men as they realized.

Adam noticed Alex scowling at his father. He flicked Alex on the arm.

"Ow." Alex rubbed his arm and pouted.

Billy shook his head as he ate, obviously sensing Alex's raging jealousy.

Stan said quietly, "Was he close to his dad?"

"Yes." Adam nodded. "I kept waiting for it to hit. He's been distracted to a fault lately. And this weekend we have Sonja's wedding to go to."

"Sonja Knight? His law partner?" Jeff asked as he took big bites of his food.

Nodding, Adam said, "Yes. It's going to be a big affair."

Billy nudged Alex. "Doll? Stop scowling at your father."

"Why does everyone go to him?" Alex dropped his fork on his plate. He gestured to Adam. "His husband is right there."

Adam chuckled. "He knows where I am, Alex."

"You don't mind Dad comforting Jack?" Alex asked.

STARTING OVER

"Of course not!" Adam laughed as he wiped his hands on his napkin. "Alex? Jack and Mark are like brothers. They've known each other since Stanford."

"Sexiest Man Alive," Alex scoffed as he picked his fork back up. "Who even gets to vote?"

Stan avoided the topic, his focus on the food.

Jeff laughed. "Aww. Wish it was you?"

"Yes!" Alex licked marinade off his finger. "I've been the headlining star in six blockbuster films; *Save a Horse* and *Snapped* with Jeremy, From *A to Zeke* with Carl, and he won an Oscar, *Bound to You* with Diesel, *Bedtime Stories* with Randy, *Bed & Breakfast* which got a nomination for a National Society award, and now I'm the top-billed celeb in *Lover Boy*! I've starred in two nighttime cable dramas, I've been nominated for tons of acting awards…what's Dad done besides look pretty for a cologne ad, star in a crappy reality show, and a guest starring role on *Forever Young*?"

Adam remembered. "Did you guys read the script?"

"What script?" Jeff asked, looking at Jack and Mark who were now laughing.

"Mark's been asked to guest star on that show in its final season." Adam chuckled. "You are gonna die when you see what they want him to do."

"Another three-way with Keith and Carl?" Billy said, smirking.

Stan sat up, his plate empty, paying attention to the conversation.

"I'll let Mark tell you." Adam giggled. "Stan? Go help yourself to seconds."

The slider opened and Mark stepped in.

Jack did as well, closing the glass door behind him. "Sorry. My fault." He kissed Adam and both he and Mark rinsed their hands in the sink.

"Are you okay, He-man?" Adam asked.

"I am." Jack gave him a loving smile and filled a plate.

Mark brushed his hair back from his face. "Well!"

"Sit." Jeff stood from the table and waved Mark over.

"No worries." Mark leaned back against the counter.

Stan got to his feet and brought his plate to the buffet. "Everything is good," he said, "Jack, take my place."

"Thanks."

Adam caught Alex pouting over his thoughts. Adam left the room and brought a folding chair and a stool into the kitchen.

Jeff helped Adam move them closer to the table so they could all sit together.

Mark put a tiny amount of food on his plate, a thimble full of the quinoa salad and a few garden vegetables. He sat on the stool as Stan piled his plate high with the great food.

Jack joined them at the table while Stan took a seat beside Mark on the folding chair

"You okay, Jack?" Billy asked, his hand on the back of Alex's chair, toying with Alex's long locks.

"Yes. Thanks." Jack appeared just fine.

Mark nibbled the food. "What were we talking about?"

"Your script for *Forever Young*." Adam laughed. "Did you read it?"

"Not really." Mark stopped eating after one bite.

Jack and Stan devoured the good food.

Adam stood up. "Hang on." He laughed as he headed to his home office to get the script he had printed. It was priceless.

~

After a wonderful run on the mountain trails, a gourmet dinner, and chatting with Alex, Tadzio sank into the hot tub in the estate's spa.

Steve stepped out of the steam-room, naked, and sat on the whirlpool's edge as he cooled down from the hot steam.

STARTING OVER

Twilight seeped into the blue-lit room and a pink and orange glow was left on the horizon of the setting sun.

Tadzio moved around the churning water to sit near Steve. He leaned his elbows on Steve's thigh and gazed up at him.

"Love the man-bun." Steve smiled at him.

"I love you." Tadzio reached up for a kiss. He got a sweet one from his husband, and sank back down to the marble bench under the churning hot water. "Steven?"

"Yes?" Steve eased himself down into the bubbling heat.

"You ask me to help wit your wardrobe. I can, of course. But, maybe we can go to Rodeo Drive? I don't know about the shopping here."

"A mall snob?" Steve laughed at him, resting his arms on the tiled ledge.

"You want top design clothes." Tadzio shrugged. "And, Mark has a modeling shoot, so he will be in LA."

"And, you miss Alex." Steve rested his head on the dry tiles and closed his eyes.

"Yes." Tadzio let him think about it. It was only Tuesday, and Tadzio imagined Mark would come here soon. Getting overheated, Tadzio climbed out of the hot whirlpool and walked closer to the wall of glass overlooking the outdoor pool, stables, and mountains.

Their groom was leading the horses into the stable as evening loomed.

Tadzio glanced back at Steve and saw the former cop eying him. Tadzio tugged at his hair, unraveling the bun, and allowed it to flow down his shoulders.

Steve's gaze became intense.

Tadzio felt sexy as hell from the hungry leer. He moved casually to the pool, holding the rail near the stairs, dipping one foot into the cool water, pointing his toe like a ballet dancer.

The former cop stood from the hot tub and made his way over.

Tadzio kept pretending he didn't realize Steve's intent. He tapped the cooler pool with his toes, making swirls on the surface.

Steve stood next to him, his cock fully aroused.

Tadzio crouched down and splashed Steve with the refreshing cool water.

Steve pulled Tadzio into his arms, and jumped into the crystal clear indoor pool.

They surfaced and Steve stood in the deep end, drawing Tadzio to a kiss. Tadzio wrapped his legs around Steve's waist, cupping the back of Steve's head and they swirled tongues sensually.

Steve moved them around the pool, then he picked Tadzio up by his waist, sat him on the ledge, and sank Tadzio's cock into his mouth.

Tadzio braced himself on his hands behind him, and watched Steve suck him off while the glow behind the horizon turned indigo and violet.

~

Mark used his fork tines to push the tiny grains of quinoa into a perfectly straight line. Although he liked being with his close friends, he wanted to be in Paradise.

Adam returned, holding two sheets of paper, a wicked smile on his face.

Jack and Stan had cleared the table after the men had finished eating.

Alex, making a sarcastic noise at his father for playing with his food instead of eating it, took the plate away from him and brought it to the sink.

"Seriously." Adam sat down in the same chair he had occupied. "This is pure Richfield gold."

STARTING OVER

"Read it." Mickey filled his tumbler glass with water from a sweating pitcher.

Outside, more firecrackers went off and whistling roman candles crackled and lit up the patio.

Jeff put his arm around Mickey, over the back of the wooden chair.

Jack and Stan stood close by, and Alex nudge Billy so he could sit on the lieutenant's lap.

Mark was bored. He stood from the table and watched the smattering of fireworks being shot off by locals.

Adam cleared his throat, "Okay. Picture the scene."

Mark took his phone out of his pocket and sent Steve a text, *'How was your day at work?'* Mark needed to be there. Not here.

Adam described the setting from the script he was holding, "A bachelor party...very drunk men." Adam chuckled.

"Uh oh." Jack laughed.

Mark didn't hear from Steve so he stuffed his phone back into his pocket.

"A scene with a dozen bachelors..." Adam kept laughing. "It takes place in a club, you get the idea; dim, loud, think disco balls."

"If Mark's in it, more like blue-balls," Jeff said.

Mickey elbowed him.

"Stage direction," Adam read, "A large table is rolled into the middle of the room."

Billy started to laugh, as if he figured it out.

Mark listened dully, not wanting to do TV at all. Someone shot a roman candle over the water, its sparking lights sizzled in the wind as muted 'pops' echoed. Children waved sparklers around in figure-eight patterns.

"The table top has an enormous layered cake on it." Adam roared with laughter. "And Mark Antonious bursts out of it, in nothing but a tiny G-string."

"Come on!" Alex scoffed. "It does not say that."

The men roared with laughter.

Mark didn't even turn to look at the table. He wanted to be home. Home in Paradise.

"Then," Adam tried to talk without cracking up, "He's passed around to the drunk men in the room and gives the bachelor a lap dance!"

Mickey and Jeff choked with hilarity.

Billy said, "Oh, fuck yeah."

Mark was humiliated.

A soft touch rested on his shoulder.

Mark focused on the glass slider's reflection. It was Stan.

"Mark! You have to do it!" Mickey shouted, "Holy shit, that's funny."

"Give me that, Adam!" Alex snatched the pages. "I don't believe it. Why Dad? They could have picked any number of guys to do that!"

Stan kissed Mark's hair softly.

Mark turned around and held onto him.

"Tired?" Stan asked, caressing his back.

"Yes."

"Let's go."

"Yes." Mark kissed Stan's lips.

Stan took his phone out of his pocket and sent Dean a text.

"Come on!" Alex shook the pages. "He's too old for that kind of shit."

"Apparently not." Adam smiled. "The Sexiest Man Alive."

"Ratings, ratings, ratings." Jack shook his head. "No wonder it's the last season. When you need Mark naked to boost the viewership, you have reached the end."

Mark walked closer to the group. "I'm very tired. Thank you for dinner."

STARTING OVER

Billy nudged Alex off his lap and the men stood from the table.

Alex flapped the script pages at his dad. "Here's your Golden Globe opportunity," he said with biting sarcasm.

"Alex, cut it out." Jack took the script from him.

Stan kissed the men goodbye, and Mark kept checking for a text from Steve.

More crackles of fireworks echoed through the open windows as they stood near the front door.

Jack pulled Mark close before he left. "Hey. Are you okay?"

Mark glanced at the men saying their goodbyes in the living room. He gazed into Jack's blue eyes. "I should write a book, yes? My life as a brainless sexual object?"

"Mark?" Jack whispered, "You're a model. And, you *are* the sexiest fucker alive. Enjoy it. Fifty is looming."

"Yes. I should be used to the constant leering by now. Nearly fifty years of groping, of being treated like a living sex-doll without a thought in his head."

Just as Mark said it, Jeff pulled him into his arms. "Get over here, you fucking god." Jeff, the magazine in his hand, dipped Mark into a 'Hollywood' kiss.

Mark felt dizzy from being tipped backwards quickly, accepted Jeff's kiss, and was set on his feet. The unexpected rush to his blood pressure made him faint.

He had not eaten well this week preparing for another modeling session. Mark began to black out.

~

Stan had a feeling Mark wasn't keen on the sexploitation of the script. He kept his eye on the top model, and after Jeff's exuberant kiss, Mark went pale as a sheet.

Stan rushed towards him as Mark's knees gave out.

"Fuck!" Jack obviously saw it as well.

Stan picked Mark up in his arms and carried him to the couch.

"Is he fainting?" Billy asked.

"Dad?"

"Fuck! Did I do that?" Jeff gasped.

Stan laid Mark out on the sofa and bent his knees, then placed a throw pillow under Mark's head.

"He's starving again, right?" Adam said, shaking his head. "Fuck these modeling shoots!"

Jack and Stan crouched low next to the couch as Mark came around slowly.

"Dad! You have to eat something! Isn't that why you smoke weed?"

Stan caressed Mark's hair back from his face and watched the color return to his cheeks.

"Hullo, baby," Mark whispered.

"Hey, Mark." Stan knew about these fainting spells. Yup. He'd been warned.

Mark appeared disoriented. "What's happened?"

"You passed out, Richfield." Billy shook his head.

A knock came to the door.

Adam answered it. Dean was there with the limo.

"Did I?" Mark sat up on the couch slowly, his feet on the floor.

Stan was still crouched in front of Mark.

Mickey handed him a bottle of water.

Mark took it, drinking thirstily.

"Dean's here to take us home." Stan tucked a strand of Mark's hair back from his face.

"Yes, love." Mark handed the water back to Mickey.

Stan stood up, reaching for Mark. Mark clasped his hand and rose up off the couch.

The men in the room were quiet as they looked on.

STARTING OVER

"Do you need to be carried out of the house, Mark?" Billy asked.

"Carried? Whatever for?" Mark ran his hand through his hair, still looking a little confused. "Goodnight, love. We'll see you soon." Mark kissed Adam and Jack.

Stan stood beside Mark, ready to catch him when/if he fell. He noticed the rest of the men giving him a concerned look. They had dealt with this from Mark for years. It was his turn. But, Stan knew something they did not. Mark had spoken to Arnold Newhouse. He was done with his modeling career, done with starving for the shoots, and wanted to be a CEO, not a 'dumb' model.

"Come on, baby." Mark hooked Stan's elbow and they followed Dean to the limousine.

~

Billy stayed behind for a minute with the others.

Jeff appeared miserable. "I had no idea I'd do that to him when I dipped him."

Mickey rubbed Jeff's back. "Hey. Don't sweat it."

Jack said, "It's fine, Jeff. This is Mark before modeling. You know that."

"Gee..." Alex said, "I guess fainting was considered an asset in choosing the sexist man alive."

"Let it go, babydoll." Billy nudged Alex towards the limo. "Goodnight," he said to the two cops, "See ya soon." He walked with Alex to the car as Dean waited near the open back door.

Alex climbed in first, then Billy.

He sat with Alex across from Mark and Stan.

Mark had his head on Stan's shoulder, his eyes closed, looking exhausted. Stan, his arm around Mark, caressed him gently.

Alex sighed loudly and folded his hands on his lap as Dean made the drive to Bel Air.

Billy stared at Mark in concern. The model was being pulled between two worlds: Richfield-Miller International, and *Dangereux*. And it was complicated by Alex's needs, which of course became Mark's problem.

He asked Stan, "When are you guys going to Paradise?"

"Tomorrow morning, early."

Alex asked, "Then, back here for the shoot?"

"Yes. It's on Sunday morning, so I figure we should come during the day on Saturday."

Billy's urge was to help Mark, somehow…But, seeing Stan's attentive care, maybe Mark was already in good hands. He put his arm around Alex and kissed his cheek. "How're you doin', superstar?"

"Wishing I was sitting by the pool with Tadzio in Paradise."

Billy smiled at Stan at Alex's wish. "We will be soon."

~

After hot sex with Tadzio in the spa, they showered in steaming heat and relaxed in bed. Steve had a message from Mark. He didn't answer him.

He curled around Tadzio under the crisp sheets and closed his eyes, sexually sated and emotionally content.

~

Alex brooded. On the way back to Bel Air, he rested on Billy's shoulder, staring at his dad and Stan across from their bench seat on the limo.

Sexiest Man Alive?

Bursting out of a cake on *Forever Young*?

Another little voice in his head said, '*Alex? Let it go. Would you miss him if he was gone?*'

It was Michael's voice. Stan's Dad.

Alex closed his eyes and held onto Billy. His Billy. Not his dad's, not Steve's…his.

The car pulled in front of Mark's home first.

STARTING OVER

Stan shook Mark gently to wake him.

Dean opened the back door.

Billy sat up. "We can walk from here."

Alex and he climbed out of the back of the car.

More crackling noise made both Billy and Alex look to the sky. Fireworks sputtered in the darkness.

Mark emerged, barely functioning.

"Goodnight." Stan held onto Mark and walked to the door of their home...Steve's home, actually.

Billy handed Dean a cash tip. "Thanks."

"No problem. Have a good night." Dean returned to the driver's side of the limo and drove off.

Alex held Billy's hand and they strolled down the block under the glow of tall streetlamps. More crackles and whistles from handheld fireworks went off overhead.

Billy turned his key in the lock of their home. Alex stepped inside this gorgeous house, one with a view and large spacious rooms. He paused before heading to the bedroom.

Billy pulled him into his arms and squeezed him close. Alex pressed his face on Billy's chest and closed his eyes.

"Stop competing, Alex."

"It's hard. He isn't working to death like I am."

"Mark is more interested in being a CEO than a celebrity. One more year, and he won't even be in the tabloids any longer." Billy kissed Alex's hair and walked towards their bedroom.

Alex wondered if that was true. For all Alex knew, Mark would be on the cover of every business journal next year, as the World's Most Beautiful Corporate Executive.

He spotted fireworks going off beyond the Getty Museum and walked closer to the glass slider, to stare at them.

Chapter 13

Very early Wednesday morning, Mark dressed in black designer skinny jeans, and a crewneck white top. While Stan was filling travel mugs with coffee, Mark emptied his sex-goody drawer into a bag. He left one tube of lubrication behind, and packed more of his items.

It was six a.m. and Mark was anxious to leave.

He took a quick look around the master bedroom and trotted down the stairs. Mark placed the bag near the garage's connecting door and surrounded Stan's waist with his arms from behind.

Stan purred and finished filling the travel mugs.

"How's my big stud this morning?" Mark rested his chin on Stan's shoulder.

Stan finished the task and then turned in Mark's embrace and kissed him.

Mark parted from the sweet kiss and asked, "Did you have a bite?"

Stan said, "I will later."

"Then, are you ready?" Mark released him and checked the slider was latched.

Stan emptied the coffee grounds, wrapped what was left of the trash under the sink to toss into the bin in the garage, and rinsed the coffee pot.

Mark made sure the front door was bolted as well, and then picked up a travel mug and his bag.

STARTING OVER

Stan threw out the trash and returned for his coffee and a backpack.

While he did, Mark tapped the button on the wall and the garage door opened to the sunshine and cool morning temperature.

Stan closed and locked the connecting door after setting the security alarm, and then he opened the Lamborghini's trunk.

Mark brought the plastic bag to it, and there were the framed photos from Arnold's office, still stacked inside it. Mark placed the small bag in it, as Stan tucked his backpack into it as well.

Then, they both sat in the low bucket seats.

While he backed out of the garage, Stan said, "Paradise, here we come."

"At last." After putting on his sunglasses, Mark rested his hand on Stan's thigh.

Waiting for the garage door to close first, Stan selected music from his sound system and he and Mark sang as they drove to the highway.

~

In just his briefs, Steve pushed suits on hangers across the rod, growing annoyed.

Tadzio leaned against him from behind.

"Fuck." Steve shook his head.

"Let me." Tadzio looked at Steve's clothing.

Backing up, letting Tadzio help, since Steve seriously needed a wardrobe upgrade, he rubbed his face and yawned.

Tadzio selected a black sports jacket, and black slacks, separates, not a suit, and then inspected the shirts.

Steve slipped the trousers on and noticed Tadzio in a smart linen beige skirt with a slit up one side showing off his amazing legs, and a brown blousy top.

Tadzio appeared to grow frustrated with Steve's outfits as well. "Let me just look someplace," Tadzio said and left the large closet.

Steve watched him walk confidently in his brown high-heeled strappy shoes. Shortly after, Tadzio returned, holding two shirts on hangers.

"Mark's?" Steve asked as he put on black socks.

"Yes. You are bigger than him?" Tadzio held up one of the shirts against Steve's chest.

Steve had never tried Mark's clothing on before. He chose a black silky button-down long-sleeved shirt, taking it off the hanger and putting it on.

Tadzio held the second top, waiting as Steve checked the fit.

Since Steve wasn't a bodybuilder, the shirt did fit well enough to wear, although maybe, he was a size larger than Mark. He buttoned it up, then looked at the cuffs. Mark's expensive tops usually needed cufflinks.

This one was no exception.

"Nice. Yes." Tadzio left the second choice, a maroon Versace shirt, on the bed. He straightened Steve's collar. "A black necktie?"

"What am I? In the mafia?" Steve cracked up.

Tadzio chuckled and entered their closet again.

Steve peeked at his reflection in the mirror over the dresser. "Huh. Nice." He put the black sports jacket on over the shirt.

Tadzio emerged with a black necktie. "Yes. Mafia-boss-Miller."

Steve cracked up. "Get the hell over here." He dragged pretty Tadzio into his arms. "I love you."

"I love you!" Tadzio blushed and placed the necktie around Steve's collar, tying it. Tadzio made a perfect Windsor knot and tightened it gently, then he straightened Steve's shirt collar and sport jacket lapels.

STARTING OVER

Once he did, he stepped back. "Oh, Steven. You are such a handsome man."

Steve adjusted the knot in the tie and had a look. A power suit, no doubt. "Huh." He touched his hair and inspected the outfit. "Blondie? You're amazing."

Tadzio chuckled and took the second shirt out of the room. "Sierra has breakfast, Steven."

"Be right there."

Steve tugged at the shirt cuffs and then checked himself out in the mirror. "Nice." He liked it. He jogged up to the second floor and into Mark's bedroom, passing Tadzio who was on his way down after replacing the second shirt.

They kissed playfully midway.

On a dresser was a small wooden box. Steve opened it, removing one pair of plain gold cufflinks from it, and managed to get his left one on, but battled with the right, since he was right-handed. Cupping it in his palm, Steve returned to his first-floor bedroom and grabbed his wallet, and phone, then found Tadzio in the kitchen. He gave Tadzio the cufflink and his wrist.

Tadzio fastened it efficiently.

Sierra paused in her preparations. "Wow. Steve. You look fantastic."

"Clothes make the man." Tadzio beamed at Steve.

"Thanks, Sierra." Steve felt like a million bucks.

"Espresso?" she asked.

"Please." Steve caught a whiff of the egg dish she had prepared, which looked like a soufflé. "Mark and Stan are coming today."

"Great." She set Steve's cup on a white porcelain saucer.

Steve brought it to the breakfast nook and sat down with Tadzio, who had a cappuccino. The two of them gazed outside as their groom brought the horses to the paddock on this picturesque July day.

Alex walked the length of the studio to the set of his nighttime cable show.

"Alex!"

Alex paused and turned around. Keith O'Leary was catching up to him. "Hi, Keith."

The two men hugged and kissed and Keith joined Alex on the way to their rehearsal, since both shows were filmed close to each other, sharing most of the crew, and the director.

"When's *Lover Boy* premiering?" Keith asked, dressed in faded jeans and a white tee.

"Not for a while. It's still in post." Alex paused before he headed to his dressing room.

"So? Is your dad doing our show?" Keith's blue eyes shined as he spoke.

Crossing his arms, Alex asked, "Why him? You want a man to jump out of a cake? I can do that."

Keith's smile faded. "Did Mark say no?"

"Keith? Dad's old!" Alex shook his head in frustration.

"Mark isn't old, Alex. A magazine just selected him as the sexist man alive. Give me a break."

"Whatever." Alex walked off, entering his dressing room.

~

Before his SWAT training course, Billy Sharpe worked out in the LAPD gym. Pumping heavy weights, Billy kept his fitness level high since he was now back where he needed to be, on the frontlines. Yes, he had taken a cut in pay, but screw it. It was a small price to pay to be happy.

Hearing other officers working out around him, Billy grunted and pushed a loaded bar off its mounts as he did bench presses.

The familiarity, the sense of coming back to where he belonged, it felt so fucking good.

He sat up between sets and caught his breath.

STARTING OVER

As men came and went, he was greeted with respect and affection.

"Good to have you back, L-T."

"Welcome back, sir."

Fist-bumps, handshakes, high-fives and broad smiles...oh, hell yes. Not one officer sneered, made a snide comment, or treated him as if he had failed. Not one.

Most cops knew the difference between a job on the front lines, and bureaucracy. Being a chief wasn't for everyone, and it certainly wasn't for him.

Billy couldn't wait to throw on his heavy gear and hit the streets to do some battle.

~

Wearing a suit and tie, Jack filled two mugs with coffee. He dropped bread into the toaster and checked the time on a wall clock in his kitchen.

Adam, dressed in navy blue slacks and a printed designer top, entered the kitchen and took the mug Jack handed him. "So, a wedding Saturday?"

"Yes." Jack lowered the toaster lever and sipped his coffee, leaning against the counter. "It'll be fun. I can't remember the last time we were social with Pete Harrison and Colt St John."

Adam smiled. "Colt. Is he still a Dom?"

"No clue." Jack set his mug down on the counter. "Jennifer Bernstein is coming as well."

"Ooo. Here come da' judge." Adam laughed.

Jack smiled. "Get the hell over here." He dragged Adam into his arms.

Adam placed his mug down beside Jack's and hugged him. "You seem better."

"I am. I guess grief was what was gnawing at me."

"Expect moments of sadness as you relapse."

Jack gazed into Adam's bedroom brown eyes. "Why don't you ever speak about your parents?"

The amusement fell from Adam's expression. He backed out of Jack's arms and picked up his mug.

"Adam." Jack shook his head.

Looking pained, Adam said, "Jack. They were murdered."

As Jack let out a soft gasp, the toaster ejected the bread behind him. "What?"

After putting the mug down, Adam placed the toast on plates and buttered them. "I don't want to talk about it."

Trying to grasp what Adam revealed, Jack was stunned and didn't know what to say. They'd been married for nearly a decade and this was the first time he'd heard it. Jack had assumed Adam's parents were simply against gay men. That was not the case.

Adam handed Jack a slice of toast and chewed his quietly, staring out at the crashing waves through the sliding glass door.

~

Climbing out of the limousine as it parked in front of their office in Sacramento, Tadzio held his purse and looked up at the tall sky-scraper. Steve put his arm around him and they entered the lobby and waited for an elevator.

Placing his sunglasses into his purse, Tadzio stepped into the lift as Steve poked the button for the executive level floor.

"Steven?"

"Yes?" Steve glanced at him as he kept an eye on the lit numbers.

"I need insurance. I have now?"

"Yes. You have insurance both through me, and through working here."

"Good."

"Why?"

STARTING OVER

Tadzio waited as the doors opened, and then he and Steve merged into the main lobby. 'Richfield-Miller' was on the wall in large gold letters behind their receptionist, along with the teddy bear logo.

"Good morning, Mr Miller, Mrs…Miller." The receptionist blushed as if she wasn't sure how to address pretty androgynous Tadzio.

Steve chuckled. "Hi." He held onto Tadzio and they continued to Steve's executive office.

Tadzio set his purse on the table near Steve's area of the spacious office. "I am still getting some hormonz, Steven. Iz okay. I can tell the doc-tour I am covered."

Steve picked up the phone on his desk, holding one finger up to Tadzio. "Hi, yes, this is Steve Miller. I need someone to get my husband his medical ID card." Steve winked at Tadzio. "Thanks. Oh. Hang on." Steve cupped the phone. "What name would you like on it?"

"Tadzio Andresen-Miller."

"You got it." Steve smiled and relayed it to the woman in personnel, and hung up.

"Steven? We have another meeting wit immigration. Iz wit our lawyer in LA."

"Okay. When?"

"Next week. I will remind you."

"What do they want to see us about?" Steve checked his cellphone and then placed it on his desk by a toy police car.

"Just follow-up he said. Just to make sure we are still husbands." Tadzio made his way to the wet-bar and filled a mug with coffee, bringing it to Steve.

"Okay." Steve thanked him, and then a knock was heard on Steve's office door. "Come in."

A buyer holding paperwork peeked in. "Mr Miller?"

"Come in, Jessie." Steve waved her closer.

Tadzio waited, because it was coming; a comment on Steve's amazing outfit.

Jessie paused and admired Steve. "You look really handsome today, Mr Miller."

Steve ran his fingers over his black tie. "Why, thank you."

Tadzio giggled mischievously.

"Right." Jessie brought him the stack of papers. "These bolts of fabric just came from Morocco and arrived in the port in Bordeaux."

Steve took the pages.

"I need to know how much the markup is since they were rushed for the designer in Paris."

"Tadzio?" Steve waved him closer.

Tadzio scampered towards them on his heels. "Yes. I can." He took the paperwork from Steve and sat at Mark's big desk with a calculator.

Steve said, "Tadzio is our new vice president of operations and production."

"Awesome!" Jessie clapped.

Tadzio stopped calculating markups and looked at Steve. He got a proud wink and a smile from the sexy hot owner of the company.

~

By noon, Stan parked his Lamborghini in front of the estate. They had made the drive in just under six hours. He had flown on the open highway at nearly ninety, ironically, keeping up with most of the traffic.

Warren, having heard the car, opened the front door.

Mark waited for the car to stop, then climbed out. After Stan popped the trunk, Mark took the bag of sex toys, not wanting Warren to deal with it.

"Hi, Mark, Stan." Warren smiled warmly.

STARTING OVER

Stan shouldered his backpack. "I brought some framed photos. Mark's modeling agent is retiring, so…"

"Wonderful!" Warren had a look. "Where would you like them?"

Mark peered at them. "Uh, what about one of the spare rooms, a den or study?"

"Very good. I'll bring them in and when you decide, let me know." Warren gathered the frames.

Stan and Mark walked into the mansion together.

Stan craned his neck at the grand foyer, always overwhelmed by this place. Mark continued up the imposing staircase to the second floor.

Behind him, Warren carried an armful of picture frames.

Stan took a deep breath and trotted up the staircase. When he entered the bedroom, Mark was changing into a suit and tie.

They still had not eaten, since, well…Mark didn't seem to eat. Stan set the backpack down and asked, "Do you need me?"

"That's a silly question." Mark zipped the fly on his suit trousers.

Stan smiled and clarified, "Do you want me to come to work with you?"

"Pet?" Mark grinned slyly at him. "You are an employee."

Chuckling, Stan took off his jeans and tee and entered the enormous closet to grab a suit off the rack. "So…uh…food?"

Mark slipped on a light blue Ralph Lauren shirt to go with his shimmering blue suit. "I can ask Sierra to fix you something to go, or we can grab a snack in Sac." Mark chose a tie off his rack, with a pinstripe pattern matching both the blue of the suit and the light blue of the shirt.

Stan stepped into the trousers, feeling rushed. "Mark. Don't you ever get hungry?"

"Not really." Mark walked off, knotting his tie.

Stan muttered, "Not really?" Picking out a shirt and tie, Stan dressed quickly and when he stepped out of the closet, Mark was searching his jewelry box.

"Where are my bloody yellow gold cufflinks?"

Stan knotted his tie as he looked into the mirror over the dresser.

"Bloody hell." Mark dumped the box onto the wooden surface and kept looking.

Stan leaned closer. "Aren't those cufflinks?"

"Yes, but...oh, never mind." Mark picked up a pair and poked it through his cuff. "Give us a hand?"

Stan pushed white gold cufflinks through Mark's cuffs, one, then the other.

"Cheers." Mark kissed him, slipped on designer loafers and rushed out. "Hurry, pet!"

Stan did, changing socks, tying shoe laces, and racing down the stairs.

Mark clapped his hands. "Chop! Chop! Warren! I need the car!"

Sierra raced into the foyer with a white paper bag. "I made some sandwiches."

Stan grabbed the bag. "Thank you!"

She winked at him sweetly.

The chauffeur stepped into the house. "I'm here, Mark."

"Good. Off we go." Mark hurried out of the house. "I really need to see to that helipad. I must be able to get to work quickly."

The chauffeur held open the back door of the limo. "Warren's working on it."

"Good. Ta, love." Mark held his phone as he sat in back of the limousine.

Stan climbed in and opened the bag. The aroma was delicious. He removed one of the sandwiches. A homemade

STARTING OVER

croissant which was still warm, with sliced turkey and Swiss cheese, sprouts and arugula. He took a big bite. "Oh, fuck, that's good."

Mark texted on his phone.

"Mark?" Stan held out the bag.

"No, love."

About to remind Mark he had fainted at Jack's house last night, Stan shut up. Nope. Not doing that. He devoured the sandwich in three huge bites, and asked, "You sure?" before he ate the second one. Sierra had added a basil aioli that was superb.

Mark giggled at him. "You eat it, big boy." He said to their new chauffeur, "Louis? Any chance you can get me an espresso en route?"

"You bet, Mark."

"Thanks, love." Mark kept texting.

Stan unwrapped the second sandwich and took a big bite, brushing crumbs off his dark suit trousers. "Damn, that's good."

Mark smiled sweetly at him.

Stan finished the food and crushed the bag. This was it...life in the fast lane. *Richfield-Miller here we come.*

Chapter 14

Mark exited the limousine with Stan, entered the lobby, and waited for the elevator. He took off his sunglasses, pocketing them and stepped into the lift with Stan.

Mark poked the correct floor number and then slowed down his manic pace since he was finally where he needed to be. He faced Stan, brushed a crumb off the handsome man's lapel and kissed him.

Stan caressed Mark's long hair gently, and appeared concerned or worried. Mark knew why and was glad Stan was not harping on him about food, like Steve always did. He was modeling Sunday. He'd eat after.

He did not lift weights like Stan to look cut and muscular. Mark appeared perfect because he starved.

The doors slid open soundlessly to their posh lobby.

"Good afternoon, Mr Richfield." The receptionist beamed at him. "Hi, Mr Richfield," she said to Stan as well.

"Good afternoon, lovely." Mark waited as she handed him a stack of mail. "How are you?"

"Great."

Mark sorted through the letters as he continued to his office. He handed them off to Stan. "It doesn't appear to be anything important."

"I'll handle it."

Mark entered his office and paused. Steve was working on his computer and a Kate Spade purse was left on Mark's desk.

STARTING OVER

"Well, well." Steve smiled as he stood from his chair. "I finally get you back."

"Hullo, handsome." Mark approached Steve and kissed him. "My. Don't you look stunning?" Mark inspected Steve's clothing. "Is this new?" He touched the shirt collar.

"It's yours." Steve laughed, holding up his hands. "So are the cufflinks."

Mark was surprised. "Pilfering my wardrobe, copper?" Mark picked Tadzio's purse up off his desk and handed it to Stan, for lack of a better place to put it.

Stan laughed and held it up higher. "And? What am I supposed to do with this?"

"It looks good on you," Steve joked and walked around the desk.

Mark tapped his computer to wake it. "Have you been working on this?"

"Tadzio has."

Mark took a second to think and stared at Steve. "Tadzio. Has been working on my computer and at my desk?"

Stan set Tadzio's purse on a chair in the lounge area, and poured Mark a cup of coffee. Stan opened the bar fridge and peered into it.

Steve sat on the corner of Mark's desk, crossing his arms. "Yes. I promoted him to veep of operations and production."

Mark choked at the news. "My word. That screams of nepotism. Is this because he gives good head, Steven?"

Stan set a steaming cup of coffee on Mark's desk as well as a tub of low fat yogurt and a spoon.

"Ha! Yes," Steve teased, then glanced at Stan and said, "Hey, uh, can you go to personnel? They need some information from you to get you medical and dental coverage."

"Okay." Stan paused. "Mark? Need anything?"

"Not at the moment." Mark picked up the yogurt and peeled back the lid.

Stan nodded and left, closing the office door.

After eating a spoonful of the yogurt, Mark narrowed his eyes at Steve. "Vice president of operations? Are you mad?"

Steve's expression became dead serious. "Mark? He's been helping me while you were in LA. Do you have any idea how much he knows about this business?"

Becoming confused, Mark said, "Tadzio. We're talking about Tadzio." Mark ate one more spoonful of the yogurt and set the pot on his desk.

"When I couldn't get a hold of you he was here to help me out. Mark? He knows this business from working in it."

"Love." Mark shook his head and picked up the coffee. "He was a runway model, not a buyer."

Steve stepped beside Mark and moved the mouse to open the program he and Tadzio were working on. "He knew the markups."

Mark tried not to panic, setting the mug down. "No! Please tell me you didn't allow him to do it!" He sat on the chair and scooted closer.

"See for yourself." Steve crouched beside Mark.

Mark read the invoices and the percentages of profit on each item. They were correct; higher margins for low cost, lower margins for the very expensive fabrics. Mark gazed at Steve's profile. "Tadzio?"

"Tadzio." Steve laughed.

"My word." Mark was stunned. "Why are you wearing my shirt?"

"I needed a makeover." Steve spun around to show Mark the black outfit, giving him a view front and back. "He wants us to go to LA with you two on the weekend so I can hit Rodeo Drive."

STARTING OVER

Mark admired his former cop. "What brought on the urge to change?"

Steve thumbed towards the purse. "He looks so good every day. Christ, I felt as if I was a schlub in rags next to him."

Mark was amused by Steve using a Yiddish word, Mark muttered, "A schlub in shmatas."

"Huh?"

"Nothing." Mark kept chuckling.

"I realized I was wearing the suit I wore to my interview with Harold Parsons. Mark? That was a decade back."

Mark shook his head. "Well, you look smashing." He sipped the strong coffee and set the mug down.

Steve sat on the corner of the desk again. "What happened with Alex at the shrink's appointment?"

"It was horrid. We shouted at each other. Then, just when I think we're all right, Alex had a snit over me being selected the sexiest man alive."

Steve made a noise in his throat and his eyebrows became expressive. "No. You did it again?"

"Steven." Mark exhaled loudly. "Those magazines are rubbish." Mark glanced at the door to the office. "I do think, however, that Stan is getting over the nasty deed. He seems better, less preoccupied."

"Keep them apart. Don't let the two of them end up alone anywhere." Steve climbed off the desk.

"Yes. Well. I said as much to our Billy. If Billy doesn't come with Alex, Alex is not welcome at the estate." Mark paused then said, "Do you know the chief is now an LAPD SWAT lieutenant once more?"

Steve smiled and shook his head. "I bet he's thrilled."

"Like a child with sweets."

The office door opened and Tadzio stepped in, his arms full of sample books. "Mark! You are here!"

"I am."

Tadzio set the samples down on the table near his purse and raced over. "I miss you! I miss you so much!"

Mark accepted the wonderful hug and kiss. "How is our newest veep doing?"

Tadzio brushed his blond hair back from his eyes. "What iz veep?"

Steve said, "Vice president."

"Oh! Yes. Mark? Iz okay?"

"Come here." Mark reached for him.

Tadzio stepped closer.

Mark pointed to the screen. "How did you know the correct markups?"

Looking shy, Tadzio tugged at his skirt and said, "My fadder was in manufacture. I work wit him when I was a boy. Iz the same. Less needs more, more needs less."

"I think I've underestimated you as well. You are more than a pretty face." Mark held Tadzio's hand and inspected his painted nails and the emerald cut diamond of his wedding set. "And, you're going to help Steven upgrade his wardrobe?"

"Yes. He iz borrowing your shirt." Tadzio blushed.

"I think our newest veep needs his own office, Steven."

"Oh?" Steve stood behind Tadzio and toyed with his long hair. "I was thinking he could sit right over there." Steve pointed to the area of the large office near the plate glass windows. "Maybe have his computer and desk with that view."

Mark watched Tadzio's pale blue eyes light up. "That sounds just fine."

"Thank you!" Tadzio hugged Mark. "I am so happy!"

Mark spotted Stan standing at the door to the office, smiling adoringly at them.

Stan held up forms. "I guess I now have medical and dental coverage."

STARTING OVER

"Me as well!" Tadzio clapped and rushed to Stan. "You are here!" He jumped into Stan's arms.

Mark gazed at Steve and they smiled at each other. "It's good to be where I belong."

Steve caressed Mark's cheek. "I can't tell you how happy I am."

Mark kissed Steve's knuckles and laughed at Tadzio snuggling with Stan.

~

"Sugarplum?" Charlotte Deavers waited for their lunch break to speak to Alex.

"Hey, Char." Alex paused before heading to the chow line.

"Has your dad made a decision on the role in *Forever Young*?"

"I don't think he's into it." Alex tried not to be distracted by the grips and crew members scurrying around.

"What did he say?" She nudged her eyeglasses higher.

"Well, last night, Adam Lewis printed the script and read it while we were at dinner at his place. Let's just say, Dad ignored him."

She made a silly face of distress. "That's not good."

"Char?" Alex sighed. "Ya want a stunner to jump out of a cake?" He opened his arms. "Here I am."

She laughed softly. "We know where you are, pumpkin. Will and Derek wanted Mark because it's like a bookend. He was there at the beginning, so him wrapping it up with Carl and Keith was for nostalgia more than anything else."

"Oh!" Alex got it. "That makes sense. I thought…oh. Okay."

"So?" she asked, "Is he willing?"

"He's back in Sac this week until his modeling shoot on Sunday."

"I need to know." She held her phone and scrolled with her fingers on it. "What if I sent another text?"

"Hang on." Alex took his phone out of his pocket and called his dad. He smiled at Charlotte as she shouted out directions to her gaffer, "Yes! Night scene. Thanks!"

"Dad?"

"Yes, Alex?"

"I'm at work with Charlotte Deavers. Can I hand my phone to her?"

"Yes."

He smiled. "Here he is."

Charlotte grabbed Alex's phone eagerly. "Mark!"

Now that Alex knew why, he was a lot less jealous.

"Look, Mr Richfield," she said, her tongue firmly planted in her cheek, "I'm calling in a special favor…no. Let me explain." She laughed loudly. "Will and Derek are bringing back a few guests from the first season…Yes." She winked at Alex. "Yes! A reunion of sorts. Since you were there in the beginning…" She tapped her finger to her lip. "Um. I don't think it will take more than one afternoon. Mark? You don't have many lines. You can certainly riff or say whatever you like. All you have to do is look scrumptious."

Alex chuckled, imagining his dad's reaction.

"Right. Leap out of a cake, lap dance, shimmy and shake." Charlotte's smile broadened. "That's why I adore you. Thank you, Mark. Yes. I will." She handed the phone to Alex. "Thanks, sugarplum."

"Did he say yes?"

"He did." She kept laughing as she walked off.

Alex put the phone to his ear. "Dad?"

"Yes, Alex?"

"You know how much fun that scene is going to be? Huh? You with Keith and Carl again?"

STARTING OVER

"Yes. Well. I suppose that's what happens when your son is starring in a nighttime cable drama with a pushy director named Charlotte Deavers."

Alex roared with laughter.

"I must go. Be good."

"Love ya, Dad."

"And you."

Alex cracked up and made his way to the craft table to get food into his belly. Now that he understood why they wanted his father, he felt a whole lot better.

~

Billy Sharpe kept to the filthy wall of a seedy apartment house hallway; one that stunk of old nicotine and cat urine. Federal agents had surrounded the exterior of the building.

His communication wire in his ear, Billy glanced back to the line of heavily armed men wearing helmets, eye protection, body armor, and holding assault rifles.

The feds radioed they were in place.

Billy hand signaled to his team.

A big bruiser with a battering ram was poised.

Holding up his gloved hand, Billy counted down from three. On 'one', the door was shattered open.

"Police! Hands where I can see them!" Billy and his team flooded the cluttered space. Men inside reached for guns but soon changed their minds and placed their hands over their heads.

Ten SWAT team members swarmed inside the two bedroom apartment.

Echoes of, "Police! Get your hands up!" made Billy's adrenalin surge to a new height.

Once all the men were rounded up, Billy let the feds know. "Entry made. Under control."

Men were handcuffed as they knelt on the floor.

Billy shouldered his rifle and had a look. Chemicals to make explosives, a cache of weapons and ammo, maps of soft targets, and stacks of cash.

The federal agents took over, leading the suspects out first, then having a look at their operation.

"Home grown terrorists," the lead agent said as he surveyed the claustrophobic space.

Billy patted the man's back. "Great work. Absolutely amazing work."

"Thanks, Sharpe."

"Okay, boys. Let's go." Billy waved to his men. Their heavy boots sounded like thunder as they plodded down the cement stairs to the outside of the building.

Dark sedans and SUVs pulled up as the suspects were patted down and then transported.

Billy took a deep breath and grinned wickedly. "Well done. Well-fucking-done."

His men gathered into a tight circle, and pressed their fists together, then roared in a military type cheer.

As they returned to their black SUVs, which were out of sight of the suspects' view, Billy was on fire. No one had been injured, and the mission had gone down perfectly.

Looking at his men, his amazing team, Billy was high. High on the adrenalin and high on the work.

He caught the smiles from Manny, Bernie, and Jim and loved it. Fucking loved it!

~

Mark stood in front of the brightly lit, large conference room. A dozen individuals were seated around it, shareholders, with folders in front of them.

"As you can see, since Steven and my takeover, our stock prices have risen nearly ten percent." Mark had to borrow reading glasses from one of the older men at the table. He held

STARTING OVER

the pamphlet up as he spoke. "Not only has our market share risen substantially, the new order percentage has doubled." Mark glanced up at the solemn faces as they read the last quarter's numbers as well as their projected growth.

"Since I have opened us up to new designs, college students, and scholarships; the advertising volume of exposure has risen whilst the cost of our advertising has dropped. This, I assume, is because the designers are promoting not only our fabrics, but they are sharing the designs on social media." Mark turned a page and adjusted the glasses. "Contrary to the past owners," and Mark meant his mother and Harry Jenkins, "We have set up accounts on the social networks. I realize we are a wholesaler, but with our top clients being household names like Vera Wang and Ralph Lauren, we need to be exposed to our target audience, as well as any future aspiring companies. I would also like to look into opening lines of credit to startup companies, especially small businesses from low income areas of our country."

Mark set the paperwork down and took off the glasses. He allowed the men and women to read the paperwork.

"And," Mark said, "Our projection as we go into the next year has been outstanding. Our stocks have quite a good outlook at the moment, encouraging buying, not selling as was the case just months ago when our stocks were being dumped as they plummeted."

Mark ran his hand through his hair. "I will continue to encourage young talent, which as you know, is our blood, our future." Mark handed the glasses off to the nice man who had loaned them to him. "Any questions or concerns?"

A middle-aged man of color held his phone in front of him. "Richfield-Miller has just crept into the top thirty largest companies on the stock market."

"Ha!" Mark was tickled pink. When his father ran this place, it was in the top ten.

Happy noises came from the stockholders.

An older man smiled at Mark. "Your father would be so proud."

"Thank you." Mark smiled sweetly at him. "If there's nothing else..." Mark picked up his paperwork and shook hands as he stood near the open door of the conference room, soaking up the accolades and thrilled that whatever he and Steve were doing, was working.

~

Two desks were set up in Mark and Steve's enormous office. Technicians were connecting computers, phones, and lighting.

Meanwhile, Stan was in the lounge area with a laptop, entering numbers on a spreadsheet, while Tadzio ordered fabric to go with the invoices he was sorting.

Steve was at his desk, video-chatting on a conference call. "Uh. I'm not certain of that..." Steve said, then called to the office door, "Mark?"

Stan and Tadzio peered up at Mark as he returned from the shareholder's meeting.

"Yes, love?" Mark handed Stan the paperwork in his hand and walked towards Steve.

"Paris office." Steve stood from his chair.

"My. It's awfully late there." Mark took his seat.

Stan and Tadzio stopped working to watch Mark in action.

"*Bonjour! Comment allex-vous?*"

Stan and Tadzio blinked at each other in surprise.

"*Oui. Je Suis au courant de ça.*"

"Holy shit." Stan stood from the couch and approached Steve, who was looking so proud of Mark he was beaming.

Mark peered at them for a second and then focused on the call.

Stan and Tadzio stood next to Steve, able to see the buyer on the video screen as Mark spoke in French.

STARTING OVER

"*Pas de probèmes. Ce'bon...Au revoir.*" Mark disconnected the call. "Right. Are we ready to go home?"

"Dumb model, huh?" Steve shook his head. "Jesus Christ, Richfield."

"Holy fuck." Stan was stunned.

Tadzio picked his purse up from the table after logging off the laptop. "Mark? *Comment se fait-il que vous parliez si bien le français?*"

"I learnt it in school, lovely." Mark buttoned his suit jacket and walked towards the door, texting on his phone.

Stan and Steve gawked at each other as Mark and Tadzio left the office ahead of them, talking in both French and English.

Stan waited for Steve to put his suit jacket on. "Did you know Tadzio could speak French?"

"I did not." Steve laughed. "Well, fuck me. I'm the only idiot in the room."

"Yeah, uh. No. That makes both of us." Stan buttoned his suit jacket as he and Steve followed the other two to the elevator. "I had a few semesters of Spanish, but I can't speak it."

"Same here." Steve closed the office door behind them and walked with Stan to the other two.

Mark cupped Tadzio's chin in his hand. "You, my love, are a great asset."

"When you will open office in Sweden, I will help," Tadzio teased. He poked Steve playfully in the chest. "You can ask me. I would have helped wit the Paris call."

"Now I know!" Steve laughed and pulled Tadzio into his arms as the elevator opened.

Stan was overwhelmed at the moment, but happy. Very happy. They rode to the street level together. Stan caressed Mark's hair. "How did the shareholder's meeting go?"

"Fabulous." Mark put his sunglasses on as they arrived at the lobby. "Whilst we chatted our company has just hit the top thirty on the stock market."

Stan choked and Steve made a noise of surprise in his throat. They stepped outside into the Delta wind as the limousine driver opened the back door. He and Steve whooped it up and high-fived.

Mark chuckled at them and he and Tadzio sat in back of the limousine.

"Holy shit, Steve." Stan was elated.

"Fuck yeah! Fuck yeah!" Steve appeared pumped.

They climbed into the limousine and Mark chuckled at them. "My two macho men."

"Mine too." Tadzio cuddled against Steve.

"Indeed." Mark held Stan's hand and rested his head on him. "What a day."

"Wow." Steve loosened his necktie. "Just wow."

Stan felt better than he had done in weeks. Steve was happy and had let go of his stranglehold on Mark, Tadzio was giddy, and Mark? He was a man on a mission.

And that mission was making an incredible life for their family. All of them, even their extended family.

Tadzio held his phone in his hand and called someone. Then, he brightened up. "Alskander!"

Mark shook his head, smiling, and kissed Stan. "How are you, baby?"

Stan replied, "I'm fucking delirious."

"Oh. Well. That's a bloody good thing."

"Alskander! I am veep!"

Steve cracked up and Stan gripped Mark's hand tightly.

Fuck yes. This is how it should be.

It was like starting over.

STARTING OVER

Chapter 15

Mark entered the mansion and loosened his tie.

Steve and Tadzio walked to their bedroom on the main floor. "Who's running with me?"

"I am!" Tadzio said joyously.

"Mark?"

He paused. "I was going to run...on Piccadilly." Mark laughed.

"Stan?" Steve waited.

"I think I need to ride Bull. I miss that beast. But, Steve? I was going to lift weights after dinner."

"Perfect." Steve led Tadzio to their room to change.

"Ha!" Thinking of Stan growing close to Steve made Mark a happy man. He held Stan's hand and they climbed the stairs together. He walked into the huge closet in their bedroom. Mark hung up his tie and suit, and changed into his britches and riding blouse.

Behind him, Stan swapped his business attire for jeans and a flannel top since the evenings were cool at the base of the mountains.

Mark buttoned his white blousy shirt and noticed Stan gazing at him. Mark took a look at himself in the skin-tight beige britches, ones with brown suede patches inside the lower thighs.

Stan dropped to his knees and stared at the bulge under Mark's zipper. Mark caressed Stan's hair gently, letting him know...yes.

Stan framed Mark's package with his big hands, admiring it. He chewed on it gently over the material, then opened Mark's zipper and groaned when Mark's cock was revealed.

Mark held onto the side wall, one with a rack for their shoes, to brace himself as Stan took his cock into his mouth.

Moaning, exposing Mark's balls and reaching under them to his ass, Stan rubbed hot friction at the root and drew strong suction on Mark's erection. A mad rush of chills washed up Mark's spine. His focus was on the blowjob, Stan's lips around his shaft and Stan's expression of pure bliss.

His young husband brought Mark up to the edge quickly. As Mark's cock pulsated and thickened, Stan whimpered and sucked deeper, rubbed boiling friction into and around Mark's rim.

"Ah!" Mark held onto the wall and Stan's shoulder as his knees gave out. He went into a powerful climax. "Ah! Yes!" Mark threw back his head and shivered.

"Mmm!" Stan pulled harder suction on Mark's cock, holding the base in his palm.

Mark rode the climax wave and clung to Stan to stop from falling over.

Stan withdrew the suction with a pop and caught his breath. "Fuck, you taste amazing. Is that from the diet of the fruit and yogurt?" Stan licked the slit of Mark's cock.

"Bloody hell." Mark tried to function after the strong orgasm.

Stan tucked Mark's soft cock behind the fabric and zipped his britches up. Then, he stood and rubbed his hard-on over his jeans.

Mark kissed him. "Can I accommodate you after? I do want to ride."

"Yes." Stan smiled. He crouched down to lace up his work-boots.

STARTING OVER

Mark picked up his high black boots and had to pause as a wave of dizziness hit.

~

Christ, you look great, you smell great, and you taste amazing. Stan was so horny he was losing it. He stood straight and was about to joke about coming in his pants when he noticed Mark appeared pale again.

Stan grabbed Mark's arm. "Hey. Are you going to faint?"

"Let me…" Mark gripped tightly to Stan. "One moment."

Stan tried to be patient, but this was absurd! *Eat! Will you eat!*

"All right." Mark seemed to battle the spell and continued on, carrying his black boots to the stairs.

Stan tried to bite back his comments, but he was beginning to understand why Steve, Alex, and Billy continually berated Mark about food.

Mark managed to walk down the enormous staircase without falling. He continued to the back of the house, into the kitchen, where Sierra was cooking dinner.

Mark sat down near the back door to put his boots on.

Stan glanced behind him as Tadzio and Steve, dressed in shorts and tees, were ready to run.

"Mmm. Smells amazing." Steve sniffed at dinner.

Tadzio tied his hair in a ponytail. "What iz dinner?"

Sierra showed off a tray. "Seafood in puffed pastry with a light butter sauce."

"Oh, hell, yeah." Steve laughed and put a ball-cap on his head. "Ready, blondie?"

"I am." Tadzio and Steve jogged out of the back door.

"Mark?" Sierra said softly.

Mark, appearing slightly disoriented, stood from the bench of the breakfast nook. "Yes, love?"

Stan had a feeling Mark was not going to eat that food.

As if she knew, Sierra said, "I've got a small salmon fillet for you. I'll broil it, no oil, no butter, and steamed asparagus."

"Thank you." Mark opened the back door and headed out.

Stan said to Sierra, "Thanks."

She winked at him knowingly.

Stan and Mark headed to the stable. Out in the distance, Steve and Tadzio jogged across the open field on a trail.

As they entered the remodeled space, Mark's horse Piccadilly leaned his long graceful neck out of his stall towards Mark.

Stan jumped out of his skin when a man emerged from Shadow of the Knight's stall.

"Hi, Mark."

Mark spun around from petting his horse. "And, who might you be?"

"Andrew Wilson." The young man reached out his hand enthusiastically. "Warren hired me to take care of the horses."

"Well. Welcome. This is my husband, Stan." Mark drew Piccadilly out of his stall.

"Hi, Stan. Can I get Shadow saddled for you?"

"No. Bull is my horse." Stan gestured to his big percheron.

"Ha. Awesome." Andrew headed to the tack wall to get the western saddle as Mark placed his English one on Piccadilly.

Stan watched Andrew prepare Bollward's Tempest for him as Mark placed a bit in Piccadilly's mouth.

Jack's black thoroughbred appeared curious, snorting and watching from his stall.

Mark mounted the graceful white Arabian stallion and waited.

Andrew tugged at the stirrup and said, "All ready."

Stan used a stool to climb onto Bull's high back, taking the rein. "Thanks."

"It's a fabulous evening. Have fun." Andrew opened the two large stable doors for them so they could leave easily.

STARTING OVER

"Ready, pet?" Mark asked, looking over his shoulder.
"Yes."
Mark squeezed his knees and Piccadilly broke into a canter.
Stan encouraged Bull to follow, and he did his best to keep up with the white speed machine.

~

Steve and Tadzio jogged to the tree line in a route that was not only incredible, but began to feel normal, away from traffic and smog, off the concrete and tarmac.

A three-beat rhythm became louder. He and Tadzio looked behind them and there was Mark, racing over the same field on his white stallion.

The incredible horse with its long silver mane and tail flew by. Behind it, Stan's massive heavy horse made the ground thunder as he also sped past. Stan made a loud, "Whoop!" as he did, and Steve and Tadzio 'whooped' in reply as they watched the two men fly.

~

Billy and Alex caught their breaths as they finished their after-work run. They entered the home and Billy continued through to the back of the house.

While still boiling from the run, and sweating profusely, Billy wrapped his knuckles with canvas straps and pounded the punching bag.

Behind him, he heard a splash.

Alex had stripped and jumped into their pool.

Billy continued working out until he was completely spent. After a full day, a morning weightlifting routine, tactical training, and helping the feds round up criminals, Billy's body was burning from the lactic acid.

He did his punching bag workout, not cutting it short, pushing his muscles to their max, then he dropped his arms and felt them vibrate and ache.

When he turned towards the pool, his gorgeous superstar was watching him, his arms on the ledge, his chin on his forearms.

Billy unwrapped his knuckles as his chest expanded from his demand for air. He toed off his shoes, tugged off his damp socks, and then stripped off his shorts and briefs.

He dove into the pool.

When he surfaced he swam to Alex and Alex locked his ankles behind Billy's back. Billy gazed into Alex's bewitching green eyes. His babydoll was back. The anger, the hate, the rage, they had vanished.

That made Billy very happy indeed. He gave Alex a smile as he drew Alex to his mouth to kiss.

While Billy bobbed with Alex in the refreshing water, they kissed, and kissed, and kissed, like they hadn't done in ages.

Billy picked Alex up by his waist, set him on the pool's smooth ledge, and sank Alex's hard cock into his mouth.

Alex spread his legs, bent his knees, placed his heels on the lip of the pool, and held onto Billy's shoulders.

Billy sucked to his heart's content, laying off the anal for a while until Alex felt ready for him.

"Oh, Christ." Alex moaned as Billy jerked his cock into his mouth.

Billy hummed as he stimulated Alex with friction at the root of Alex's dick.

"Ah!" Alex's legs jerked and he came. "Ah! Billy!"

Billy took the load into his mouth. He then, hoisted himself out of the pool, straddling Alex's hips as the handsome star dropped to his back on the white cement patio. After he spat the cum into his palm, Billy used it to jerk off, gazing at Alex as he did. His eyes were drawn to the lieutenant badge on Alex's pelvis. Billy worked his cock vigorously and spattered cream on Alex's cock and balls, while the taste of Alex's cum lingered on his tongue.

STARTING OVER

"Oh, fuck, yes." Alex admired Billy as he came.

Billy released his cock and caught his breath, lying beside Alex on the patio, staring at the cloudless sky.

"I fucking love you." Alex held Billy's hand.

"I fucking love you too, doll." Billy relaxed and held Alex's hand, hoping this was it. A new start. And a drama free life.

~

Adam signed off of his computer at work. He checked his phone and then closed his office door behind him. Logan was logging off his computer as well, and Natalie was standing by her desk, reading her phone, giggling.

"Yes?" Adam stood next to her.

"I think I'm in love." She blushed.

"Oh?" Adam tried to recall Natalie behaving like this before.

Logan approached them. "When's the hot date?"

"It's supposed to be Friday but we've been texting every day and calling every night before bed." Natalie was glowing.

Adam chuckled as they left the agency. "Do I know this person?"

"Yes. Remember? I asked you about Becca McKenna? Stan's friend?"

Adam held open the elevator door. "You...you mean, you and Becca are becoming a thing?"

"I hope so. She's so cute." Natalie faced the elevator door as it closed. "Did you know she's carrying Mark's baby?"

Adam did, but didn't say anything to Natalie about it previously. "Yes."

"I adore her." Natalie looked completely love struck.

"Huh." Adam tried to wrap his head around it.

Logan laughed. "So? Does that make you the stepmom or the aunt for Mark's baby?"

"Neither!" Natalie cracked up.

"Wow." Adam waited as the other two left the elevator first. "You just blew my mind."

Before they headed to their cars, Natalie said to Adam, "Tell Mark to not worry. Becca's in good hands."

"Ha. Okay." Adam had no idea what that meant, or what he should think about it. He sat in his BMW and sent Jack a text, *'on my way home.'*

'okay, same here.'

~

Jack logged off his office computer and left a few files on his desk he had to deal with tomorrow. As he locked his office door, he ran into Pete Harrison, one of the lawyers working in his firm.

"Hey." Pete smiled at Jack.

"Hey, Pete." Jack and Pete walked to the elevators together. "Ready for Sonja's wedding?"

"I am. I'm looking forward to it." Pete held the elevator door open as he and Jack joined the few office employees leaving for the day.

"Is Donny coming?" Jack asked.

"Danny." Pete laughed. "Donny is the other twin."

His cheeks heated up in embarrassment. "I knew that." Jack felt stupid since Donny and Danny Rothschild were identical twins who worked for Parsons and Company, Mark and Steve's old firm. Jack left the elevator and stood outside the lobby's glass doors. "Is *Danny* coming," he corrected.

"He is." Pete laughed.

"Do you know if Colt is?" Jack loosened his necktie.

"As far as I know. He said Ash is back in rehab. I think Colt has had enough of him going in and out of clinics."

"Oh. I'm sorry to hear that." Jack didn't know Colt's boyfriend very well.

"Has Sonja invited Mark?" Pete asked, the Santa Ana winds blowing the handsome man's necktie.

STARTING OVER

"No. She doesn't really know Mark well, and Steve isn't coming either."

"Well, it should be a bash. See ya tomorrow." Pete patted Jack's arm.

"See ya." Jack walked to his Jaguar and dropped onto the low bucket seat. As he drove to his home in Malibu, Jack was happy to attend Sonja's wedding, but wished he was going to Paradise to ride his horse and hang out with Mark. Soon. He and Adam would go soon.

~

With just the four of them present; Mark, Stan, Steve, and Tadzio ate in the nook in the kitchen.

The small salmon fillet was perfect, with just a touch of garlic and dill. Mark managed to clean his plate, which made the three men he was dining with very happy.

"How was dinner?" Sierra picked up the empty dishes.

"Fantastic." Steve patted his belly.

Mark chuckled.

Warren held up a bottle of sherry. "May I pour?"

"Yes." Tadzio smiled.

Mark tapped Stan. "Can I get up?"

Stan slid out of the bench seat and allowed Mark out.

Mark took the tiny sherry glass from Warren and stepped outside his home.

As night deepened the velvety sky, the blue lights of the outdoor pool glowed like luminous gemstones. The wind felt refreshing, almost chilly.

Mark gazed up to the heavens.

The door behind him opened and the other three men stepped outside with him.

"Look at that." Steve gestured to the sky and the pinpoints of light.

Warren shut off the outside spotlights, allowing the ambient light to vanish so they could admire the cosmos.

Sipping the sherry, Mark craned his neck to the view.

"There iz so many stars."

Stan put his arm around Mark and enjoyed the sky with him. "Amazing." Stan gazed upwards.

Remembering lying out in the fields as a boy, not only to admire the sky but to escape his father, Mark rested his head on Stan's shoulder and tried to identify the constellations.

"That iz Orion." Tadzio pointed.

"My God. You can see the Milky Way." Steve made a soft sound of awe.

Finishing the sherry, Mark set the tiny glass on the deck table and held onto Stan in the cold wind.

"What an amazing place this is, Mark." Stan's gaze was aimed at the sky.

"Iz truly paradize."

"Oh!" Steve pointed. "A falling star! Did you see it?"

"Yes!" Tadzio inhaled in surprise.

"Did you make a wish, Mark Antonious?" Stan whispered into Mark's ear.

"Oh, my pet. All of my wishes have come true." Mark hugged Stan and stared at the black velvet sky blanketed with stars.

STARTING OVER

Chapter 16

Saturday morning, Stan stirred from a fantastic night's rest. Stretching his legs under the crisp cotton sheets, Stan stared through the wall of glass to the mountain view.

Silver and gold sunlight flooded into the massive bedroom.

He read the time on his new watch. It was before seven. Praline was sitting on the night table, smiling.

Stan chuckled at him and then rolled over.

The 'sexiest man alive' was sleeping beside him.

Crushing the pillow under his cheek, Stan stared at Mark.

Mark was on his side, facing him, his smooth shoulder exposed from the white sheet.

A whinny from one of the horses floated to their open window.

My God.

Stan had no idea what he had done in a past life, but…

He must have been a very good boy.

Dark masculine stubble grew on the top model's jaw, his soft brown hair was deliciously mussed from his slumber. Mark's full lips, his black thick eyelashes, his straight nose, his high cheekbones…

Stan could only marvel at how gorgeous he was. Stan's cock engorged and pulsated.

The gold chai charm had stayed around Mark's neck since Stan had given it to him. Their matching sapphire and diamond wedding rings shimmered in the light.

Fuck…fuck, fuck, fuck…I wanna fuck you.

Today all four of them were going to fly to LA in Mark's private jet. He and Mark had a modeling shoot early tomorrow morning, and Steve and Tadzio were going to shop in Beverly Hills to buy the former cop a new wardrobe.

Stan touched himself as he gazed at this glamorous beauty. After dinner and stargazing every night this week, he and Steve worked out together in the spa. Tadzio was content watching him and Steve lift weights, helping to spot when he needed to, while Mark relaxed, reading in the library with a cup of tea and classical music; in a room with thousands of books from the floor to the ceiling. A relic from Mark's mom that was so outstanding, Jason and Ewan had left it intact.

Mark began to move, shifting on the soft pillows.

As Stan anticipated the sight of Mark's emerald eyes, he squeezed his own dick, hungry for sex.

Those thick eyelashes fluttered and Mark opened his eyes.

Chills washed over Stan's spine. "Good morning, gorgeous."

As Mark became lucid, he peeked at the digital clock and then relaxed.

Stan shifted closer, running his hand over Mark's smooth chest, down to his low abdomen.

"Mmm." Mark appeared drowsy and sexy as hell.

Stan nibbled Mark's shoulder, touching Mark's cock.

"Let me…" Mark yawned and gestured to the bathroom.

He allowed Mark to climb out of bed, seeing his tight ass and long legs as Mark took his turn to freshen up.

Stan rolled to his back and needed release. Sleeping with Mark had him pent up, and all he'd need to do to come is jerk his dick a few times.

While Mark got ready, Stan reached into the nightstand's top drawer. Mark had dumped their toys into it, as well as the lube.

STARTING OVER

Stan took it out of the drawer and placed it close to him on the bed.

His phone hummed.

Stan peered at the bathroom door and then picked it up.

Oswald had sent a text, '*so you guys are going to be in LA today until late Sunday?*'

'*Yes.*'

'*dinner? paintball tag?*'

'*definitely dinner, no tag. Mark and I are modeling tomorrow so no bruising.*'

'*any idea where? in Bel Air?*'

'*can I let you know?*'

'*yup!*'

Stan set the phone back down on the nightstand and touched himself since his dick had softened slightly with the distraction.

The bathroom door opened and Mark emerged.

Oh fuck yes.

Stan tossed off the sheet and jerked himself as he watched Mark strut over. Mark rested one knee on the bed and ran his fingers down his chest to his cock.

At the sensual leer from Mark, Stan went crazy. He scrambled over towards him and took Mark's dick into his mouth. He had no idea if it was Mark's pheromones or just his natural scent, but...

Stan was addicted.

"That's it, baby." Mark crooned as he petted Stan's hair.

Wanting to taste Mark's cum, Stan held Mark's hips and drew Mark to the bed. Mark relaxed on his back and bent his knees.

Stan camped out between his legs. He burrowed in, using his face against Mark's balls and inner thighs, holding the base of Mark's cock in two fingers.

Mark purred and straddled wider.

The scent of clean skin and soap came from the top model. Stan pushed Mark's legs backwards to his chest and went for Mark's rim.

Stan darted his tongue into Mark's ass and was about to blow his load. He knelt upright and gazed at Mark.

"Fuck." Stan couldn't get over him. Whatever the doctor was doing was simply beyond belief. Mark looked thirty, not a day older.

Holding the base, Mark aimed his cock towards Stan.

Stan whimpered and sucked as much of it into his mouth as he could manage. He snatched the lube from the bed and used it on his fingers, then he pushed into Mark's ass with two slick fingers.

"Ah!" Mark arched his back and pre-cum coated Stan's tongue.

The rush to Stan's groin was unbearable. He jerked Mark's cock into his mouth, driving Mark crazy, while he worked the lubrication into Mark's rim.

"Ah!" Mark clawed the bedding.

Stan released the suction on Mark's cock and dove onto him, aiming his cock at Mark's slick hole. He put the head of his dick on target and thrust in, deep and hard.

"Ah! Bloody hell!" Mark threw his head back into the pillow.

"Damn! Fuck." Stan hammered in, seeing Mark going insane under him, Mark's cock blushing deeply and dripping pre-cum which was running in a string to his taut belly.

Stan came. He couldn't hold back if he wanted to, and he didn't want to. He continued to slide in and out, staring at his hard cock as it dipped into Mark.

Mark moaned and his hips rocked against Stan. "More..." Mark purred.

STARTING OVER

Stan toyed with Mark's length while gliding inside him. He could see goose bumps rise on Mark's forearms. Stan swiped at the tip and sucked his finger. "Oh, fuck, you taste good."

Mark touched the tip of his cock and held his finger out to Stan wickedly.

Stan grabbed Mark's wrist and sucked his finger, swirling around it like it was a cock.

"Ah! Ah!" The top model went into a climax. "Yes!"

Creamy ropes of cum spattered Mark's chest. Stan drove in once more, about to hit the stratosphere.

Mark tore at the bedding, his body tensed and his cock leaking more cum onto his bronze skin.

"Oh, fuck. *Fuck!*" Stan came a second time and choked on the intensity. It was so strong he couldn't function for a few seconds, feeling the tight throbbing from both of their groins as his toes curled and his teeth clenched.

Mark gasped and went limp under him.

Stan pulled out and sat on his heels, shaking his head in disbelief.

Mark moaned and stretched out his long lean legs.

Stan braced himself over Mark's chest, and lapped at Mark's cum.

He felt and heard Mark's sensual chuckle as he did.

Stan sat heavily beside Mark on the enormous bed and tried to recover. "Jesus Christ."

Mark touched himself gently and sighed. "That cock on you…my word."

Stan dropped to his back beside Mark, touching Mark's hip with his fingertips. "The sex. Mark. The sex."

"I know. I know." Mark patted Stan's arm.

Stan finally felt as if he could think. He rolled to his side and drew Mark's lips against his. Mark cupped Stan's jaw and they kissed sensually, purring and humming in passion.

~

Tadzio opened his eyes.

Bright sunshine was flooding the gorgeous bedroom.

He looked towards Steve's side of the bed and then heard the shower running. Tadzio sat up, stretched his back and spotted the pink 'pussytat' on the floor. He chuckled and picked him up, putting him on the bed, then skipped to the marble bathroom.

Steam had filled the space as Steve stood under a massaging showerhead.

Tadzio waited as the toilet lid raised up automatically. He relieved himself and it also flushed on its own.

Tadzio brushed his teeth and then climbed into the enormous shower stall, one with a large head on either side.

Steve backed up from the one he was using. "Good morning. I didn't want to wake you."

"I am up!" Tadzio wetted down under the soothing spray.

"How did you sleep?" Steve asked as he shampooed.

"Like baby." Tadzio dropped to his knees and took Steve's soft cock into his mouth.

"Oh, hell, yes." Steve laughed and held onto the tile wall.

Tadzio giggled and gazed up at Steve while he gave him a nice morning blowjob.

"I love you, blondie." Steve spread his feet on the marble bottom and relaxed.

With his mouth full of cock, Tadzio said, "I luff you doo, Steffen."

~

Alex woke from a bizarre dream, one where he was having sex with Stan while Tadzio spanked Billy's rump with the pink stuffed cat.

He had no doubt the valium was responsible for his strange dreams. He was using them to sleep lately.

STARTING OVER

Rolling over, brushing his mop of hair out of his face, Alex noticed his police lieutenant still sleeping. Billy's large hand was exposed from the bedding, near the pillow. Alex inspected the knuckles. They were callused like Billy's palms, from the punching bag workout and the weightlifting. Billy's cuticles had traces of either gunpowder or gun oil, which didn't scrub off easily.

Alex admired him, stared at the gray hair at Billy's temples, on his sideburns, and a smattering of gray hairs now on his chest as well.

The military man had a few scars on him, nothing scary, but it was obvious Billy had injured himself over the decades.

Alex recalled Billy being shot in the vest during a particularly horrendous LAPD hostage situation. Although Alex checked, he did not see any scars from that incident. Luckily the vest had done its job and Billy had been bruised, but…that was all.

Alex next inspected the barbed wire tattoo on Billy's biceps. The amount he loved this guy was limitless.

Even after simulating sex with some of the hottest movie stars in Hollywood, Alex knew nothing compared to his lieutenant.

Slowly, Billy's eyes opened, showing off the ring of blue around his irises.

Alex smiled and his cock thickened. Billy had laid off anal sex for the past few days to give him time to recover, but, Alex was ready to play once more.

Billy rolled to his back and rubbed his face and the corners of his eyes. As if he were struggling to come out of the deep slumber, Billy gazed in the direction of his gun and badge, and then the digital clock.

Alex rested his chin on Billy's broad chest.

"Hey, doll." Billy caressed Alex's hair.

"Wanna make love?"

"Sure." Billy cupped Alex's cheek. "Let me just brush my teeth." He gestured to the bathroom.

Alex sucked Billy's nipple into his mouth and then released him. Billy stood from the bed and entered the bathroom.

As he did, Alex gazed at his wide muscular shoulders and narrow waist.

"Oh, fuck, yeah." Alex relaxed on the bed and played with himself until his police lieutenant returned, and claimed what he owned. Him.

~

Stan scampered down the grand staircase to the foyer. The scent of bacon and coffee made his stomach growl.

"Stan?" Warren caught him before he joined the others.

"Yes?" Stan tucked his T-shirt into his skinny jeans.

"Come see what you think." Warren beckoned him down the long corridor.

Stan followed, gazing into Steve and Tadzio's bedroom, seeing the bed made, and the silly pink cat on it. He chuckled and kept going, walking by the library, several more guest bedrooms, and the theater and spa.

Warren gestured to a study with several computer screens on a long desk near glass doors which opened to a terrace.

Stan entered and had a look. Warren had arranged Mark's modeling photos on one massive wall. "Wow." Stan stopped short and took in the display.

Centered were Mark's *Dangereux* ads; Mark with Piccadilly, Mark with Alex, Mark with a Santa hat and his wicked smile, and then, Mark's Red Cologne ads, including his motorcycle ads, and then, his…he and Mark paired up together.

Along the perimeter of those sexy ads were Mark's automobile ads; Mark in skintight white leggings on the front seat of a white sports car, Mark in gold stretch pants in a gold

STARTING OVER

sports car…Mark in a tailored business suit in front of luxury sedans…

Okay. I can jerk off in here. Stan chuckled to himself.

"Stan?"

"Huh?" Stan was lost on Mark's cock, visible in many of the car ads. Then, he recalled it may be a phallus, not Mark.

"Stan?" Warren laughed, since Stan was mesmerized.

"Sorry." Stan tried to focus on the older man.

Warren smiled wryly. "There was also a box of photos from Steve. His academy graduation and swearing in as well as some with him and Alex's husband."

"Sure. Yes. Add them to the room. I can't think of a better place to put them than in here with Mark's photos." Stan drew closer to the ad he and Mark did together, and then inspected one Mark did with Alex. Mark looked exactly the same even though years separated the two shoots.

The wedding photo from Katie Tice was hanging in a special place in their bedroom.

"Do you have any from Obsession?"

"Huh?" Stan discreetly touched himself since staring at Mark in spandex was making him insane.

Warren chuckled. "Never mind. Go have breakfast. I know you're all heading to LA."

Stan tried to tame his erection. "Great job, Warren. I love it. Thanks for doing this."

"No problem. It was fun."

As Stan returned to the kitchen, he tugged at his tight pants and tried to calm down.

"There you are." Mark patted the bench beside him as the three of them had breakfast in the cozy nook.

Mark was nibbling a fruit and yogurt parfait Sierra had made, while Tadzio and Steve devoured bacon and eggs.

Mark's gaze darted to Stan's crotch. "What's got you all excited?"

Stan sat down on the bench and Sierra brought him a loaded plate of food and his coffee. "Thanks. Is this homemade bread?"

"It is! Mark? More espresso?" she asked.

"Please."

Tadzio, wearing red jeans and a white lace shirt, chewed on a crispy bacon slice. "We will have dinner today wit Alec?"

Stan began eating the great food. "My buddies wanted to know what we're doing as well."

Steve wiped his hands on his napkin. "We still have the house in Bel Air. Or do you want to go out?"

"Where are we sleeping?" Stan asked as Sierra brought Mark more coffee.

"I'm not bothered," Mark said as he moved the half-eaten parfait aside and held his coffee. "But, we have no vehicle if we fly. So, we have to depend on our chauffeur."

"Shit." Steve handed Sierra his empty plate. "Thanks, it was amazing."

"My pleasure."

Steve checked the time. "Should we drive?"

"Drive?" Mark narrowed his eyes at Steve. "That's too long round trip."

"We can rent a car." Stan used a crusty homemade slice of walnut wheat bread to soak up the runny yolks.

Steve appeared to think about it. "Okay. You two need to model when?"

Mark relaxed on the bench seat as Stan gobbled the meal. "I've my and Stan's shoot tomorrow at ten. Stan's cologne shoot is right after we do *Dangereux* Red."

"And Tadzio and I have no timeline for shopping." Steve put his arm behind Tadzio after Tadzio had finished eating. "So, why

STARTING OVER

don't we just have Dean drop you guys off on Sunday for your photo shoot, and we can have him today for shopping?"

"Then, perhaps we need to stay in Bel Air." Mark ran his hand through his hair. "Otherwise we'll be making it harder on Dean if we want to see Alex and Billy."

Stan sat back as Sierra cleared the empty plates. He said to her, "It was fantastic. Thanks."

"You are very welcome." She smiled sweetly.

"Right," Mark said, "And if Jackie would like to come for dinner…"

"He has Sonja's wedding today." Steve gazed outside.

Stan had a look and the horses were already out in the paddock.

"Still. He may want to come by for an hour." Mark checked the time. "Okay. Well, our jet is going to be leaving soon."

Stan slid out of the bench seat and let Mark out.

Tadzio said, "I will just be a minute." He left the kitchen.

Steve thumbed behind him towards his bedroom. "Pit stop, then we go."

"Yes." Mark finished his coffee and patted Stan's bottom. "Let me just freshen up."

Stan followed Mark to the staircase. "Mark? Warren has arranged the photos from Arnold's office in a study near the spa."

"All right." Mark climbed the stairs.

Following him, Stan gazed at his ass in his tight black trousers.

They had left enough items in Bel Air and West Hollywood, that they didn't need to pack. Mark entered their bedroom and walked through it to the master bathroom.

Stan leaned on the doorframe to watch Mark as he relieved himself and brushed his teeth.

~

Mark rinsed his mouth and ran a brush over his hair, then noticed his husband was gazing at him. "You all right?"

Stan drew Mark into his arms.

Mark felt Stan's cock pulsating against his groin. "We don't have much time now, love."

"It's okay. I just enjoy staring at you."

"Flattery." Mark chuckled. "Are you ready?"

After releasing Mark, Stan touched himself. "Yeah. Let me just calm down so I can pee."

Shaking his head at his horny husband, Mark gathered his keys, phone, and wallet from the dresser, and returned to the foyer. As he waited for the other three, Mark wandered down the long hallway.

He stepped into the study and had a look.

The photos were hung in a symmetrical pattern, pleasantly arranged. Since the room was twenty by twenty, it was large enough to accommodate the display.

Mark inspected the older ads he'd done with Alex, knowing Alexander did not want to take his place. He gazed at the racy automobile ads, trying to forget how horrendous they had been for him and just allow Stan to enjoy them.

Steve's academy class photo had found a place as well, including Steve and Billy's mugging for Armand during one of his photo shoots, as well as one from his first wedding; Adam, Jack, Steve, and himself in tuxedos, taken here, at the estate.

He heard Steve calling for him.

Mark made his way back to the foyer and found them ready to head to the airport.

"You okay?" Steve asked.

"Yes." Mark held Stan's hand and they exited the columned entry, to the waiting limousine driver. "Good morning, Louis."

"Hello, Mark."

STARTING OVER

Mark took a seat in the back of the limousine and tried to prepare himself for LA and the traffic, smog, and chaos.

Chapter 17

"I now pronounce you, husband and wife...you may kiss the bride."

Jack held Adam's hand as they sat in a church full of friends and family.

Sonja, looking gorgeous in her satin, off-the-shoulder wedding gown, her hair decorated with tiny white flowers, kissed her new husband, an attorney that worked with Sonja's father at the NAACP, Frank Williams.

Lively music began to play and the room full of attendees stood as Sonja and Frank walked down the aisle, followed by her wedding party.

The church service had been around an hour long, and next they were going to have the celebration in a hall on the same street, able to leave their cars and walk.

Jack adjusted his necktie as he waited for their row to empty so they could follow. Pete and Danny, Colt St John, and Jennifer Bernstein and her husband were in their row.

As they met up in the aisle and made their way to the front of the church, Danny caught up to Jack. "Hey."

"Hey." Jack smiled at the handsome twin.

"How're Mark and Steve managing?"

"Good. They're coming to LA this weekend. They live in Paradise now."

Adam released his hold on Jack's hand to read his phone.

STARTING OVER

Danny checked on the mob of people laughing and discussing the beautiful service. "I miss them at Parsons and Company. It's not the same since they left."

"I thought you got Richfield-Miller's ad account." Jack spotted a limousine with balloons and streamers on it, taking Sonja and Frank to the reception even though it was walking distance.

"We did. But we're not working with Mark or Steve directly." Danny waved at Pete, letting him know he was coming. "Tell them we miss them."

"I will." Jack put his arm around Adam.

"They're here," Adam said, holding his phone. "Steve asked if we'd be free this evening for dinner in Bel Air."

Since it was early afternoon, Jack replied, "I'd like that."

"Me too." Adam walked with the rest of the group to the reception's location.

"She seems very happy," Jack said about Sonja.

"She does." Adam interlaced their fingers.

Jack noticed Colt walking on his own and gestured to him. Adam and he approached the handsome man.

"Still doing the BDSM shit?" Jack asked, smirking.

"Not so much anymore." Colt put on sunglasses in the glare.

"Where's Ash?" Adam asked.

"Back in rehab." Colt didn't appear happy about it.

"Oh. Sorry to hear that." Adam shot Jack an expression of regret.

"Meh. I tried." Colt paused out in front of the reception hall as the limo parked and Sonja and Frank climbed out to the cheering of the group.

"Know anyone who's single you can fix me up with?" Colt asked.

"Huh." Adam appeared to think about it.

A passing thought of Stan's friends came to Jack's mind, but, they were much younger than Colt, who was in his thirties.

"Jack?" Colt asked him, "Any of Mark's friends?"

Adam replied, "We're all paired up at the moment."

"Logan?" Jack asked Adam.

"No. He's been living with the same man for nearly a decade."

Jack gestured to the jubilant crowd. "Maybe there's someone here."

"Ha." Colt didn't look hopeful. "I don't think I'll discuss my BDSM past after a church wedding."

Adam cracked up. "Maybe not. I'll think about it and let you know."

"Sounds good. Let's get some booze." Colt led the way into the reception hall, where music was playing and guests found their places at large round tables.

~

After an hour flight and a forty minute drive, Mark climbed out of the limousine with Stan.

"So, we'll see you in a few hours." Steve stayed behind with Tadzio since they were heading to Rodeo Drive.

"Have fun." Mark closed the door for Dean so he didn't have to move from the driver's seat.

The limousine drove down the street, passing his son's home.

Stan noticed Mark's distraction. "Do you want to go say hi?"

"Shall I go alone?" Mark didn't want to subject Stan to his son.

"Mark." Stan held Mark's shoulders and waited for Mark to search his eyes. "Alex isn't going to do anything to me again."

"Can you blame me for being wary?"

"No. But, I wouldn't mind seeing Billy."

Mark glanced at the vacant home behind him and held Stan's hand as they continued on down the street. Not able to see

STARTING OVER

anyone inside the house through the front windows, Mark knocked, but had a key.

He hadn't texted his son since Alex had contacted him for Charlotte Deavers, earlier this week.

The door opened and the lieutenant was there, in jeans and a T-shirt. "Hey!"

"Hullo." Mark embraced him and squeezed tight.

"Hi, Stan."

"Hi, Billy." Stan gave Billy a warm hug.

"Alex is on an audition." Billy waved them in. "Come in. Are you hungry?"

"Sierra made us breakfast." Stan walked deeper into the spacious open-planned home.

"Mark? Coffee? Water?"

"Water, ta, love." Mark followed Billy to the kitchen, seeing the smog over the horizon as a few fires still burned in the hills.

"Here ya go." Billy handed each man a bottle of water. "Want to sit outside?" He thumbed to the pool and patio.

"What part is Alex auditioning for?" Stan opened the plastic bottle cap and drank the water.

"Uh...one where he's a pirate." Billy laughed, looking happy and energetic.

"A pirate?" Stan chuckled. "Classic. Yes, I can see Alex as a swashbuckling romance hero."

"Mark?" Billy asked, "Want to sit in the living room or outside?"

Mark approached the slider, looking at the brown haze hanging over LA. Even coming back here for a weekend was unsettling.

~

Billy gave Stan a curious glance at Mark's odd mood.

Stan didn't say anything, but they exchanged silent expressions of concern. Stan opened the slider. "Let's sit outside."

Mark drank from the bottle of water and stood near the pool, looking out at the distance.

Billy closed the slider behind them. "Still smoky out there on the horizon."

"You should see the sky at night in Paradise." Stan set his bottle on the patio table. "It's so clear, you can barely make out the constellations. There're just too many stars visible."

"So, modeling tomorrow?" Billy ran his fingers up Mark's back.

It sent a shiver down Mark's spine and he wiggled from it.

"Yes." Stan seemed to be answering for Mark, since Mark was quiet. "Uh. Both of us in the morning for Red, and mine right after."

"Mark?" Billy ran his fingers over the nape of Mark's neck.

Mark finally snapped out of his daydream. "Yes. Well. I am hoping this is my last."

"You've tried to get out of the contract before." Billy gestured to the lounge chairs.

"Yes. Well." Mark ran his fingers through his hair. "I can't. I simply cannot do it any longer."

"Arnold Newhouse is retiring." Stan sat on one of the cushioned lounge chairs. "He told us the contract was up soon. Mark's was. Not mine."

Billy stretched out on the lounge chair next to Stan's. "Are you still auditioning for roles?"

"No."

At Stan's shake of the head and flat out denial, Billy had a feeling Stan was happier in Paradise, than here, in the smoggy Los Angeles rat race. "Richfield? Sit down."

STARTING OVER

Mark sat on the foot of Stan's chair, facing Billy. "So? Are you back to busting down doors and playing superman?"

"Yup." Billy grinned wickedly.

Stan laughed. "I think you like it."

"I fucking do." Billy crossed his bare feet at the ankle.

Mark pouted.

"Why do you look so unhappy?" Billy asked.

"I bloody miss you." Mark ran his hand over Stan's shin absently. "I was hoping you detested being back on the street and would come to Paradise."

At that admission from the 'sexiest man alive', Billy took a minute to absorb the comment. Mark Antonious, model-ready, looked as if he fell off the pages of his own glamour advertisements.

What he and Mark had was a powerful bond.

If Stan wasn't sitting right there, Billy would have acted on his impulse to pull Mark into his arms.

~

He may not have known Billy for as long a Mark did, but Stan missed him as well. Missed their runs, missed Billy's dry humor and common sense.

Seeing these two men gazing at each other, Stan was well aware of their past. Mark and Billy had indeed shared everything together, including their bodies. "Uh." Stan pointed to the kitchen. "I need a pit stop." Sensing these two wanted a minute alone, Stan climbed off the chair and caressed Mark's hair gently.

He entered the home and closed the slider, letting Mark and Billy have a moment of privacy.

~

"Love," Mark whispered.

Billy glanced at the slider and reached out to Mark, grasping Mark's shirt.

Mark moved from one chair to the other and Billy drew Mark into his arms, against his chest. While Billy kissed Mark's hair, combing his fingers through it, Mark missed him so much.

"Okay…it's okay." Billy rubbed Mark's back affectionately.

"I am so worried for you." Mark knew how Alex felt. "It's as if we're now safely tucked away from this mad city, and you are back on its blue line."

"What am I supposed to do?" Billy brushed Mark's hair away from his face so they could see eye to eye. "Alex's work is here. I'm not even fifty. I can't sit in a mansion and get fat and lazy."

Mark dabbed at the corner of his eye in upset. "What about at my office?"

A low choke of sarcasm came from Billy. "No. I can't take sitting in an office or at a computer. No way."

Mark sat up higher so they could converse. "You should see Steven and Tadzio race across the meadows." Mark ran his hand up Billy's leg. "Oh, pet. They are delirious."

"I'll bet." Billy smiled and tucked a strand of hair behind Mark's ear.

"I hate it without you. Hate it." Mark touched Billy's jaw tenderly. "You. Jackie. Adam." Mark shook his head. "You are the missing ingredients."

"And?" Billy raised an eyebrow. "Alex? You didn't mention your son."

"Of course. Alex." Mark didn't mean to exclude him intentionally. He traced Billy's sternum with his index finger. "Has he settled down?"

"He has."

"Is he taking pills?"

"As far as I know, just to help him sleep." Billy cupped Mark's hand and kissed his palm.

"And his TV show? All good?"

STARTING OVER

"Yes. Alex is very happy to be back into a routine. But, Adam sent him several movie auditions. I told Alex to go, to try to get them, since this blip, this popularity, may not last."

Mark gazed into Billy's intelligent blue eyes. "You are quite right. Fans are fickle. They have the attention span of a gnat."

Billy laughed heartily. "Oh, Mark…Mark, Mark, Mark."

Seeing Billy's smile made Mark smile.

"How's Stan?" Billy whispered, "Any lasting bullshit from Alex's attack?"

"No. He seems to be himself again." Mark peeked at the slider.

"Does he treat you well?" Billy's jovial smile fell and he touched Mark's lower lip with his thumb.

"Yes. Like gold. He's a treasure."

"So, he's content to be your PA and that's it?"

"Yes. For now. He mentioned to me his top priority is our relationship."

"Fuck. He's smart." Billy ran his fingers over Mark's neck. "If you weren't his top priority, he'd be insane."

"Love. He's a very young man with ambition. Although I do appreciate it, I hate to think I'm preventing him from attaining his goals."

Billy choked at the comment. "His goals?"

"Yes. Stardom."

Billy peered behind him to the slider and then said, "Stan is married to you. He has achieved a very high bar, Richfield. And Stan's not crazy. He knows what he has. He's very aware of how lucky he is. That's why I don't kick his ass."

Mark blinked and then roared with laughter. "I do adore you."

"Come 'ere." Billy drew Mark to his lips.

~

Tadzio sorted through racks of clothing with an enthusiastic salesman while Steve was in a dressing room.

"Dis...here." Tadzio held up another sleek designer suit. "Put this one wit the odders."

The salesman and he were gathering a large amount of both business attire as well as smart casual, something Steve lacked completely. He either had ten year old suits, or jeans and T-shirts.

The curtain moved and Steve stepped out of the dressing room wearing a dark blue suit with a shimmering silky finish and a narrow lapel.

Tadzio made his way closer as Steve stood in his socks at the triple mirror. "What do you think, Steven?" Tadzio checked the fit of the shoulders and waist.

"I feel like Mark." Steve laughed and ran his hand over the sleeve.

"It fits nicely," the salesman said as he crouched low to check the length of the pants.

"Should I put on shoes?" Steve asked.

"Only if you like it." Tadzio stepped back to decide if he did.

"This color blue really accents your eyes," the salesman said as he folded the hem.

"I like it." Steve buttoned the jacket. "But, it's up to my designer hubby."

Tadzio picked up a shirt and tie and brought it to Steve. He lay both on Steve's chest. "I like it wit this maybe. I think it need something to make it pop. Yes?"

"Oh, that's a nice combo." The salesman nodded. "Can you take off the top half?"

Steve allowed the man to remove his jacket and then Steve unbuttoned the light blue shirt.

A woman approached them. "Can I get you more drinks?"

STARTING OVER

Tadzio had a glass of champagne, while Steve stuck to sparkling water. "No. Iz enough for me."

"I'm good." Steve took the bold-patterned navy and white shirt from Tadzio, and put it on. He winced. "Um. Not really me."

"I know." Tadzio laughed. "That iz the idea."

Steve put the jacket back on and took the necktie Tadzio handed him. It was dark navy blue, so only the shirt had pattern to it. "Okay. I see where you're going."

The salesman brought over a dark red suit, and held it up.

Steve made a comic face of fear.

"No?" The salesman appeared disappointed. "You'd be amazed how hot this is with a white shirt and black tie."

"He can try." Tadzio pointed to the outfit Steve now wore. "Iz very handsome."

Steve did a sweep of his front and back in the triple mirror. "I can handle this."

"You see this jacket?" Tadzio touched the sleeve. "It can be used for separate. This blue can be wit dark, light, white, peach, lavender and even very light moss green. This…yes, and the dark gray pinstrip. We will make you find one more suit, and then choose slacks and tops for smart casual."

"I did like the pinstripe suit." Steve took off the jacket and shirt.

"Pin-stripe. Yes," Tadzio corrected himself. He nudged Steve back into the dressing room. "You must try the red. You will be surprise."

"Red." Steve made another silly face.

"Yes!" Tadzio pushed him, laughing, and the salesman hung up the dark red suit inside the dressing room with Steve.

Once Steve was busy changing, Tadzio had a look at the selection of smart casual clothing.

The salesman whispered, "Thank gawd you came with him."

"He iz former police. So? He thinks everything must be a dark blue uniform." Tadzio laughed and held up a pink shirt. *No. He'll never go for pink.* He hung it back on the rack.

~

Giving Mark and Billy their alone time, Stan inspected the home. He'd been here before, but had never been left alone to snoop. He paused after using a hall bathroom and was near the master bedroom suite. Stan took a look into the pleasant space.

A handgun in a holster was on the dresser, near a lieutenant badge in a leather holder. Stan peered behind him, then entered the room. It was neat, the bed made, nothing left on the nightstand but a phone charger.

He was about to return to the kitchen slider when he spotted a strip of photos; like the ones you took at a carnival or fair. He picked it up to inspect. Mark and his son.

Smiling at the love that was so obviously shared between them, Stan shook his head, since they looked like mirror images, especially when they kissed.

He set the strip down and heard rumbling coming from somewhere in the house. When he left the bedroom, it was then he could hear a loud car motor. The Ferrari. Alexander was home.

Stan left the bedroom and returned to the kitchen to go outside to Mark, when the door connecting the kitchen to the garage opened, and the superstar appeared.

"Oh." Alex looked shy. "Hi."

"Hi." Stan gestured to the patio. "Mark and Billy are outside."

"Cool. Modeling tomorrow?" Alex set his phone down and took off his shoes.

"Yes."

The slider opened and Mark stepped in first, then Billy. "Look what the cat dragged in."

STARTING OVER

Alex gave his father a silly expression and rinsed his hands in the kitchen sink. "What's up?"

"How did the audition go?" Billy asked as he put two empty water bottles into the recycling bin.

"I probably got it." Alex dried his hands and flipped his hair back.

"Arg, avast ye matey." Billy cracked himself up.

"Ha. Ha." Alex chuckled. "Keep laughing, lieutenant, since if I do get it, it's being filmed in the Bahamas."

Stan didn't think Billy thought it was funny any longer.

"Where's Steve?" Alex hugged Billy, snuggling.

Billy kissed Alex's hair and squeezed him close.

"Tadzio took him to Rodeo Drive for a wardrobe upgrade." Mark checked the time.

"Oh yeah. He mentioned that. But, dinner tonight together?" Alex asked, resting against Billy.

Mark gazed at Stan. "Are your mates coming by?"

Stan took his phone out of his pocket, reading texts. "They're waiting for a plan, but yes, they're into it."

Mark looked tired. He sat on a kitchen chair.

"Dad? When did you last eat?" Alex released Billy and stood behind his father, drawing Mark's hair into a ponytail and toying with it.

"I don't recall." Mark sent a text on his phone.

"Dinner last night," Stan said, "Sierra made him a tiny piece of salmon."

Billy checked his watch. "She didn't make breakfast?"

"She did. Mark barely touched his yogurt parfait."

"Oy!" Mark narrowed his eyes at Stan.

"He asked." Stan held up his hand defensively.

Alex laughed. "Yeah, he's finally on to you, Dad."

"One more day. All right?" Mark shook his head. "I can eat after tomorrow."

"Are you fainting?" Billy asked, opening the refrigerator.

Stan crossed his arms, wanting Mark to be honest, but...Mark kept texting.

"Jackie and Adam are free too. They said they are going home after the wedding and will come after." Mark read his phone. "And Steven and Tadzio said they're having lunch in Beverly Hills."

"Let's go." Alex shrugged. "I'm starving."

So was Stan. "We need the limo."

"Okay." Billy left the room.

"Mark?" Stan asked before he sent his old limousine company a text, since both Alex and Billy's cars sat two.

Mark appeared distracted.

"Dad?" Alex hugged him from behind, resting his chin on Mark's shoulder. "Please eat? Please?"

The care from Alex, witnessing his concern about Mark, seeing that sweet strip of photos from a booth at a fair, Stan gave in a little. Alex adored his dad, and maybe, just maybe, he had created a wedge there.

"Stop clinging." Mark nudged Alex.

"No. I need to get my dad fix. You'll be in LA less and less."

Mark shifted on the chair and drew Alex to his lap. "All right, baby."

Alex sat across Mark's thighs and rested his arms around Mark's neck, his head against Mark's.

Stan smiled at the sight, imagining their future children doing that.

Billy returned and had his gun on his waist near his badge. "Did you call for the limo?"

"I can." Stan sent a text to both Dean and his former dispatcher. He got a text from his workplace that one was now on its way.

STARTING OVER

Mark, sounding tired, said, "Alex, text Tadzio and let him know six for lunch."

"Okay." Alex held the phone while still surrounding Mark with one arm.

Billy asked Stan, "How's Becca?"

"Good." Stan smiled and nodded. "She'd be thrilled to see you again tonight. I think she's your number one fan."

Billy appeared flattered. "Sounds like a plan."

Stan gazed at Billy as he laughed at Alex's attachment to his dad.

"Too cute, Richfields." Billy held up his phone and took their picture. "Smile, Mark."

And when Mark did, so did his son.

Stan held his phone up as well, since, it was just too nice an image to pass up.

Chapter 18

Steve, wearing a shirt and pair of slacks from his new 'smart casual' purchases, sat at a table for six in a posh Beverly Hills eatery. Sipping a cup of coffee while he and Tadzio waited, Steve felt like a celebrity with his gorgeous Swedish runway model keeping him company; both of them wearing expensive designer clothing.

They may have appeared to be famous as well, since people were checking them out as they walked by.

Steve set his cup down on his saucer, and caressed Tadzio's cheek. "Hey, blondie."

Tadzio, looking stylish in his lavender slacks and indigo top, his blond hair cascading down his shoulders, gave Steve a kiss.

At the sound of Mark's voice, Steve looked up from their smooch.

"Yes, they are right there. Thank you." Mark held Stan's hand as Billy and Alex walked into the dining area behind them.

Steve stood up to greet them politely.

Mark paused before he kissed Steve. "My. Look at you, copper. You look fabulous."

Steve kissed Mark's lips. "You wouldn't believe my new wardrobe."

"I can't wait to see it." Mark cupped Tadzio's cheek. "Hullo, lovely."

"Hi, Mark."

Steve kissed Alex and Billy and gazed at Stan. Stan reached out his hand in greeting.

STARTING OVER

Steve clasped it and pulled Stan into his arms. He kissed Stan's cheek.

Stan appeared surprised and touched the spot Steve had kissed.

They found a place around the table as two waiters rushed over to fill water glasses and ask for drink orders.

"Wow. Steve." Alex held a menu as he sat beside Tadzio and adjacent to Billy. "You look great."

"He iz so handsome." Tadzio kept hugging Alex as if he had missed him very much.

Mark sat back as a waiter filled his glass with water. "Thank you."

"My pleasure, Mark. Can I get you a cocktail?"

Mark noticed Steve's coffee cup. "An espresso, love?"

"You got it." The waiter took requests from the rest.

Mark leaned closer to Steve. "I must say, copper, I am impressed with you staying on the wagon."

Steve looked into his coffee cup. "I thought I'd miss the booze more. I don't." Steve relaxed while the other four decided what to order for lunch. As he gazed at the patrons around them he spotted a few taking notice of them. After all, it was a celebrity packed table; superstar Alex Richfield, former Police Chief William P Sharpe, hot models Stan Richfield and Tadzio Andresen, not to mention…the Sexiest Man Alive…

And him…CEO of one of the top thirty companies on the stock market. For a change, Steve didn't feel inferior.

"Alskander? Did you get the part for the pirate?" Tadzio held Alex's hand tightly, resting it on the table.

"Probably." Alex laughed.

"Arg," Steve said, laughing, "Ahoy, pretty boy."

Stan cracked up.

Billy smiled. "A gay pirate?"

"Weren't they all?" Alex asked.

A waiter brought coffee and soft drinks to their table. "Are you ready to order?"

Mark gestured to Steve and Tadzio. "Begin with them."

Before Steve commented on Mark eating something and not just drinking coffee, Stan pointed to the menu. "Mark? They have low cal meals."

Steve was happy Mark was now someone else's problem. He addressed the server, "I'll have the Kobe beef burger, medium."

"With fries or peanut coleslaw?"

"Fries." Steve folded the menu.

Billy laughed, his reading glasses on his nose. "Still getting burgers and fries, Mr CEO?"

"You bet." Steve unfolded his cloth napkin on his lap.

Alex said, "This time with truffle mayo." He chuckled.

Billy gave Steve a silly grin and said, "Same for me."

Stan laughed loudly. "Ditto!" He handed the waiter the menu.

Tadzio giggled. "Ahi tuna taco for me."

Alex asked the waiter, "What's the chicken hash like?"

As the waiter described the dish, Steve watched Mark. He was rubbing his stomach and appeared uninterested in the menu.

After Alex ordered the gourmet 'hash' the waiter stood patiently next to the top model.

Steve had a running bet in his head Mark ordered…nothing.

Looking upset, Mark folded the menu and handed it to the waiter. "Nothing for me, ta."

"Dad!" Alex sounded exasperated.

Steve knew it. He picked up a roll from out of a basket and buttered it.

"Mark?" Stan asked quietly.

Mark shot both his son and husband a glare and they shut up.

Steve waited for the waiter to leave and then he cracked up with laughter.

STARTING OVER

"What?" Tadzio asked as he took a roll and passed the basket to Stan.

While Mark and Billy chatted quietly at the other end of the table, Steve gave Stan a smile. "Welcome to my world."

Stan leaned closer to Steve so Mark couldn't hear him. "He is fainting."

Steve chewed the roll and shook his head. "Of course he is."

Tadzio brushed crumbs off his hands and whispered, "Af-tar this modeling you can come for longer to the estate?"

"I'm hoping we can live there. This commuting sucks." Stan took another roll to butter.

"Imagine if you were driving or using a commercial airline." Steve was about to ask the waiter for more bread when he anticipated it and set a basket down. "Thanks."

"My pleasure." He topped up the water glasses. "More coffee?"

"I'm good. Mark?" Steve asked.

Mark glanced at Steve.

"More coffee?" Steve pointed to the waiter.

"Yes, love." Mark went back to Billy's conversation.

The waiter picked up Steve's empty cup and left.

"Alex?" Steve asked while Billy was busy, "How are you doing now that Billy's back in SWAT?"

~

Sitting across from his son, next to Stan, and adjacent to Billy, Mark ran his hand over Billy's leg under the table discreetly. "If Alex gets a part in a film that's shooting in the Bahamas, you must stay with us."

"As inviting as that sounds, I can't. I'm on call for the hostage negotiation team as well as any civil unrest." Billy parted a warm roll and spread butter on it.

"Can't you work part-time?"

Billy choked on his laugh and covered his mouth.

"What?" Alex asked, glancing at them after chatting with Steve.

"Nothing." Billy winked at Alex and then stared at Mark. "Richfield?"

"Yes, lieutenant?" Mark squeezed Billy's thigh.

"Eat a goddamn roll." He held his bread up to Mark.

Sitting back, giving Billy a sly smile, Mark said, "All right. I shall leave you be. But if I hear you have one cut or bruise on you..."

"Cut or bruise? I get those just from training." Billy stuffed the roll into his mouth.

Mark worried. He looked at his son, who was across the table from him. Alex was staring at him. "How are you, baby?"

"I'm as upset about him being back in SWAT as you are." Alex flipped his long hair back from his face. "Do you know he took a cut in pay as well?"

"Hey." Billy narrowed his gaze at Alex. "That's my business."

Alex didn't let up. "You make less money for a more dangerous job."

Mark exhaled and tried not to deal with it, since he had a headache. The waiter brought him another espresso, removing his empty cup.

"Thank you." Mark waited for him to leave, then rubbed his temples.

"Are you okay?" Stan asked, his arm around the back of Mark's chair.

"A headache."

"That's from starving!" Alex threw up his hands.

Tadzio opened his purse and said, "I have something."

Stan took the aspirin bottle from Tadzio and handed it to Mark. Mark shook out two pills, drinking them down with his water, then he gave the bottle back to Stan. "Thank you, Tadzio."

STARTING OVER

After twenty minutes of catching up, a group of servers appeared with their food. They set the meals around the table.

Mark sat back patiently, feeling sick to his stomach at the sight and smells.

"Wow. That looks amazing," Stan said.

"Mmm." Alex inhaled the food.

Mark finished his water and wanted to leave.

Billy and Steve took huge bites of their burgers, consuming them quickly. Stan also had a hearty appetite, since his workout regime was brutal.

"Iz very good." Tadzio ate his tuna tacos. "Mark? A taste?"

Feeling more nauseated and uncomfortable by the moment, Mark needed to leave. He scooted out his chair.

Everyone at the table stopped eating to stare at him.

Mark set his napkin on the table. "I just…" He pointed to the exit. "The restroom," he said.

"Dad…" Alex narrowed his gaze.

Mark stood from the table and looked for either the men's room or the door.

~

"Goddamn it." Steve shook his head.

Stan watched the direction Mark took.

Alex sighed loudly. "Whose turn is it to babysit Dad?"

Stan set his napkin on the table and hurried after Mark. He followed him into the men's room and quickly assessed the space for occupants. It was empty.

Mark stood at a sink and splashed his face.

Stan rubbed Mark's upper back gently, feeling heat coming from Mark as if he were burning up. What was he supposed to do? Beg? Beg Mark to please eat?

Mark dried his face and hands and inhaled deeply a few times.

"Mark?" Stan kept close in case Mark fainted, which he expected.

"I...can't stay here. I feel ill."

Calculating the caloric intake of this model for a twenty-four hour period, Stan couldn't believe Mark could function. If Mark had three hundred calories of food he'd be amazed.

Mark's phone shook in his hand.

"Who are you texting?" Stan asked.

"Our driver."

Stan did it for him. "Okay."

"Love? Go back out and finish your meal." Mark held his stomach.

"I'm not leaving you alone." *Fuck these modeling shoots! Fuck them!*

Mark grew pale as a sheet.

"Goddamn it." Stan knew he was passing out. He pulled Mark into a stall for privacy and forced him to sit down on the seat, pushing Mark's head between his knees.

~

Alex gazed at the food left on Stan's plate. "Well, Steve? You're off the hook." He had finished his lunch as well as the other three men.

"Bag it." Billy gestured to Stan's plate. "Poor kid."

"He knew what he was getting when he married Mark," Steve said.

Tadzio signaled to a waiter. "Could you put this in a bag?"

"Sure." He took Stan's plate. "Can I get anyone dessert?"

"No. Just the check." Steve removed his wallet.

Alex took a peek behind him in the direction of both the men's room and the exit. "They're not coming back."

"No. I don't think they are." Billy tossed cash on the table.

Tadzio held his purse on his lap. "Why can he not eat one roll?"

STARTING OVER

Alex muttered, "Because he's an idiot."

"Alex." Steve shook his head in admonishment. "He starves for the shoot, and, because he's not eating, he can't stomach the sight or smell of food. It's the same broken record I've been dealing with for ten years."

"No more model for Mark." Tadzio shook his head. "Iz too much to do. Why does Mark not just exer-size like you?" He pointed to Billy.

"He likes being sleek. He doesn't want brawn." Billy sat back as the waiter brought both, the check and a bag of Stan's leftovers.

Alex stood from the table as Billy and Steve figured out the tab. He and Tadzio looked for Mark. They peered into the men's room. "Dad?"

Stan opened a stall door. "In here, Alex."

Tadzio and Alex approached Stan. "Is he taking a shit?"

Mark glared at his son.

Tadzio leaned in. "You must go home. You can't stay here."

"The limousine should be outside." Stan exhaled deeply. "Mark? Can you walk?"

Tadzio held up the bag. "I have your food, Stan."

"Thanks." Stan hauled Mark up to his feet.

Alex was not happy with how ill his father appeared. He held Mark on the opposite side as Stan, following Tadzio out of the men's room.

"Let's not make a scene, please." Mark tried to walk on his own.

Alex met up with Steve and Billy as they stood near the exit. The six of them left the restaurant and stepped out into the sunny, breezy day. The limousine was already there.

Billy opened the back door and let Stan help Mark into it.

Alex shook his head in frustration.

Tadzio held Steve's hand, also looking upset at Mark's constant starving for modeling shoots.

Alex gazed at Billy. "Fuck."

Billy pulled Alex into his arms. "Okay. He's trying to get out of modeling. He has to quit." Billy nudged Alex into the limousine.

Alex sat across from his dad as Stan held onto Mark. Mark, his eyes closed, was resting on Stan's shoulder.

Tadzio, Steve, Billy, and Alex exchanged worried looks as Stan took the responsibility, quite literally, shouldering the load.

~

Adam swayed in Jack's arms. As the reception wrapped up, and a few last slow songs were played by the band, he and Jack danced together.

Since they had married at Mark's estate with Mark and Steve, and ironically, with Mark's mother and Harry, Adam and Jack didn't have a wedding like this.

Maybe they should have. But, at the time, who was there to invite? Jack hadn't told his parents he was gay, and Adam didn't have anyone left in his immediate family.

But, this was very nice; the meal, the music, the romance, and the connecting of two families as one.

As the song wrapped up and servers cleared the tables, Adam parted from the dancing and smiled at Jack.

Jack gave him a loving smile in return and a commotion drew their attention. Sonja and Frank were leaving the hall, headed to the decorated limousine.

A crowd of attendees threw rice and flower petals at their car as the newly married couple headed out on their honeymoon.

Cheers, waves, and even a few happy tears were shed by both families as the car, complete with signs and streamers, drove off.

"Time to go home." Adam needed a nap before they joined Mark in Bel Air with their friends.

STARTING OVER

Jack waved at Pete, Jennifer, and Colt, then walked with Adam to his car. Adam sat in the passenger's side and held his phone as Jack started the Jaguar. He sent Steve a text, '*Dinner at six? Seven?*'

'*Either. We're already home, so just come by whenever you'd like.*'

'*okay.*'

Adam loosened his necktie and top shirt button, rubbing Jack's thigh as he drove them to Malibu. "Steve said to stop by whenever. They're all home now."

"I feel like I need a nap."

"Me too." Adam gazed at the cars lined up at traffic signals. LA. Cars. Too many cars. "Jack?"

"Hmm?"

"Do you ever think of retiring?"

"In our forties?"

"Yes. Or…semi?"

"We could sit with a financial advisor and see what we need to do it by fifty." Jack ran his hand along Adam's leg. "Why?"

"I can work remotely." Adam thought about living in Paradise.

"From…" Jack sounded amused.

"From…" Adam mimicked him and laughed.

"Uh huh."

"I would think Sacramento needs lawyers too." Adam grinned and held Jack's hand. "Ya know, since it's the state capitol."

"Uh huh." Jack cracked up.

"Yes? No?"

"Adam. Leave our beach house? That's a tough choice."

It was. Adam loved their home on the Malibu beach. "I fucking miss our weekends with them."

Jack slowed for another line of cars at an intersection. He kissed Adam's hand.

"And…you'd have Shadow to ride…maybe Mark could use another attorney at Richfield-Miller."

Jack made a noise in his throat.

"No?" Adam was surprised. He imagined Jack would jump at the chance.

"I don't know." Jack drove to Highway 1.

Adam let him be, wondering if eventually, that massive home was going to be like a retirement retreat for them. He didn't realize just how much he missed seeing Mark and Steve until, they moved away.

STARTING OVER

Chapter 19

Stan helped Mark out of the limousine and into the house. Behind him, Tadzio and Steve gathered their purchases from the trunk of the limo; suits in garment bags, large shopping bags with shoes, tops, ties, and even socks.

Billy helped carry the load with Alex, into the house.

Stan urged Mark up to their bedroom. Mark appeared to be running on fumes. He sat the top model down and took Mark's shoes off for him.

Mark had stopped functioning, looking woozy.

While he helped Mark undress so he could rest, Stan was cursing in his head, furious that Mark did this to himself in order to appear sleek and cut.

"Let me..." Mark gestured to the bathroom.

Stan backed up, allowing Mark to go. He picked up Mark's designer slacks and top and folded them, putting them on top of the dresser.

Alex poked his head into the room. "You okay?"

Stan was not. He made sure Mark couldn't hear and approached Alex. "What the fuck? Why does he do this?"

"He thinks he has to. He thinks he looks best when he starves for a week." Alex ran his hand through his hair keeping his voice low. "Stan? Dad can't model any longer. Look what he does to himself."

"He doesn't want to. We stopped by his agent, Arnold Newhouse's office. Arnold is retiring. He told Mark he was done, so? Mark can quit without—"

A noise of something clattering to the floor in the bathroom made both him and Alex rush towards it. They opened the door and Mark was crouched down, holding the edge of the vanity, his hairbrush on the tiled floor.

"Dad!" Alex yelled at him.

Stan picked Mark up in his arms and lay him on the bed.

"Fuck!" Alex panicked. "Billy! Steve!"

Thundering noise came from the carpeted stairs and Steve and Billy burst through the door, Tadzio right behind them.

Stan sat next to Mark on the bed. The top model was snow white and sweat beaded on his top lip.

"Goddamn it!" Steve grabbed the cordless phone on the nightstand.

"Are you calling 9-11?" Billy asked.

"Yes."

"Steven." Mark reached out to him. "No."

"Mark!" Steve roared in fury.

Stan was frantic.

"Let me try Blake and Hunter first." Billy stood with his cellphone, taking his glasses out of his pocket to text.

Tadzio climbed on the bed. "I will make tea? Mark. Tea. Just tea?"

"Yes." Mark tried to sit up higher against the headboard. "Billy. No. Do not bother our firemen."

"Dad?" Alex pouted.

Tadzio hurried down the stairs.

"I'm fine." Mark brushed his hair back from his forehead.

"You are not fine!" Steve screamed at Mark.

Stan winced and stood from the bed. He corralled Steve. "Hey," he spoke softly, "Steve."

Steve clenched his teeth, balled his fists and looked so enraged, Stan thought he may punch a wall.

STARTING OVER

Steve pointed to Mark in warning. "This is the last shoot! Do you hear me?"

"Yes, Steven."

Billy said, "Blake is texting me. I want him here."

"Dad? It's just Blake. At least let him check you out." Alex curled up with his father on the bed.

Billy said, "He's on his way."

Stan held Steve by the shoulder, very well aware the former cop's love for Mark was limitless, and this was pure concern, nothing more. "Steve...he doesn't want this anymore. You don't have to convince him."

"I can't stand seeing him this way."

At that moment, Stan felt so much affection for Steve, he couldn't prevent pulling Steve into his arms. They had a common bond; Mark's wellbeing.

Steve held onto Stan tightly, rubbing his back.

In Steve's ear, Stan whispered, "I'm going to make it clear to Bob Sutter and TJ Brown, this is it. No more."

Steve leaned back to see into Stan's gaze. "Thank you."

"Do you think I like seeing him this way?"

As both Stan and Steve broke their embrace to look at Mark, Tadzio entered the room carrying a small tray. Billy headed down the stairs to wait for Blake, as Tadzio placed the tray on Mark's lap and Alex stuffed one of the pillows behind Mark's back.

Stan and Steve stayed quiet as Tadzio worked his magic.

"Milky tea, as you like." Tadzio blew on the steaming mug. "And toast. You must eat."

Steve shot Stan a sweet smile at Tadzio's care, since, well, Mark took the bread, which appeared to have 'gasp!' butter on it!

Mark ate the toast, chewing as if he hated every second of it.

While Alex and Tadzio nursed Mark, Steve tapped Stan and they left the room, headed down the stairs.

Billy had left the front door ajar and was sunk low on the living room sofa, his feet on the coffee table.

Stan and Steve dropped down on either side of him and exhaled a sigh in harmony.

"I'm sick to death of this." Billy rested his head on the back of the sofa.

Stan and Steve mirrored Billy's position, head back, feet up. "He wants to be in Paradise working for his company. He doesn't want this anymore," Stan said.

"We tried to extricate him from this contract before," Steve said, "But it was tied to Harold Parsons' account."

Shaking his head, Billy said, "No. I don't care if Mark breaches the contract. Enough."

"I have no idea how he does it." Stan yawned and rubbed his face. "I have to eat. I don't get starving. He's already skinny enough."

"It's in his head, Stan." Steve stared at the far wall of the living room, which no longer had photos hanging on it. "It's like anyone with an eating disorder. They don't see what they're doing."

"An eating disorder." Stan thought about it. "You think he genuinely has one?"

Both Steve and Billy turned to look at him, and their expressions said it all.

At the sound of a car door, they all sat up. Billy jumped to his feet and stood at the door to the house.

Blake and Hunter made their way to him, carrying kits with their medical gear.

Blake entered first. "Is he upstairs?"

"Yes." Billy gestured to the staircase.

Hunter and Blake trotted up.

Stan felt numb, but it beat sending Mark to the hospital. Steve put his arm around Stan and gave him a reassuring squeeze.

STARTING OVER

~

Mark managed to eat a half a slice of buttered toast. While his son caressed his hair lightly, Mark held the warm cup. Tadzio watched Mark like a hawk, making sure he kept drinking the tea.

Blake and Hunter entered the bedroom.

Tadzio stood to give them access to Mark.

Alex took Mark's teacup as the two firemen removed a blood pressure cuff and stethoscopes out of their bags.

"Mark Antonious?" Blake raised an eyebrow at him. "I thought we'd left this behavior behind." He wrapped the cuff around Mark's biceps.

"We have to stop meeting like this," Mark teased. He smiled at Hunter. "Hullo, handsome."

Hunter crouched next to Mark and checked Mark's pupils while Blake took his blood pressure. "Don't hello handsome me. Stop starving, Richfield."

Billy, Steve, and Stan stood near the bedroom door on the top landing.

Blake muttered to Hunter, "Ninety over sixty." Blake unwrapped the cuff and held Mark's wrist to take his pulse. "Forty." Blake took Mark's temperature, using a gauge for Mark's ear.

"Enough fussing." Mark tried to shift back.

Hunter waited for Blake to get his baseline numbers. "What do you weigh, Richfield?"

"None of your bloody business."

Alex laughed. "You don't know, do ya, Dad?"

Steve said, "He's never owned a scale."

"Why would he have to?" Blake read the thermometer, "Ninety-eight-point-six."

Hunter took his turn at the top model. He sat where Blake had been and listened to Mark's heart and lungs with his stethoscope.

"This is absurd." Mark found them all staring at him.

Hunter shifted his position, nudging Mark forward so he could listen to his lungs from behind.

"Enough!" Mark threw up his hands. "Bloody hell!"

Hunter wrapped up his stethoscope. "Clear breathing."

Blake sat beside Hunter on the bed. "What have you eaten today?"

"I've a modeling shoot tomorrow. I will eat after." Mark checked the time on the digital clock on the nightstand. It was three.

Stan said, "He ate two bites of yogurt this morning, and since then, all I've seen him consume is water and coffee."

Mark noticed Blake glance at the half a slice of toast. "You can't finish that?"

"It's not sitting well." Mark rubbed his stomach.

"Jesus Christ," Billy said, shaking his head. "Toast? You can't eat toast?"

"Will you all leave me be?" Mark was frustrated. "I don't know why they drag you here each time. I'm fine! This is normal for pre-photo-shoot. For pity sake! How many years must I do this before you stop worrying?"

Tadzio walked closer. "You will eat dis or I will insert it elsewhere." He held the toast closer to Mark.

Alex snickered.

Blake said, "Eat the fucking piece of toast!"

Mark grumbled and picked it up. "It's cold."

A chorus of "Mark!" came from the men in the room.

Mark took a bite and chewed. "Happy now?"

"Unreal." Billy threw up his hands in disbelief.

Mark forced himself to eat the bread, then drank the rest of the tea.

Alex laughed at Stan. "Don't you love this side of the glamour, Stan?"

"He's done." Stan shook his head. "This is it."

STARTING OVER

Mark shoved the empty plate at Tadzio. "There. Happy?"

"You will eat dinner. I am not happy." Tadzio wagged his finger at Mark.

"He'll eat wonton soup." Steve stood near the firemen. "Can you stay for dinner?"

Hunter packed their kits. "We have a late shift tonight."

Blake leaned over Mark's legs, one hand braced on the bed. "I know you think this is nothing, Mark, but doing this constantly to your heart, your brain…it's not good."

"Do you think I enjoy this?" Mark gazed into Blake's dark eyes. "This is why I am battling to get out of it. I can't take it either."

"Get some rest." Blake kissed Mark and stood from the bed.

Hunter cupped Mark's cheek and pecked him on the lips. "We'll make plans for when you're feeling better, and we're not working."

"Come to the estate." Mark sank in the bedding. "I don't know how much longer I'm going to be coming to LA."

"Okay." Blake picked up his kit and left with Hunter.

Steve and Billy followed them out.

Tadzio held the tray with the dishes on it and pouted at Mark. "You will be okay for dinner."

"Yes."

Tadzio left the room.

Alex and Stan lingered with him. Mark drew the sheet up and felt exhausted.

"Dad…" Alex stood next to him. "I can't handle you sick."

"I'm not sick. Stop spouting rubbish."

"Mark?" Stan moved next to Alex. "You made yourself sick. It's not rubbish."

Seeing Stan and Alex on the same side for a change, Mark started to laugh. Alex and Stan exchanged confused glances.

238

"The two of you." Mark shook his head. "I prefer you this way."

"And we prefer you stoned and eating." Alex poked his father's chest.

"Tomorrow. After." Mark closed his eyes.

"Coming down?" Alex asked Stan.

"I think I'll stay with Mark."

Mark opened his eyes before he tried to nap. Alex gave Stan a big hug, and then left the bedroom.

Mark watched Stan as he closed the door and drew the curtains to darken the room, then he undressed to his briefs and crawled into bed. Mark nestled against him, his cheek on Stan's chest.

"Are you going to be up for dinner with Jack, Adam, and my friends?" Stan caressed Mark's hair.

"Of course. No worries, pet." Mark needed to shut down. He was beyond exhausted.

As Stan caressed him, lulling Mark to slumber, Mark heard the comforting sound of the low murmur of men's voices coming from below.

~

"Ya have a few minutes?" Steve asked the firemen.

"Sure." Blake set his kit by the door and took Hunter's to do the same. The two men, wearing their dark blue uniform trousers and T-shirts with the LAFD logo on the chest, sat down together on the couch.

"Can I get you something?" Steve thumbed to the kitchen.

"I can." Tadzio brought Mark's tray to the kitchen counter. "Coffee?" he asked.

"Sure." Hunter put his arm around Blake on the back of the couch. "How are you, Miller?"

Steve gathered his thoughts as Alex and Billy sat on the loveseat. "Good. Love living at the estate."

STARTING OVER

Blake gave Steve's outfit a onceover. "You're all dressed up."

"Tadzio took me on a shopping spree. I needed an update." Steve looked down at his outfit, considering changing into his jeans.

"The CEO," Hunter said, smiling, "Nice. You're starting to look the part."

Alex laughed. "His husband is a fashionista. Tadzio dragged Steve kicking and screaming."

"I did not!" Tadzio called from the kitchen.

Steve chuckled.

"Billy?" Blake asked in a quiet whisper, "We saw your resignation speech. That was fucked up."

Alex scooted closer to Billy on the cushions and tugged his shirt. "He's back in LAPD SWAT."

"No!" Hunter looked stunned.

Steve asked, "Jeff and Mickey didn't tell you?"

Blake shook his head. "They must be over the moon you're back."

Tadzio brought in a tray with cups, sugar, and cream, and set it on the open coffee table.

"Want help?" Steve asked him, caressing his soft hair.

"I am good." He returned to the kitchen.

When Steve looked at Blake and Hunter, he found them both watching the interaction. Steve sat down on a chair near the sofa.

Blake said, "So? You and Tadzio?"

Nodding, Steve glanced at the kitchen and said, "I'm crazy about him."

Alex giggled and cuddled on Billy.

Steve continued, "You have no idea how big an asset he is to not only Miller-Richfield, but to me."

"Richfield-Miller," Billy corrected, chuckling.

"Good for you," Hunter kept his voice low, "It's nice to see you guys doing well after…"

All of them looked in the direction of the stairs.

Steve leaned over his lap, his elbows on his knees, so he could continue to speak quietly. "That shit?" He pointed to the upper floor. "Not my problem. It's Stan's."

Tadzio brought in the coffee pot and held it up.

Hunter picked up a mug as Tadzio filled it, and one more for Blake.

Tadzio set the coffee pot down on the tray and sat on Steve's lap. "So? What did you find about Mark? He iz well or sick?"

Hunter stirred milk into his mug. "His blood pressure is very low, which is why he keeps getting lightheaded."

"Low?" Billy asked, "So, that's better than high, right?"

Steve said, "Mark's an athlete. It's not uncommon for runners to have slow heart rates and low pressure."

"Dad? An athlete?" Alex reached for a mug and poured himself a cup of coffee.

"Yes." Steve shifted Tadzio's legs so he was sitting across his lap. "Mark runs, he does yoga, he's fit."

"But," Tadzio said, "He does not need a doctor?"

Hunter rested his mug on his knee. "If this is just because he's starving for his shoot, and he isn't sick when he eats, then…"

Blake sipped the hot coffee. "Men need physicals at least once a year, and that includes prostate exams."

"Billy gives me those every night."

Steve shook his head at Alex as Billy chuckled.

Hunter looked around the living room at the nearly bare walls. "What are you going to do with this house?"

Steve kissed Tadzio's hair as Tadzio camped out on him, his head on Steve's shoulder. "Not really sure yet. I guess when

STARTING OVER

Mark finally stops needing to come back to LA, we'll see about selling it."

"How much?" Blake asked.

"Blake? We can't afford a five bedroom home in Bel Air." Hunter set his mug on the tray.

"Miller? Is it millions?" Blake asked.

Steve had no idea. He and Mark had lived here for nearly ten years. The housing market had jumped since then, quite a bit.

"Would you rent it?" Hunter asked.

"It's paid for." Steve toyed with Tadzio's hair gently. "I don't see why we can't figure something out if you guys want to live here."

"I fucking love this place." Hunter looked around. "Always have."

Blake added, "And if you and Mark do need to come back to LA, you can stay."

"They have our place for that." Billy picked up a mug and tipped coffee into it for himself.

"And, I think Stan still has an apartment in West Hollywood." Steve felt Tadzio shift.

The young man took a look into the coffee pot and then stood up with it. "I will make more?"

"I'm good." Blake and Hunter shook their heads.

Alex said, "Nah. This is enough."

"Billy?" Tadzio asked.

"All good, blondie."

Tadzio took the tray out of the living room.

It grew quiet, and then Steve asked, "So, when can you guys come up? Adam and Jack told us they want to spend every free weekend with us."

Hunter took his phone out of his pocket. "Let me check our schedule."

"We should have a party there," Alex said, "With Jeff, Mick, Josh, Tanner…"

Billy poked Alex's shoulder. "You shouldn't be inviting people to your dad and Steve's house. It's not your place."

Steve said, "Billy. Alex is welcome."

Blake appeared confused. "Why on earth shouldn't Alex be welcome?"

Alex appeared sheepish and no one said why.

Steve stood from the chair. "I need to be in jeans. I can only take so much of this smart casual shit."

Blake set his mug down on the coffee table. "We need to head out. I wanted to get a workout in before shift." They stood from the sofa.

Tadzio returned to kiss them goodbye.

Blake pulled Steve aside and asked, "What did Alex do to Mark?"

"He had issues with Stan. It's been resolved."

As if he got it, Blake nodded and finished saying goodbye.

"Thanks for always coming through for Mark." Billy hugged the two men.

"Hopefully this was the last of the starving." Hunter shouldered his kit and opened the door. "See you soon."

"Bye."

Steve walked up the stairs and paused at the master bedroom. He peered in.

Mark was asleep and Stan raised his head off the pillow to see him.

"How's he doing?" Steve whispered.

"Okay." Stan tried to slip off the bed so they didn't wake Mark.

Steve waited in the hallway.

Stan stood beside him, wearing just his briefs. "We should wake him before dinner. Otherwise he won't sleep tonight."

STARTING OVER

Steve checked the time. "It's four-thirty. Why don't we give him another half hour?"

"Sounds good. He will eat wanton soup, or I'll spank him." Stan glanced back into the room.

Steve took a look at Stan's body and couldn't quite get over how fit he was. He thumbed down the hall. "Gonna get out of these duds. It's so not me."

Stan gave Steve a sweet smile. "It will be, Mr CEO."

"Ha." Steve patted Stan's cheek and continued to the bedroom down the hall.

~

Coming out of a dream, Mark stirred. Stan was shaking him gently by the shoulder. He opened his eyes to see Stan was dressed in a cotton shirt and jeans.

"Hey." Stan kissed Mark's cheek. "Adam and Jack are here."

"Yes." Mark rolled to his back and rubbed his face.

Stan waited, watching Mark.

He sat up and climbed off the bed slowly, trying not to feel faint. As if he needed to catch Mark if he fell, Stan hovered.

Mark freshened up in the bathroom and dressed in jeans and a cotton crewneck. He nodded he was fine. Stan held onto his hand and they descended the stairs.

"There he is," Adam said, a wineglass in his hand.

Mark reached out for Jack giving him a warm hug. Then, he greeted Adam.

"Modeling tomorrow?" Adam asked.

"Hopefully my final shoot." Mark entered the kitchen for water.

Tadzio and Steve were setting up the counter for a buffet.

"How was your nap?" Tadzio asked.

"Good." Mark opened the fridge and took out a bottle of water. He heard commotion at the front door and stood at the arched threshold between the living room and kitchen. Stan's friends had arrived as did the chief and Alex, who Mark assumed had gone home for a few hours.

Seeing Becca, Mark brightened up and set his water down. She hugged and kissing everyone hello. An older woman with purple hair and tattoos was with the group.

Becca approached Mark. "Hi."

Mark drew her into his arms. "Hullo, sweetness." He rocked her.

"Hi, Mark," the woman said.

"Hullo." Mark reached out to shake her hand.

"Mark? You know Natalie, right?" Becca introduced them. "She works for Adam."

"Yes. Well." Mark tried to put two and two together but was struggling. "Very nice to see you."

"Natalie!" Tadzio raced towards her and they gave each other a playful hug and air kisses on each cheek, giggling.

Mark greeted Stan's friends, sharing hugs and kisses. He made his way to Adam and watched as everyone became excited to see each other.

"Your Natalie?" Mark asked him.

"Yes. Tadzio set up Becca and Nat. And, well, here they are."

"Oh my. We have a lesbian couple amongst us now? How remarkable."

"Hey," Adam spoke softly, "If you were worried about Becca and her pregnancy? Don't. Because Natalie will be her bodyguard if they manage to stay together."

Mark inspected Natalie's appearance, her tattooed sleeves, and her piercings. "Yes. That is a comfort."

Stan drew Mark's attention.

"Excuse me," Mark said to Adam and approached Stan.

He held a menu for Chinese food. "You will have wanton soup. Anything else?"

STARTING OVER

"No." Mark took a look at the selection Stan was ordering. "Do you need my credit card?"

"Up to you."

"My wallet is on the nightstand."

Stan kissed him and left the kitchen.

Mark picked up his water bottle and observed as Stan's friends mingled with his own. The more the groups united, the closer they became.

Mark leaned on the archway and enjoyed the noise and happiness around him.

~

Alex couldn't believe Becca was gay. Didn't she have sex with his dad? When he stopped paying attention to them, he realized he was being stared at. "Hi."

"Hi."

"Lou." Alex remembered his name. "The comic."

"Alex…the superstar."

Alex grinned. "Yes. I suppose."

"I'm not going to get all fan-girl on you, but…" Lou expressed his excitement, "Alexander-fucking-Richfield! Aaaah!" He waved his arms up in the air in glee.

Alex cracked up with laughter. "Thanks."

"What's celebrity feel like?" Lou asked, as the noise of chatting and laughter filled the house.

"You want the attention. You want to be recognized. And then." Alex exaggerated fear. "You don't."

Lou glanced around the room at all the activity, and then said, "You've kissed a lot of leading men. Which one was your favorite?"

Alex thought about it, then spotted Stan coming down the stairs from the bedroom. Alex gestured to him.

Lou, sensing Alex was teasing, laughed. "Better than Jeremy Runner and Diesel VanDen?"

"He was the youngest."

"You don't like 'em young." Lou elbowed Alex and stared at Billy. "Dude? Billy's freakin' awesome."

Alex admired his man. "Yeah. He should be a movie star."

One of Stan's friends, Fred, was trying to get their attention. He held up a joint.

Lou acknowledged him. "Wanna toke? Your dad needs an appetite and we want to get a head-buzz."

"I can't smoke." Alex touched his chest. "Bad lungs."

"Late'…" Lou walked to the stairs behind Fred and Mark.

Alex joined Billy's conversation. He was standing with Steve, Jack, and Adam. He hugged Billy and rested against him.

Billy put his arm around Alex and held tight.

As Alex relaxed, taking in the house full of people, he had a feeling things were going to be just fine now. Just fine.

STARTING OVER

Chapter 20

"Beautiful, Mark, absolutely beautiful." Armand Legrand moved around Mark as he posed in front of a green screen, a fan blowing his long hair.

Stan, also wearing leather pants, topless, and ready, waited for Armand's signal.

"Okay." Armand gestured for Stan to join him. "Spotlight on the left side, please!"

Stan pulled Mark into his arms. Mark's eyes were heavily lined with black, his skin shimmered, and his hair was full and wild. They fell into their poses easily, having modeled together for months now.

Knowing Mark was going to quit after this shoot was bittersweet for Stan. Mark was model-ready, but…

His usual spark and sizzle were missing. Mark's exhaustion and frustration with being here in LA, when he needed to be in Sacramento, was easy for Stan to read.

Although Mark looked spectacular, cut, sleek and perfect, Stan knew the method Mark had used to get here. Starvation. That had to stop.

"Okay!" Armand held his hand up as he reviewed his photos on his camera and then a list of shots he had to take.

Stan held onto Mark between photographs, knowing Mark felt ill and was ready to eat a real meal. Last night he did manage the soup, but…that was hardly enough.

Armand signaled towards another backdrop, one behind a red Ducati motorcycle.

Hearing Mark inhale deeply, seeing his body language, Stan had a feeling Mark was wearing thin already.

"Okay. Stan? On the bike. Mark, face him at the front wheel."

Stan straddled the Ducati, his heavy boots on the floor.

Mark flipped his hair away from his face as if it irritated him, and his stylist raced in to fix it. Mark tolerated it, and said, "Enough," to Danielle.

Armand shot Stan a concerned look over Mark's mood.

Mark took his place facing the handlebars.

There was no doubt in Stan's mind, Mark wanted this shoot over with.

"Mark?" Armand walked closer to him.

"I'm fine. Please. Can we get on with it?" Mark gave him an imploring look.

"Yes." Armand retreated. "Okay, let's go."

As Armand instructed his assistants to correct the lighting, Stan and Mark tried their best to get through this, because right after Stan had his solo shoot, Mark could rest.

~

Mark battled to smile and wipe the scowl from his lips. A week of starving was taking its toll. Maybe he could behave this way in his thirties, but not in his forties.

Shaking off the exhaustion, Mark focused on Stan. Stan, looking gorgeous, powerful and cut, gave Mark a sultry grin.

As Mark fought his way through this last session, he noticed two men enter the room through the back.

TJ Brown and Bob Sutter.

Mark didn't know why they were here, but he was glad they were. He needed to quit, and they were the two men he needed to talk to about it.

After Armand took a few more photos for the print ads, he said, "It's a wrap!"

STARTING OVER

Mark felt unsteady as he and Stan moved away from the motorcycle prop.

"Mark." Bob extended his hand.

"Hullo." Mark shook it, and then TJ's, as Stan greeted the two men as well.

"You look sensational." TJ admired Mark.

"Yes. Well." Mark waited as Bob spoke to Stan about his solo photo shoot which was next, and then said, "May I have a word with you two?"

Stan lowered his head and thumbed to the changing area. "I'll get my gear on." Stan walked off.

Bob smiled brightly at Mark. "Mark! You look fabulous! That Sexiest Man Alive bit really boosted our sales. I have you and Stan booked for the next tour…"

Mark glanced at TJ, who appeared concerned as if he were reading Mark before Bob managed to do the same. "Love." Mark shook his head.

TJ asked, "What's wrong?"

Bob's smile fell.

Mark gestured to folding chairs, since he was about to drop to his knees he was so tired. The three of them opened up the chairs and Mark moved his to face backwards, towards the other two. He straddled the seat and rested his forearms on the back.

TJ shook his head. "No. You're not quitting. No."

Bob turned his head to look at TJ. "What? Quitting? No! Mark?"

Mark ran his hand over his hair. "Gents? I'm a CEO. I am the co-owner of Richfield-Miller International."

"Fuck. I knew this was coming." TJ appeared upset.

Bob shook his head adamantly. "Your contract—"

"Love," Mark implored, "Have pity on me. I can no longer starve for these shoots. I don't have the time. I am needed up north."

"No way." Bob was the chairman of the board for *Dangereux*, while TJ was the ad exec. "Mark, you are the face of *Dangereux*. There's no way we can replace you."

Stan emerged from the dressing room, wearing SWAT gear, holding his helmet under his arm.

Mark gestured to him. "You have an ideal replacement."

The men turned to look at Stan.

"If you continue to use Stan in both, the *Dangereux* Red and Obsession, making the transition gradually over this holiday season, you will maintain your sales." Mark had worked in advertising for seven years. He knew how things worked. "I do understand. I do. But, I am forty—" Mark muttered his exact age incoherently under his fingers, "And simply cannot continue. Your market demographic is much younger than I." Mark watched as Stan stood in front of a backdrop with police cars projected on it, their light bars lit.

He gestured to Stan. "He, is your future. And if you want a pretty boy, someone to replace me, all you need do is a talent search. Please. I am begging you. Let me pass on the torch."

The two men took a moment to watch Stan model. The big man looked like he should be teamed up with Lt Sharpe.

Bob stared at Mark. "And, there's no negotiation?"

"I have negotiated." Mark needed to either eat or sleep, he was losing his patience and his focus. "I gave you last year against my wishes. I can't keep starving. It is making me very ill."

As if he were upset, Bob stood from the chair and walked closer to Stan.

TJ stayed behind. "He's devastated."

Mark rubbed his forehead and battled to keep alert. "I can't. TJ, you saw how ill I became during one of our tours. I had to cut it short and go home. I am fed up to the back teeth with

STARTING OVER

passing out. Done with the dizzy spells. Done with the fasting. Please. I beg of you to understand."

"Mark."

Mark tried to stay strong and not give in.

"You're like a comet. Models like you come along once in a lifetime. There's no replacing you. There is no finding another pretty boy. If we continue, we will have to shift gears completely."

"I understand."

TJ stood and signaled for Mark to follow.

Mark climbed off the chair with an effort and they watched Stan pose.

The big man, in full SWAT gear, had his face-shield up and was holding a mock assault rifle.

"Wonderful!" Armand gushed, "Now aim the gun at me."

Stan settled the rifle's butt against his broad body and pointed the barrel.

Mark studied Bob's expression as he observed, then he whispered to TJ, "*That* is your future," as he gestured to Stan.

~

Billy, Steve, Alex, and Tadzio ran a long weekend route.

The weather was perfect; cool mornings were coming as fall finally appeared on the horizon.

Billy stopped at Steve's driveway and they caught their breaths, bending over after a ten mile run.

Steve plopped down on the cement retaining wall and unlaced his shoes.

Tadzio, his hair in a ponytail, a cap on his head, put his hands on his hips and looked towards Alex's home. "We will wash and have breakfast wit you?"

"Sounds good." Alex, also wearing a cap, ponytail, and sunglasses, inhaled deeply.

"I'm going to hit the bag for a bit, and then shower." Billy wiped the running sweat off his face.

"Okay." Steve stood from the wall and said, "An hour?"

"That'll work." Billy coaxed Alex to keep going. They did a quick jog to their own home and Billy unlocked the door and walked through the house. He opened the slider, slipped on gloves, and pounded the hanging bag.

Alex stepped outside as well, drinking from bottled water. He took off his cap, yanked the rubber band out of his hair and watched Billy.

Billy kept glancing at Alex as he worked the bag, getting into a rhythm. Seeing Alex back to himself again, looking good, less angry, made Billy a happy man. As he worked out, he said, "A pirate?"

Alex cracked up and wiped his mouth. "Yup. Gay pirate, in love with a stowaway kid."

Billy continued his workout, his arms beginning to get that burn he loved. "A kid."

"Yeah. I guess they'll make him eighteen, even though back in those days, who knows how young the boys were that they fucked."

Billy stopped the bag from moving and stared at Alex. "Hang on. You're playing the older man in this romance?"

"Yup." Alex tipped up the water bottle.

"Son of a gun." Billy rapped the bag again, thinking about Alex turning twenty-nine in November, the same month as his dad's birthday.

After fifteen minutes of pounding the bag, Billy dropped his arms to his sides and shook them out, then tossed the gloves aside. He toed off his shoes, took off his socks, shorts, and briefs, and dove into the pool.

When he surfaced, Alex was smiling at him. "I'll be in the shower. And...I want to get fucked."

STARTING OVER

Billy walked over to him in the deep end. He hauled himself out of the pool and stalked Alex. "Ya do, do ya?"

"Oh, hell, yes!" Alex grabbed his own crotch. He roared with laughter and tried to outrun Billy to the bedroom.

Billy sprinted after him, dripping wet, and cracked up with hilarity as they played. Alex made it to the bedroom but, just before he got the bathroom door shut between them, Billy stopped it, pushing it back against Alex's weight.

"Holy shit!" Alex was no match.

Billy entered the bathroom and Alex appeared wild, his hair a mane of brown waves, his green eyes bright and shining, and his smile, a Hollywood smile if Billy had ever seen one.

He scooped Alex into his arms.

Alex wrapped his legs around Billy's hips, crossed at the ankle. Billy tried to get his cock into Alex, yanking the material of Alex's skimpy shorts aside. Alex kissed Billy, swirling his tongue around Billy's.

Billy set Alex on his feet, spun him around, and yanked Alex's lower half of clothing to his ankles. Alex bent over the sink and spread his legs, shaking off the clothing to get one leg free.

Billy snatched lube from the vanity and used it. He held Alex's hips and sank in deep. "Oh, fuck."

Alex whimpered and rested his cheek on his forearm.

Billy slid in and out of his babydoll, watching the act, horny as hell from the workout.

Alex groaned and reached for his own cock.

Billy amped up the tempo and hammered in, seeking his own satisfaction. Hearing Alex grunting and moaning, Billy came. He thrust in and held Alex's waist as the orgasmic rush raced over him.

"Oh, fuck yeah." Alex arched his back.

Billy pulled out, spun Alex around, and dropped to his knees. He sucked Alex's cock, staring at Alex's tattoo, that lieutenant badge.

Alex cupped Billy's head in his hands and came. Billy swallowed, peered up at Alex's sexy expression, and stood tall, drawing Alex into his arms. As their sweat and scents mingled, Billy rocked Alex against him. His Alexander was back.

It was like starting over.

And Billy could not be happier.

"Love you, babydoll." Billy held him tight.

"Love you, L-T."

The End

STARTING OVER

"Mark?"

"One moment." Mark held up his finger and turned around. "*Psst. You. Yes, you. If you've read just one or all thirty-five books in the Action! Series...I want to extend my personal 'Thank-you'. Thank you for allowing myself and my lovers into your lives.*"

"Mark?"

"*Shhh. Your secret is safe with me.*" Mark winked. "Coming, pet!"

G.A. HAUSER

Don't miss the next book in the series,
NOTHING TO LOSE coming this fall!

STARTING OVER

About the Author

Author G.A. Hauser is from Fair Lawn, New Jersey, USA. She attended university at The Fashion Institute of Technology in NYC, and has a BA in Fine Art from William Paterson College in Wayne NJ where she graduated Cum Laude. As well as degrees in art, G.A. is a Graduate Gemologist from the Gemological Institute of America (GIA). In 1994 G.A. graduated the Washington State Police academy as a Peace Officer for the Seattle Police Department in Washington where she worked on the patrol division. She was awarded Officer of the Month in February 2000 for her work with recovering stolen vehicles and fingerprint matches to auto-theft and bank robbery suspects. After working for the Seattle Police, G.A. moved to Hertfordshire, England where she began to write full length gay romance novels. Now a full-time writer, G.A. has penned over 170 novels and short stories. Breaking into independent film, G. A. was the executive producer for her first feature film, CAPITAL GAMES which included TV star Shane Keough in its cast. CAPITAL GAMES had its Film Festival Premiere at Philly's Qfest, and its television premiere on OutTV. G.A. is the director and executive producer for her second film NAKED DRAGON, which is an interracial gay police/FBI drama filmed in Los Angeles with the outstanding cinematographer, Pete Borosh. (also the Cinematographer for Capital Games)

The cover photographs of G.A.'s novels have been selected from talented and prolific photographers such as Dennis Dean, Dan Skinner, Michael Stokes, Tuta Veloso, Hans Withoos, and CJC Photography, as well as graphic comic artist, Arlen Schumer. Her cover designs have featured actors Chris Salvatore, Jeffery Patrick Olson, Tom Wolfe, and models Brian James Bradley, Bryan Feiss, Jimmy Thomas, Andre Flagger, Grigoris Drakakis, among many others.

Her advertisements have been printed in Attitude Magazine, LA Frontiers, and Gay Times.

G. A. has won awards from All Romance eBooks for Best Author 2009, Best Novel 2008, *Mile High*, Best Author 2008, Best Novel 2007, *Secrets and Misdemeanors*, and Best Author 2007.

G.A. was the guest speaker at the SLA conference in San Diego, in 2013, where she discussed women writing gay erotica and has attended numerous writers' conventions across the country.

G.A. HAUSER

The G.A. Hauser Collection
FEATURE FILMS
NAKED DRAGON
CAPITAL GAMES
Single Titles
Riding Time
The Perfect man
Highway Drifter
You Can't Make This Sh*t Up
My Name is Karma
Footprints in the Snow
The Cowboy Nanny
Don't Judge Me
The Fix-Up
The Lies Your Father Told Me
The Odd Couple
Between a Rock & a Hard Place
These Four Walls
Showboys
Something to Believe in
Jealousy
The Prom Date
I Don't Know Why
Someone Like You
Venetian Blue
I'll Say I'm Sorry Now
Cry Like an Angel
Gay for Pay
Away and Back
A Matter of Minutes
Along Comes a Man
The Fall of Rome
Lover Boy
Bound to You
Whether or Not
From A to Zeke
Lost
My Super Boyfriend
Trent is a Slut
Aroused and Awakened
What Happens in Vegas…
Snapped
I'd Kill For You

The Reunion
The Ugly Truth
Bedtime Stories
Three Wishes
One Two Three
The Farmer's Son
Marry Me
I Love You I Hate You
Band of Brothers
Boys
Born to be Wilde
Taking Ryan
The Last Hard Man
Happy Endings
Hot Rod
Mr. Right
Living Dangerously
Lancelot in Love
Midnight in London
Down and Dirty
Unnecessary Roughness
My Best Friend's Boyfriend
The Diamond Stud
The Hard Way
Games Men Play
Born to Please
Got Men?
Heart of Steele
All Man
Julian
In The Dark and What Should Never Be
A Man's Best Friend
Blind Ambition
For Love and Money
The Kiss
Secrets and Misdemeanors
To Have and To Hostage
The Boy Next Door
Exposure
Murphy's Hero
Calling Dr Love
The Rape of St. Peter
The Wedding Planner
Going Deep

STARTING OVER

Teacher's Pet

Historic Books
Mark Antonious deMontford
Pirates
In the Shadow of Alexander
The Rise and Fall of the Sacred Band of Thebes

Cowboy Books
Cowboy Blues
Rough Ride
Hardcore Houston
Save a Horse…

Interracial Books
Miller's Tale
Naked Dragon
Code Red
It Takes a Man

Paranormal/Vampire Books
Ghost Hunter
The Vampire and the Man-eater
Lie With Me
Vampire Nights
London, Bloody, London
Dude! Did You Just Bite Me?
Giving Up the Ghost
Black Leather Phoenix

Fantasy Books
The Adonis of WeHo
Prince of Servitude
Timeless (Sci-Fi)

The Action! Series
Acting Naughty
Playing Dirty
Getting it in the End
Behaving Badly
Dripping Hot
Packing Heat
Being Screwed
Something Sexy

Going Wild
Having it All!
Bending the Rules
Keeping it Up
Making Love
Staying Power
Saying Goodbye
Coming Home
Knowing Better
Becoming Alex
Doing the Dirty
Anything But
Mark & Billy
Changing Times
Mark Antonious Richfield Obsession
California Dreaming
Loving Stan
Moving On
Falling Hard
Waiting to Breathe
Sons & Lovers
Holding Tight
Living in Paradise
Still Standing
Starting Over
Nothing to Lose
Finding Hope
L.A. Masquerade

Prequels & related books for The Action Series
Capital Games
Mark and Sharon
Miller's Tale
COPS
Double Trouble
Love you, Loveday
When Adam Met Jack
(The **Heroes Series***)*

Military Men
Bound to You
It Takes a Man
All Man
I'd Kill For You

G.A. HAUSER

Living Dangerously
The Last Hard Man
Happy Endings

Men in Motion Series
Mile High
Cruising
Driving Hard
Leather Boys

Heroes Series (Men in Uniform)
Man to Man
Two In Two Out
Top Men

Wolf Shifter Series
Of Wolves and Men
The Order of Wolves
Among Wolves

G.A. Hauser
Writing as Amanda Winters
Sister Moonshine
Nothing Like Romance
Silent Reign
Butterfly Suicide
Mutley's Crew
Orion in the Sky
Free Reads!
(available through my website)
Dude! Did You Just Bite Me?
L.A. Masquerade
Lie With Me
Exchange of Hearts
Live, Love…Last
Strangers With Candy
Dark Angel

STARTING OVER

LIGHTS, CAMERA, ACTION!
Catch up on all your Action! Series books!

Acting Naughty; Book 1

Keith O'Leary has been trying to break into acting for ages. When a part in the newest cable television drama, *Forever Young*, is offered, Keith struggles with the idea of playing a gay man. Adam Lewis, his agent, persuades Keith to accept the role, knowing it's a chance to star in the biggest new hit on TV. Keith reluctantly agrees, dreading working in a diner like his roommate/girlfriend, Patty, to make the rent money. When Keith meets his fabulous co-star, Carl Bronson, his anxiety is piqued. He has to kiss this man on camera, and much more.

Luckily for Keith, Carl is warm, understanding and willing to coach Keith during some nerve-wracking scenes. Soon the episodes sizzle with their erotic contact and declarations of love.

For Keith those words are beginning to feel like the truth as he grows to love the man he is kissing and touching in very passionate ways. And going through the same exact experience, Carl feels the same way.

As their romance blossoms on and off camera, someone threatens to expose them as real lovers, putting a shadow of doubt on their future in the business. Will they follow the advice of Adam Lewis, and *deny, deny, deny*, their true feelings to the tabloids? Or take the chance and expose themselves and their love and possibly risk their careers? In part one of two, Carl and Keith learn there's more to a relationship, than acting.

Playing Dirty; Book 2

Keith O'Leary and Carl Bronson thought they had it made. Having landed roles in a top racy television cable drama, *Forever Young*, both handsome aspiring actors began to believe their dreams of becoming celebrities had come true. While playing a gay couple in the show, Keith and Carl form a genuine attraction to each other, which grows into a loving, trusting relationship. The only problem is, Adam Lewis, Keith's gay agent, warns them about being seen as a couple in public, and the repercussions down the line after their top rated show, *Forever Young* ends. Both men struggle to keep their private lives discreet, while someone on the inside is trying desperately to out them to boost the show's ratings.

Agonizing over having to pretend they are straight for any possibility of a leading man part in a motion picture, both men have to come to a decision as to what they value most. Their love or their careers. This sequel to Actors shows just how bad the Hollywood hypocrisy could be when it comes to gay men coming out of the closet. It appears that playing dirty, is the only choice they have.

Getting it in the End: Book 3

You know him. You've seen him attempt to marry Sharon Tice in *Mark and Sharon*, be swept off his feet by the ex-LAPD cop, Steve Miller in *Capital Games*, begging forgiveness from his best friend Jack Larsen in *When Adam Met Jack*, seduced by two young handsome television stars in *Playing Dirty*, but who is Mark Antonious Richfield? In Los Angeles, California where everyone is a ten, Mark is an *eleven*. Too gorgeous for everyone's good, Mark is terribly flawed, and knows it. Beating himself up constantly for making bad decisions, Mark tries to please everyone to their peril.

But what on earth is going on with Mark now? Still working at Parsons and Company with his loyal lover, Steve, Mark begins modeling on the side. At one of his sessions he meets an old friend who stirs up some forbidden passion. And as usual, Mark Richfield is in the middle of a quagmire without the social skills to make a good decision. Other than his fantastic sex appeal, Mark has one other problem. He loves too much, has too much heart, and craves to be loved in return like he breathes air. Desperately.

Find out Mark's side of the story, and fly with him as he falters through his life, trying, pleading, and usually not succeeding. Mark Richfield. Love him or hate him, he is a fascinating study in human nature.

Behaving Badly; Book 4

For once, Mark Antonious Richfield thought everything was going well in his life. His full time job at Parsons and Company was fulfilling and his side career of modeling for a cologne ad was enjoyable. He and the love of his life, ex-LAPD officer, Steve Miller, as well as their best friends Jack Larsen and Adam Lewis, seemed to be getting along perfectly. What could possibly go wrong?

When a young eighteen year old man appears at their door, their whole world turns on its head. Though Mark at first couldn't see anything unusual about the teenager, the minute Steve set eyes on Alexander Lehman, he knew he was a Richfield clone. Mark had an illegitimate son, one as sensual, gorgeous, and mischievous as himself.

As Steve and Jack struggle to come to terms with the younger version of the hot model they fell madly in love with, Alexander becomes infatuated with the handsome cop, making life unbearably complicated and miserable for Mark.

With the new addition to their household, Mark and Steve take a crash course in the lessons of fatherhood, all of them learning right from wrong the hard way.

Can the young sexy 'Mark junior' manage to control his voracious appetite for older men? Or will Mark and Steve's relationship collapse with the struggle for power between sons and lovers? Follow the tale of Generation seX as the youth begin to take over for their fathers.

Dripping Hot; Book 5

With the Christmas party approaching, Mark Richfield is trying to cope with the pressure of the holidays, his out of control son, Alex, and too many men involved in his life to keep his sanity intact. It seems the popular idea at Parsons and Company is to have Mark play Santa Claus at the office gala. His latest ad for cologne has all of LA buzzing as his image hit all the billboards on Santa Monica Boulevard and the Sunset Strip; a half

STARTING OVER

naked sexpot, Mark Antonious is exposed to entice the masses, not to mention the gay men in his office.

Trying to come to terms with Alexander becoming independent and keeping the attraction between Steve and Alex under careful scrutiny, Mark, as usual, comes apart at the seams.

When Alex goes missing during an event of the battle of the bands where Alex's lover, Oliver Loveday, and his musical group are playing near the Rose Bowl stadium, Mark nearly has a nervous breakdown until a group of heroes comes to his aid.

The lifeguards from Man to Man, the firemen from Two in Two out, LAPD's finest officers from Top Men and Sergeant Billy Sharpe, and his partner Angel Loveday, and even the stars of Forever Young, Keith O'Leary and Carl Bronson, are on the scene to find the missing teenager.

Meanwhile Steve is fighting his own internal battles as his father and mother become aware that he has married a man and has a son. The fact that they know about Mark and Alex terrifies Steve as he hopes his homophobic father will not harm the ones he loves.

It all occurs during the week prior to Christmas when one's faith and hope are tested, only to be redeemed by the greatest gift; the loyal friends you have made.

Packing Heat; Book 6

Mark Antonious Richfield has become a name synonymous with both beauty and chaos. Though Mark has accomplished much in his life, despite a rocky start from an abusive childhood and living in denial about his sexuality, he has come only so far. Mark is forever conflicted with his advancing years stealing his beauty away.

Though he perceives himself as shallow and useless, Mark's circle of lovers know otherwise. Steve Miller, the ex-LAPD cop, and forever guardian angel to Mark, Jack Larsen, Mark's long-time and closest friend, and Adam Lewis, Jack's husband, all stand firm to protect Mark from his own demons.

And though Mark's son Alexander is not a bad boy, he's a very naughty boy. Mark thought his problems with Alexander were finished when Alex met Angel Loveday's son, Oliver. But perhaps Mark wishing his nineteen year old son was in a relationship that would last a lifetime was a bit premature.

As Mark's internal war rages on, he once again learns that age does indeed come before beauty, and his friends are the best weapon he has against his own wounded self-esteem.

Join Mark and his friends on another wild sexual romp and revisit all your old favorite characters from GA Hauser's Erotic Universe.

Being Screwed; Book 7

In Book 7 of the Action! Series the tale comes full circle, back to the first novel, *Acting Naughty* and the dilemma of the lead characters Keith O'Leary and Carl Bronson on whether it is prudent for an up and coming actor to expose their sexuality to the public.

Mark Antonious Richfield is turning the dreaded 4-0 and is going out of his mind, as usual, with hitting a milestone he assumed he'd never admit to hitting.

Steven Jay Miller, the ex-LAPD cop, is doing all he can to get Mark and Alex through their personal crisis, but other than being supportive, Steve can't do a thing to prevent the life changing decisions both Mark and Alex are destined to make.

Having to prove he is still young and vital, Mark reunites with the mega-stars of *Forever Young*, Keith and Carl, in a television episode that becomes unforgettable as Mark and the two celebrities get naughty again, much to the producers' and director's delight.

Alexander Mark Lehman-Richfield is twenty-one, in college and still seeing Oliver Loveday loyally. To everyone's astonishment (and fear), Alex gets his big break in Hollywood as the number one star of his own racy cable TV drama, *Being Screwed*. And though Adam Lewis, Alex's agent and close friend begs Alex to deny his sexual preference in public, like he had done with Keith and Carl, Alexander is too outspoken to even consider hiding in the closet. But is the world ready? Or is being an 'out' gay actor in Hollywood still a deterrent for men to get leading roles in blockbuster movies?

Revisit with all your favorite men, Jack Larson, Adam Lewis, the cops from *Top Men*, Mickey and Jeff, as well as many others you have grown to know and love from Hauser's Erotic Universe.

And learn how **Being Screwed**, is not necessarily a bad thing...

Something Sexy; Book 8

Having hit the milestone of 40 years old, Mark Antonious Richfield seems to have survived. But on a trip to London to join his mother, Leslie and step-father Harry for the wedding of Harry's son, Luke, Mark decides perhaps this is a good time to 'reinvent' himself.

Ex- LAPD cop, Steve Miller, Mark's husband, and truest love, embark on a journey to London to let down their hair and go wild. Or at least that's Mark's idea of a good time.

During a session at a fetish club one evening, Mark's beauty captivates the editor of an erotic gay men's magazine. Adrian McKenzie asks Mark to do a centerfold for his latest edition.

Assuming this will be anonymous and thrilling, Mark agrees to his own peril.

Meanwhile, Alexander, Mark's incorrigible son, makes his own bad decisions while trying to cope with school and a new career. Though Alex is continuing his acting role in *Being Screwed*, the racy nighttime cable drama, his behavior is increasingly unstable during the time his father is away.

Both father and son, though they try their best to do what's right, end up complicating their lives eternally.

But one thing is never in doubt. When it comes to Mark Antonious Richfield, his Action! will be *Something Sexy*. Very sexy indeed!

Going Wild; Book 9

In this latest G.A. Hauser Action! novel find out how Mark and the gang are truly 'Going Wild' with all of your favorite men finding love in all the wrong places!

STARTING OVER

After their forbidden affair, twenty-two year old Alexander Richfield and the forty-two year old LAPD SWAT lieutenant, Billy Sharpe, can't seem to keep away from each other. Billy's love and attention towards the rising Hollywood star give Alexander just what he craves.

Attorney extraordinaire Jack Larsen introduces his husbands, Adam Lewis, Mark Richfield and Steve Miller to his new law associate, the professional Dom Colt St. John. Mark's new found love of all things leather and latex brings the men to Colt's penthouse loft for a BDSM session they will never forget.

Meanwhile Adam Lewis struggles to find work for award winning actors Keith O'Leary and Carl Bronson on the heels of the news that their top-rated cable drama *Forever Young* has been canceled; a victim of the rising intolerance in society for gay men. In the beginning of Keith and Carl's stint of the racy drama, Adam begged them to deny they were a gay couple and keep their sexuality a secret. With the pressure from the tabloids and their producers to come out, Keith and Carl succumbed to the exposure and admitted publicly they were gay. Now the test will come if their decision costs them their careers.

Will the affair between Billy Sharpe and Alex Richfield be nothing more than a sexual fling? And will Adam be able to battle against the growing tide of homophobia in the media?

In Book 9 of the best selling Action! Series, we see each of your favorite men *Going Wild* in their search to achieve happiness and true love.

Having it All!; Book 10

In a town where *having it all* is what everyone strives for, Mark Richfield and his son Alex, already seem to be living the highlife in LA. But are they?

Jack Larsen, Mark's closest friend begins to fantasize having Mark play Dom instead of his absolute submissive behavior. This dream becomes an obsession for Jack as he tries to lure Mark into a one on one evening.

SWAT Lt. Billy Sharpe is adjusting to life as Alex-The-Superstar's sugar daddy and bodyguard, dealing with constant tabloid gossip, paparazzi and life post-Angel Loveday, his partner, who has since moved onto another relationship.

In the bizarre crossroads where the Hollywood elite intersects Gay men, life is never easy, nor simple.

Come join Mark and all your Action! Series favorites as they learn *Having it All* is really about finding trust, hope, and true love.

Bending the Rules; Book 11

Top model Mark Antonious Richfield didn't want to let go of his family estate in Paradise, CA. Though his childhood home brought both good and bad memories, Mark struggled with a decision on selling it. On a visit to the mansion with his husband, Steve Miller and their closest friends, Jack Larsen and Adam Lewis, Mark begins to recall memories about his father he had repressed for decades. Dark, painful recollections that overwhelmed him.

His son Alexander Richfield, and his fiancée SWAT Lt Billy Sharpe of the LAPD adjust to their new home in Bel Air as well as trying to plan a wedding in New York, which is constantly put on hold because of their busy schedules.

When a sexy androgynous newcomer Tadzio Andresen is cast as Alex's love interest on the hit vampire series, *Being Screwed*, Alex and Billy's love and trust is put to the test.

In Book 11 of the Action! Series, delve into the darkness of Mark's early years, and his son's determination to withstand the forces that try to tear him and Billy apart.

Sometimes you don't have to break the rules to survive- when just *Bending the Rules* is enough to give you a boost in the right direction.

Keeping it Up: Book 12

Top Model Mark Antonious Richfield made the decision to sell the mansion, in Paradise, CA where he grew up as a young boy. His prim-proper English mother had remarried and moved on to live in London, and Mark's homophobic abusive father, Milt Richfield was dead. In order to send off the estate with a defiant 'bang!' -literally- Mark invites all his good friends for a proper boy's weekend. As your *Action! Series* favorites get together for a final fling, find out how they mix emotional closure with pure pleasure, and of course, Mark is the main course. But not before Mark is forced into shooting a controversial modeling session with his newest account, a luxury car company, which is setting LA gossip columns on fire.

With grueling pressure from the producers of *Being Screwed*, the hot vampire cable TV drama starring Mark's superstar son, Alexander, to make their wedding a worldwide spectacle, Alex and LAPD Lieutenant Billy Sharpe who is twenty years older than Alex, finally find the time to take the leap to get married in New York. But the two men want a private affair, not a media frenzy.

See how memories of the day Mark left Sharon Tice at the altar for the love of his life, ex-LAPD cop Steve Miller, haunts Jack Larsen, Mark's oldest and best friend. Find out how Jack copes with the ill will it begins to stir in him much to Jack's husband Adam Lewis' annoyance.

Keeping it Up. When it comes to *Acting Naughty* and *Behaving Badly*, the men of the *Action! Series* will manage to keep it up for a long time to 'come'.

Making Love: Book 13

In this newest edition to the Action! Series novels, Mark Antonious Richfield begins to question his high pressure LA lifestyle, made even more evident with the sale of his family's estate in Paradise, California. Although Mark has always had mixed emotions about the home he grew up in, the emptiness of its loss has left more sadness in his heart.

Meanwhile, Lt Billy Sharpe of the LAPD, has been called to the scene of a hostage situation. Yes, Billy thought he had left the action of the SWAT team behind when he was transferred to internal affairs, but somehow he became swept up in the drama and

STARTING OVER

risks his own life and the lives of his old SWAT team members. When Alexander Richfield, Mark's son-Billy's new husband, finds out that Billy has placed his life in jeopardy, Alex finds the act selfish and unforgivable.

As tensions mount between the couples and Mark's stress level becomes impossible for him to handle, the friction between partners begins to get hostile. When Mark realizes the impact Billy's actions have on his son, Mark is immediately drawn in as peacemaker between the two, and forbidden attractions begin to form.

Adam Lewis and his husband, Jack Larsen, Mark's longtime companion, realize something must change or Mark will self-destruct as he has done in the past. But this time it's impossible for either man to make a difference in anyone's lives but their own, and they too, nearly suffer from the consequences of the fallout from Lt Sharpe's life-changing decisions. Consequences which originate from Billy's on duty police incident start to have a domino effect; the actions which began from Billy putting his life on the line and directly into a shoot-out with a heavily armed suspect.

Another day in the life of the Action! Men...Superheroes or madmen- the one thing they can count on is love. And without Making Love, and holding onto their priorities, their relationships would fall apart.

Be anxious, laugh, cry, and enjoy another chapter in the lives of the men of the Action! Series you have grown to adore.

Staying Power; Book 14

In Book 14 of the Action! Series, ex-LAPD cop, Steve Miller thinks going to his husband's therapy appointments is a good idea. But he soon finds out Mark Antonious Richfield, may not be telling his shrink everything the doctor needs to know.

Meanwhile, Mark's son, Alexander, is offered the chance of a lifetime when a big named Hollywood director approaches him for a starring role in a block buster film, 'Bedtime Stories'.

While Alex and Adam Lewis, Alex's agent and one of Mark's dearest friends, tries to iron out a solid contract for Alex, Alex's husband, Lt Billy Sharpe makes the Captain's list for the LAPD. So big changes are on the way for the newlyweds. But when Mark mentions he is nervous about Alexander leaving for Rome for filming, alone, Steve and Billy both take it upon themselves to confront Alex's leading man and co-star, nearly derailing Alex's chances for his break in Hollywood.

Conflict, jealousy, self-sacrifice and ego, in Book 14 of the Action! Series, the men's emotions are put to the test, and in the end, it's all about Staying Power- and the power of love.

Saying Goodbye; Book 15

When trust is shattered and bonds are broken, sometimes forgiveness simply isn't enough.

The men of the Action! Series have always been sexually driven- powerful and loyal. But that loyalty has been put to the ultimate test.

With twenty-four year old Alexander Richfield away in Rome starring in his first feature film,

Bedtime Stories, his husband, forty-four year old, LAPD Captain Billy Sharpe's frustration and anger over rumors in the tabloid press about Alex's supposed exploits, bring Billy to a breaking point.

Adam Lewis, agent to the stars, and husband of Jack Larsen, feels obligated to invite a group of their close friends to the mansion in Paradise, California. The estate his and Jack's lover, Mark Antonious Richfield grew up in, which was recently bought by Adam's client and friend, Ewan Gallagher. Knowing the estate creates stress for Mark, Adam tries his best to pretend this is a weekend with the boys, and it's all in good fun.

Steven Jay Miller, Mark's husband, is still raw over Mark's actions to keep his son Alexander's role in the feature film secure. Mark had to grant sexual favors to Alex's co-star, Randy Dawson to right a wrong Steve and Billy had stupidly made, threatening Randy to keep away from Alex. An act Steve cannot move on from.

And as the men around him suffer from his actions, Mark Antonious Richfield begins to deteriorate and self-destruct.

Trust shatters...love is tested...and even the strongest ties can be severed.

Coming Home; Book 16

In Book 15, Saying Goodbye- Trust was shattered, lives were at risk, and the world had turned upside down for the men of the Action! Series.

Coming home...rebuilding relationships that had been severed to the point of fury, Mark Antonious Richfield finds moving on, trying to keep his sanity after his last suicide attempt, and his husband and his own, infidelity, a difficult task.

As Mark begins a journey of self-discovery, he again becomes entangled in the mess his husband, Steve Miller, and his son-in-law, Captain Billy Sharpe, have created. By intervening in Mark's son, Alexander's, acting career, Billy, Alex's husband, and Steve, instilled hostilities that begin to rear their ugly head even after Alex's film is premiered.

Mark is forced to face more deep-rooted fears, and bears the brunt of the cleanup effort of the mess the two men had made.

Coming home. A sweet sentiment that makes one's heart warm. For Mark and his boys, it's a long journey to make.

Knowing Better; Book 17

In Book 17, 'Knowing Better', Mark Antonious Richfield has a birthday coming up. And growing older is something Mark wishes was a choice, not mandatory. As his stress over the increasingly racy ads for the car company begin to have an impact on Mark, Mark learns some terrible news. Someone very close to him has died.

As Mark's life once again becomes a pressure-cooker of doubt and confusion, Alexander, Mark's son, is asked to audition for yet another big blockbuster film, with a close friend, Carl Bronson.

Watching Alexander blossom into a superstar, Mark is both thrilled, yet

STARTING OVER

slightly overwhelmed, since Alex seems to have it all, and that includes a powerful LAPD Captain husband, Billy Sharpe.

Knowing better, Mark tries to do the right thing, but as his patience is once again put to the test, and his husband, Steve Miller, is at a loss on how to keep Mark from self-destruction, life for the Action! men once again begins to grow complicated.

Knowing Better.

Knowing better and doing the right thing, sadly, are not always the same path.

Becoming Alex; Book 18

Alexander Mark Lehman-Richfield. What can you say about a young man who grew up surrounded by lies? His mother, Iris, had a one-night-stand, with a handsome man when she was single and working as a stripper to support her college tuition. His mother, who was now married and a primary school teacher, never even knew the man's name.

Eighteen years later, after coming out, living his life as a gay high-school student and withstanding bullying at the same time he was satisfying older men, Alex spotted a cologne ad in a glamour magazine.

It was then, he knew.

Mark Antonious Richfield, the Nation's Top Male Model, was his real father.

From the moment Alex stood at the front door of his birth father's home, as well as Mark's husband, former LAPD cop, Steve Miller, Alex's life changed forever.

From an unknown androgynous nymph, to a superstar in blockbuster films, Alex had done the unimaginable. He had accomplished his goals. And that included, marrying a gorgeous police officer, twenty years his senior, Captain Billy Sharpe.

But there was one flaw in the plan. Trust.

Alex hoped his life would be trouble free from now on.

Becoming Alex...

The present for Alex was already tough, the future? Impossible to predict. But one thing was certain, Alexander Mark Richfield, was destined for superstardom.

Doing the Dirty; Book 19

In book 18 of the Action! Series, Mark Antonious Richfield, Top Model, and ad executive for large firm in LA, was living his sexual fantasies in his head, much to the chagrin of his former LAPD police officer/advertising coworker husband, Steve Miller.

When the media begins to spin sordid gossip and lies, the men of the Action! Series, battle jealousy, emotional setbacks, and of course, fight for their true love.

While Alexander, Mark's twenty-six year old son, begins to rocket to superstardom, his forty-six year old LAPD police captain husband, Billy Sharpe's own ambitions to be the top cop begins to create more friction between the two.

With tempers flaring and Mark getting a motorcycle endorsement for his new Red cologne ads, everyone is once more, in a tailspin.

Doing the Dirty, fun or flirting with disaster?

Are you ready for another wild ride? Hold on to your helmets, because the men of the Action! Series are back for more adventure.

Anything But; Book 20

In Book 20 of the Action! Series, events come full circle.

As Carl Bronson waits for his next movie audition, the haunting warning of his talent agent, Adam Lewis, to deny, deny, deny, he was gay, was now becoming a reality. Carl's film work dries up and his husband and costar of their TV series, Keith O'Leary, has a dismal film debut.

Meanwhile, Alexander Mark Richfield seems to have the Midas touch. And his police captain husband, a man twenty years older than Alex, finds out he just may get everything he wants in life (or maybe not.)

As the men of the Action! Series come back together for a grand reunion, it seems as if things are finally falling into place.

But be prepared…

In the universe where Mark Antonious Richfield reigns as the World's Top Male Model, life is *anything but*…boring. For fans of the series, or a newcomer, enjoy another sex-filled romp with wild adventures.

The Action! Series; where dreams come true, men love men, superstars are made, and the media circus continues to be *anything but*- kind.

Mark & Billy; 21

For fans of the series-

The undeniable attraction between Chief of Police William P Sharpe, and top model Mark Antonious Richfield is a force more powerful than nature. Mark's superstar son, Alexander Richfield, a man twenty years younger than his husband, Billy Sharpe, shares his father's fetish for men in uniform, particularly Police Officers. Mark's husband, Steven J Miller, a former LAPD cop, and now a co-worker with Mark at an advertising firm, has a lot in common with the new Chief of Police. Both of them are former military, police officers, top dogs, and both, enamored with Mark and Alex.

When father and son begin to imagine what it would be like for the two dominant alpha males in their lives to play, it opens up an opportunity- to explore their options.

Love, strong bonds, and no limits…

This book is for Action! Series fans who have always wanted…but didn't get- enough of Mark & Billy.

This book contains married men having sexual relations with other married men.

Changing Times; 22

As we catch up with Mark Antonious Richfield and his friends and lovers, it becomes clear that life has changed for everyone in their close circle. Gone are the illusions of a rosy, bright future, and in its place, conflict hits.

Alexander, Mark's son, has a reunion with an old frenemy, a fabulous costar who manages to create a huge impact on Mark, Alex's Chief-of-Police husband, Billy Sharpe, as well as Mark's husband, former LAPD cop, Steve Miller.

Through the turmoil and frustration of life in the fast-lane, comes love. Love so powerful, it conquers all, or at least if not all, it becomes a support system for a fragile

STARTING OVER

world; A world of mistrust, anguish, and loss.

Get ready for another adventure with the wild men of the Action! Series.

Changing Times...
"You once told me you would never share Alexander."
"I'm not sharing Alex. They're sharing me."

There's an exception to every rule.

Mark Antonious Richfield; 23

Mark Antonious. The anchor, the star, and the center of the Action! Series universe.

What happens when Mark leaves for a *Dangereux* Cologne company's convention tour?

As Alexander, Mark's son, begins a new feature film in Oregon, Billy, Steve, Jack, Adam, and now Tadzio, the newest planet to begin to orbit Mark, are left without father and son.

What occurs next isn't what you'd expect.

As the men in Mark's world find out just how life would be in his absence, it becomes clear to all that the Nation's Top Male Model is the powerhouse everyone clings to, including the former LAPD cop, Steve Miller, and Alexander's husband, Chief of Police Billy Sharpe.

You don't know what you have...until you lose it.

With the weight of the world on his shoulders, and regrets looming, Mark's loyalties are clear.

The last thing you want is Mark as your enemy.

Mark Antonious Richfield; much more than just a pretty face.

Obsession; 24

New to the Action! Series? This book is a great place to start your adventure!

All of the Action! Series books can be read as 'stand-alone' novels.

A week in the life of the Action! men is always entertaining. While Mark Antonious Richfield is about to be paired up with a masculine hunk for his cologne modeling shoot, Mark is enjoying his new found friend. With the sexual tension at its usual high, Chief of Police Billy Sharpe and Mark's husband, the former cop, Steve Miller, grow closer, sharing common ground.

Battling for sanity and a good night's rest, Mark discovers something that may ease his insomnia, as well as give him a hearty appetite. But his decision is weighed heavily by the police officers in his life.

With pressure from all sides, as well as bad news hitting their extended family of lovers and friends, Mark and the gang are busy with the thing we call...life.

Share the trials and tribulations of the men you have grown to know and love...

The Action! Series...where love conquers all.

California Dreaming; Book 25

(minor cliffhanger)

In this latest installment of the Action! Series, we journey with the men you've grown to adore through more trials and tribulations of their complex world.

As the lives of the many couples in the Action! Series universe moves on to yet another year's end, we find one of the pairs is in trouble.

After a decade of marriage, taking each other for granted, and opening up their options to explore has created a rift that may lead to an end.

In Book 25, *California Dreaming*, we find love is not always unconditional, and bitterness between two Action! characters creates a divide which may be permanent.

Ride the rollercoaster of love, sex, pain, and friendship, with the cast of characters you've grown to adore.

And, hold on tight, for this story will give you the ride of your life.

Loving Stan; Book 26

All things must change.

In book 26 of the Action! Series, an infatuation grows to deep love.

As Mark and Stan fly to New York City for a *Dangereux* Cologne promotional tour, their affection blossoms to an inseparable bond. As rumors fly and their attachment becomes public, family and friends react to the news.

Mark's husband, Steve Miller, is left with the fallout, on his own while Mark spends time with a man twenty years his junior.

But, Steve refuses to crumble in the face of the catastrophe. Instead, he goes on a sexual tear, which distracts him from reality.

With love being tested and life moving forward, both Mark and Steve face a decision that rocks the men of the Action! Series.

Loving Stan.
Mark can't help himself. While the two men share secrets and their bodies with each other, Mark and Stan brave the coming upheaval.

Love. The heart simply goes where it desires. *Loving Stan*, part of a trilogy inside a series.

'*Obsession, California Dreaming, & Loving Stan*' three books which complete a story on their own.

Moving On; Book 27
Moving on; Book 27

After the traumatic upheaval of Book 26- Loving Stan; the men of the Action! Series battle to recover and gain normalcy. Mark Antonious Richfield, faced with friction from every direction for his choices, craves a drama-free life, but with a man like Mark, it never is.

Steven Jay Miller, Mark's husband, is still reeling from the backlash and anger of Mark's decisions. He finds living on the periphery of Mark's life infuriating.

Is it possible for the two men to reconcile? Or have their lives been changed forever?

STARTING OVER

Moving on...
It's a desire but not always reality, when couples who have loved for a decade, fall apart.

Falling Hard; Book 28

As things ramp up for the men of the Action! Series, the fallout from Mark and Steve's separation continues to play havoc on the group. What has become intolerable friction between them, splits the close knit men apart, choosing sides.

As Mark Antonious Richfield battles to gain what he lost, his father's billion dollar business, his husband Steven Jay Miller, forces himself to come to terms with reality.

But all is not lost for the two men...
The dust will settle...the love remains.
And...an even stronger partnership has been made between them.

Mark & Steve- Falling Hard...we skinned our knees when we did it as kids.
As adults, we fall for another reason. Passion and loyalty.
And it's both of those traits that keep the men of the Action! Series from falling...apart.

Richfield-Miller International: Book 29

As spring arrives, bringing hope and nourishing rains to Southern California, the men of the Action! Series also find a little relief from the chaos.

In the midst of their divorce, Mark Antonious Richfield and Steven Jay Miller join forces to take over the mega company Mark's father had owned. Both men are inspired by the potential of a bright future, but...they aren't in the clear yet.

The Swedish model, Tadzio Andresen, is losing hope he will get to remain in LA much longer.

The superstar, Mark's son, Alexander, runs himself into the ground from fear and overworking.

The police chief, Billy Sharpe, ends up in hot water.

And, the new kid on the block, Stan Charles, brings Mark a step closer to his dream of having children.

While the corporate world reacts with rising stock to the announcement of a new partnership, the lives of the men of the Action! Series continue to spin out of control.

But, by placing one foot in front of the other, they battle forward...against all odds.

Waiting to Breathe; Book 30

It seems as if everyone surrounding Mark Antonious Richfield is waiting.
Waiting for love, waiting for success, waiting to be married.

Steven Jay Miller, Mark's ex-husband is waiting for a sign. One he may never get, from the top model.
The fabulous blond Swedish twink, Tadzio Andresen is waiting...for Steve to make a decision.

Chief of Police Billy Sharpe, is once again in trouble, waiting for break from the chaos, and Alexander Mark

Richfield appears to be losing the battle for sanity while he waits for his father and Steve to reconcile.

Life in Los Angeles with the men of the Action! Series can be challenging. Yet, hopefully, worthwhile.

In reality, Mark is just waiting for the chance…to breathe.

Waiting…sometimes the things we want most in life are worth that wait. With the men of the Action! Series, only time will tell.

Sons & Lovers; Book 31

Mark Antonious Richfield is still powering on- at full speed- getting his father's billion dollar manufacturing company into the future, with Steven Jay Miller, his new partner, right by his side.

Alexander Mark Richfield is losing his mind over the new guy in his dad's life, Stan Charles.
Chief of Police Billy Sharpe gets a lucky break at work, and Jack Larsen receives some bad news from Florida.

The boys from LA are back!
Get into the Action! groove, as Mark creates havoc with his son, and his many lovers.

Holding Tight; Book 32

In book 32 of the Action! Series, we catch up with the gang from LA. Mark Antonious Richfield and his ex-husband Steven Jay Miller work as a dynamic duo getting the mega corporation, RICHIELD-MILLER INTERNATIONAL back to its prime.

And, as Mark's formal wedding ceremony looms, they are contacted by a style magazine to cover it. He and his twenty-six year old modeling partner, Stan Charles, are set to celebrate their union for Stan's family in New York, even though the couple has eloped; both men eager to move forward, with babies on the brain.

Stan and Alexander Richfield, Mark's son, end up cast in a steamy gay romance film, and are forced to do simulated sex scenes, which the two of them dread.

Mark and his son spend some quality father/son time in hopes of helping Alex's anger at the divorce.

Holding tight. Whether it's for love, or for control, sometimes you can't get what you want, until you loosen the noose and set your fears free.

Living in Paradise; Book 33

Living in paradise…
It was a dream. A dream each of the men in Mark Richfield's orbit, wanted.

As Alex and Stan suffer through filming the on-location scenes in Manhattan's Diamond District, Steve Miller, Mark's ex-husband and business partner, plans on reigniting their passion, in Paris.

Tadzio Andresen, the hot Swedish runway model continues to feel left behind, but ends up staying with Chief of Police Billy Sharpe when Alexander leaves for New York.

STARTING OVER

Jack Larsen and his husband Adam Lewis, sadly, receive more bad news from Florida.

Mark Antonious Richfield continues to battle to get his life back; A life that the impetuous former cop had stolen from Mark that day he had swept Mark off the wedding altar, away from Sharon Tice. That fateful day, when Mark sacrificed everything for Steve, had come back to haunt him.

But he will get it back. Oh, yes. He will.

Come along on a journey as the men from LA continue to make the best of it, and find their way to Paradise.

Still Standing; Book 34

In Book 34 of the Action! Series we find the boys from LA still battling to feel normal after the upheaval.

Alexander Richfield, Mark's impetuous son, acts out one last time in rebellion. The fallout from Mark and Steve's divorce hit the young superstar hard. But...Alexander is finally coming back to himself after a last troubling act of aggression, one aimed at Mark's new man.

Meanwhile, Steven Jay Miller, the former cop turned CEO continues to power through life, finding love for his new sexy Swedish runway model, Tadzio Andresen. With everything Steve has ever dreamed of now in his grasp, Steve has never been happier.

Sadly, the Chief of Police, Billy Sharpe, cannot say the same. Billy is hit with more grief and accusations when a video shows up of him, broadcasted on a local news station, causing the career law enforcer to reassess his life.

And, then there's the Top Model Mark Antonious Richfield. As Mark's dream of being a new father becomes a reality, Mark and his new husband, Stan Charles...Richfield, push through the hate and rage that surrounds them. And Mark's relationship with his son, Alex, has never been more tenuous.

But, through the chaos, all of the men of the series are still standing; not discouraged and not giving up.

Join the characters you have grown to adore in the Action! Series as they continue to battle for sanity, love, and peace of mind.

Starting Over; Book 35

After a summer from hell, the boys from LA are finally settling down. The Chief of Police, Billy Sharpe, makes a life-changing decision, but one he can live with.

Father and son, Top-Model Mark Antonious Richfield and superstar Alexander Richfield, battle through their issues, having it out finally during a session with Alex's psychiatrist. Mark is determined to get his son to finally accept Mark's new young husband, Stan, once and for all.

Steve Miller is not only in love with his fabulous Swedish runway model husband, Tadzio Andresen- who is full of surprises; he is also finding out how much he loves his life working at Richfield-Miller International, and living in a massive, posh estate in Paradise, California.

For the fans who have survived what was a chaotic upheaval from the men of the Action! Series the reward is happiness and acceptance, not to mention, loads of sexy fun.

Join the characters you've come to cherish as family members, as they start their lives over again, trying desperately to get it right.

Printed in Great Britain
by Amazon